I0761007

THE GREATER MASSAPEQUAS
SHORT STORIES BY
RICHARD DAUB

This is a work of fiction. The characters, organizations, and events in these stories are either products of the author's imagination or are portrayed in a fictional manner.

Cover design by Richard Daub.

"You Be Illin' " was published by *Maudlin House*, October 2020

"The Huffy" was published by *New Pop Lit*, December 2020

"Showdown at the Old Sam" was published by *The Dillydoun Review*, April 2022

None of these works have appeared in *The Best American Short Stories.*

ISBN: 978-1-946094-08-7

First Edition Hardback, 2024 Clay Road Press

www.richarddaub.com

@rdaub82

THE GREATER MASSAPEQUAS

THE GREATER MASSAPEQUAS

BIRCH LANE

Carl had not once in his life thought about his wardrobe until the first day of fifth grade, when he walked into the classroom of his new school, Birch Lane Elementary in Massapequa, NY, a hamlet that, until a month ago, he'd never set foot in, and had only known as one of the stops on the Babylon branch of the Long Island Rail Road, which had the green timetables. Most of his new classmates were wearing Ocean Pacific—"OP"—designer shirts, windbreakers, tanks, sweatshirts, all with silkscreened images of surfboards and beach life, stylish apparel of the like he'd never seen back in West Hempstead. Some were wearing "parachute pants" with zippers all over them, while he was clad in a pair of brown Toughskins jeans from Sears, the same brand he'd been wearing since kindergarten, and a Bob's Auto Body t-shirt from the man the kids in his old neighborhood knew as "Bobo", who gave the shirts away to anyone who asked, even if he'd given you one the day before.

By the end of fourth grade, heading into the summer of 1983, his freshly divorced mother's affair with his soon-to-be "stepfather", Rick—the suburban cowboy with Burt Reynolds mustache, custom van, and country music, a stark contrast to his government employee "father" with the petal-pusher, the VW Bug, and the oldies-station—was no longer an "affair", but an "engagement", the wedding to take place in late autumn. She had not, though, said anything about moving away from West Hempstead until August, blindsiding Carl, who, until then, had no idea he was about to be taken from his life and his friends forever, many of whom he'd known since Happy Time Nursery School, and begin an entirely different life in a faraway place with this scary man. It made no sense that they would move fifteen miles out to Massapequa, almost Suffolk, when Rick's kids would still live in West Hempstead with his now ex-wife, and Carl's father was already long gone, having moved back into the basement of "Big Grandma's" house, his childhood home in Lynbrook. The lovers could have just bought a nicer house in a different part of town, but, islands in the stream they were, they longed to begin anew in exotic Biltmore Shores, two blocks from the legendary Biltmore Beach Club, where, back in the day, Long Island underworld figures would mingle with aging stars of stage and screen, fringe Rat Packers, Brill Building songwriters, female impersonators, and South Shore socialites. Like Carl's rich cousins up in Old Greenwich with their "Yacht Club", the whole household would become members, including his soon-to-be "stepbrothers".

They were all staring. Carl had never been a "new kid", and he'd always felt bad for them, outsiders for at least a couple of grades before the "new kid" label finally started to wear off. But this was even worse than he'd imagined, worse than his parents screaming at each other every night, worse than the day his father moved out—

The teacher, Mrs. Simons, and the class, reading from the chalkboard, mumbled, "Welcome to Birch Lane, Carl."

Mrs. Simons then asked him to tell everyone where he was from and a little about himself, which was one of the things he was afraid would happen on the first day. A few gasped when he said he was from West Hempstead, the

Massapequan children thinking the new kid was ripe from "the ghetto", but safe now in these greener, whiter, waterfront pastures—

Carl ate lunch by himself at the end of his class's long picnic-style cafeteria table. Down towards the middle were two girls sitting near but not with each other, neither wearing "OP", one a skinny girl clad in kid clothes from Sears—Carl realizing he must look like the boy version of her—and a girl with a Simon Le Bon haircut with her head buried in her arms on the table. Down at the opposite end, beyond the rest of the nobodies and marginally cool, the popular surfer kids were talking and laughing like they'd known each other their whole lives, which they probably had, the way Carl had known his old friends, who said they'd come visit, but he already knew they never would.

Across the aisle, at the end of another class's table, sat alone a kid in a blue and white-striped short-sleeve shirt exactly like one he had at home, also from Sears, and a pair of Toughskins, but a louder, mismatched alpine green.

That afternoon, Mrs. Simons gave the class 45 minutes of free time. Since no homework had been assigned, Carl browsed the meager selection on the classroom bookshelf—no *Choose Your Own Adventure*, no *Hardy Boys*, not even any *Nancy Drew* or *Archie* comics. He eventually settled on *Aesop's Fables*, which he brought back to his desk and opened to "The Cock and The Pearl". He got about halfway through it before Zack—who referred to himself as "Zaxxon", and was not clad in "OP" but in an Ozzy Osbourne *Diary of a Madman* t-shirt with the sleeves torn off—snuck up on him from behind and slapped him hard on the back, partially knocking the wind out of him—

"Welcome, new kid!" he said with a big smile, which, at first, Carl thought was a show of kindness from a fellow outcast. Then a really tanned girl named *Randi*, puka beads around her neck and a hot pink "OP" long sleeve tee with distressed white print graphic of an old school longboard draped in Hawaiian leis, said, "Hey, new kid, come over here—"

She was pretty. Most of the girls were pretty, but there was a group of five surfer girls who were really hot and well-tanned after an endless summer of boogie-boarding at Gilgo. Carl put the *Aesop's Fables* face down on his desk so he wouldn't lose his place, which Zaxxon swiped to the floor, laughing derisively. When Carl bent over to pick up the book, one of the hot girls gave him a swift kick in the ass, then another one kicked him, and everywhere he moved there was another hot girl waiting, the hotter she was, the harder she kicked, until the "KICK ME" sign fell to the floor at his feet—

He picked it up and crumpled it, dropping it coolly into the wastepaper basket next to Mrs. Simons' desk, struggling not to betray that he was on the verge of crying, and asked for a pass to the bathroom.

He ignored their snickering as he headed towards the classroom door, and felt better in the dim quiet of the corridor. The boys' room was two doors down, and, to his relief, empty.

After splashing cold water on his face, he stood in front of the sink for several minutes trying not to look in the mirror, until the door opened, and in walked the kid from the cafeteria with the green Toughskins—

"Hey," the kid said.

"Hey," Carl said.

"Uh, you're new here."

"Yeah."

"Why did you move here?"

"My parents got divorced and we moved here."

"That sucks."

"Yeah."

"This place sucks."

"Yeah, I noticed."

"You'll have to spend the next seven years working on getting out of here by going to a college far away. Like UCLA."

"Or Hawaii."

"Yeah, like *Magnum, P.I.*"

"Yeah."

"I'm Eric."

"I'm Carl."

"Well, uh, later."

"Yeah, later."

TILL DEATH DO THEY PART, PT. II

On a cold Sunday evening in late January 1983, two weeks after his Father had moved out, Carl, now ten, having enjoyed his brief tenure as man of the house, headed downstairs in his pajamas to retrieve his Hardy Boys book, #39, *The Mystery of the Chinese Junk,* which he had left in the TV den. His younger brother and sister were in bed and his mother was in her bedroom, thus the den light was off, but he knew the book was on top of the radiator cover and did not bother to turn it on.

In the dark, just as his hand had taken hold of the book, a man's voice said, "Howdy, Carl."

Carl screamed and ran out of the room yelling, "Intruder! Intruder! Call 9-1-1!"

Upstairs, the door to his mother's bedroom opened—

"It's me, babe," the man called from the den.

"Carl, stop!" his mother ordered.

Carl stopped, but was still scared out of his mind. The man stepped into the light of the living room, a short but muscular guy with black hair and a Burt Reynolds mustache, blue jeans and a pack of Kent cigarettes rolled into the sleeve of his v-neck like Schneider on the edge of town—

"Carl, this is Rick," his mother said, her son realizing that this was the man who'd cuckolded his father.

They were engaged in March, with a "wedding" planned for late autumn.

* * *

On a scorching Saturday afternoon in August, Rick had his two sons at the house—Carl's future "stepbrothers", who were the same age as he and his sister, she two years younger—and they all piled into Rick's Disco-era custom van with the yellow, brown, and orange paint job and the waterbed in the back, and headed out on the Southern State Parkway to "look at a house in Massapequa".

At first, Carl thought nothing of the expedition, assuming they were just doing some weird boring shit like they usually did on the days Rick had his kids—bird watching, digging for worms, going to Radio Shack, driving out to Shoreham to see the nuclear power plant under construction—but, during the half-hour ride, he realized what was happening and started growing concerned—

They stopped at the 7-Eleven on Merrick Road in Massapequa to get sodas for the kids, and, for the adults, a carton of Kent and a twelve-pack of Pabst Blue Ribbon, which they would pour into empty Coca-Cola cans while on the road. Unlike Carl's tightfisted government employee father, Rick was a high-salaried corporate executive and loose with his wallet, allowing each of the kids their own 128-ounce Big Gulp, Carl mixing every kind of non-diet soda into his, while the other children took theirs straight.

Ten minutes later, on Fox Boulevard in swank Biltmore Shores, home of the legendary Biltmore Beach Club, Rick had to pull over and hurriedly slide open the door to allow his youngest son to puke up his gallon of Dr. Pepper on someone's driveway, then hurry back behind the wheel and roar away—

A couple of minutes later they turned onto Shoreham Road, where, waiting in the driveway of a house in the middle of the block, smoking a cigarette, was a woman in her 40s wearing a mustard Century 21 blazer over a leather miniskirt and high-heels—

"Howdy," said Rick, clad in flowery red Hawaiian shirt, white shorts, and sandals, extending his hand, a freshly lit Kent dangling from his lips—

There was a large side yard that looked good for Wiffle Ball. The house itself seemed nothing special—a ranch with a big dormer on the back side, a concrete patio in the back overlooking a koi pond with a waterfall, and an attached garage. The interior was early 1960s suburbia, but nice, including a high-ceilinged living room with three skylights that flooded the room with light, and a finished basement with rock walls and a fully-equipped bar with working soda fountain and beer taps—

"Neil Diamond used to mingle in this very basement," the real estate lady said. "He used to live over on Frankel, right around the block, and belonged to the Beach Club. He was friends with the current owners, who are retiring to Islamorada."

"Really," Rick said, sounding impressed, another Kent dangling from his lips as he spoke, creating a Burma cloud of smoke in front of his face.

"Oh, yes," the woman said, a bit flirtatiously, which was noticed by Carl's mother, who'd never had to worry about this sort of thing with her first husband. "He wrote 'Love on the Rocks' right on that very bar over there. Also, two houses down, there's a house full of musicians who were fired from Billy Joel's band. You can hear them when you drive by, even when you have the windows rolled up and the radio on."

They moved in three weeks later. A few days into the unpacking, their mother took Carl and his siblings to Birch

Lane Elementary and enrolled them. Carl would never see his West Hempstead friends again.

* * *

On the Saturday after Thanksgiving, in their new living room, officiated by six-foot-ten Pastor Luther Roller from the closest Lutheran church in the area—"Our Redeemer" in Seaford, Massapequa's neighbor to the west—his mother wed husband No. 2.

Carl, his brother, and Rick's two sons were clad in matching light blue button-downs with navy-blue clip-on ties, gray trousers, and black oxfords from Sears, and his sister in a white and pink dress and black shoes, also from Sears.

As bride and groom kissed, the room dimmed, and a torrential rain began to fall. Moments later, the power went out in the entire neighborhood. Three blocks over, on Lagoon Boulevard, the downpour had flushed the snapper right out of the canal, covering the road with flopping, diesel-coated fish.

ZAXXON AND THE EMPEROR'S ROYAL GUARD

In the toy aisle of the Genovese drug store, Carl removed the unopened *Return of the Jedi* "Emperor's Royal Guard" action figure manufactured by the Kenner toy company from the hook and held it closer, inspecting the red-frocked figure's very cool helmet with black visor and force pike accessory. He wasn't that into *Star Wars,* but even he'd seen the latest installment in the theater three times over the summer, and these guys, and also Boba Fett, were the coolest.

"Hey, New Kid," said a voice behind him.

Carl turned and saw Zack, a.k.a. "Zaxxon", the scary kid from his fifth-grade class at his new school, wearing an Ozzy Osbourne *Diary of a Madman* t-shirt with the sleeves torn off.

"Hey, Zaxxon," Carl said.

"Still playing with toys?"

"Uh, no. My little brother is into this stuff."

"Yeah, right. Hey, why don't you steal it for him? Oh, yeah, you don't have the balls. See ya, New Kid."

He turned and left before Carl could come up with a response that didn't sound wuss-like. Alone in the aisle, he imagined how impressed Zaxxon would be if he saw the red figure standing on his desk the next day, and how it might earn him enough respect to be left alone. He didn't have any money on him, and though he had some at home, that was a mile-and-a-half away, which, even though he was a fast bike rider, wouldn't give him enough time to get home and back and home again before dinner. If he asked his mother to drive him, she would likely tell him to wait until the weekend when she wouldn't have to load all three kids into the car when it was time to start preparing dinner.

He turned the package over and pretended to be looking at the images of other *Return of the Jedi* action figures available from Kenner, while, on the other side, he began peeling the plastic shell from the cardboard backing, just enough to remove figure and force pike, which he then slipped down his shorts inside his tightie-whities.

The plastic shell was still attached to the cardboard. He removed the remaining three Emperor's Royal Guard packages from the hook and put the empty one back, then put the others in front of it. Satisfied it would be days or weeks before anyone noticed, he headed towards the front of the store.

The cashiers paid him no mind as he glided through one of the closed lanes. This seemed too easy.

Then, in the glass-enclosed vestibule where the gumball machines were, a slick, darkhaired man with hockey stick sideburns hurrying out of the store through the "IN" door nearly knocked over an elderly woman, to whom he hastily apologized and kept going. Carl noticed the rude man, but, in his reverie of red figure and force pike on his desk the next day for Zaxxon to see, he didn't pay him much mind and continued floating towards the golden afternoon sunlight, which seemed a little brighter than it had since his family moved to this place.

The noisy automatic door opened slowly before him. Just as he stepped over the threshold onto the sidewalk, his progress was halted by a strong hand clamping his upper arm.

"You're coming with me, thief," said the man who'd nearly knocked over the elderly woman.

"Help!" Carl called out as the man pulled him towards the "IN" door.

"That ain't gonna work, chico," he said, shoving him into the vestibule while the automatic door was still opening.

The man, styled in button-down shirt with wide lapels, brown bellbottom slacks, brown leather boots, and ankle holster with loaded Glock, was strong and pulled Carl towards the back of the store, to a door with an "EMPLOYEES ONLY" sign on it. The man used one of the keys from the janitor's keyring on his belt loop to open the door, then shoved Carl into a short corridor leading to a small, wood-paneled room that smelled of cigarette smoke.

There were two desks, behind one of which sat a younger man dressed in similar fashion as Carl's captor and a nameplate on his desk with the Genovese logo and "DEPUTY SECURITY GUARD". The vacant desk had the same nameplate except it said "CHIEF SECURITY GUARD". On the wall behind the Chief's desk were numerous framed photographs of the cast of the recently cancelled ABC sitcom *Barney Miller*.

"Lean forward, palms on the desk," the Chief ordered Carl.

"Well, what do we have here?" asked the Deputy, chewing on a toothpick, as the Chief began patting Carl down.

"Another dumb, stupid thief coming into my store thinking he can just steal my merchandise. The stupidity! What is this world coming to? Yesterday we caught an eighty-year-old lady trying to steal a hundred dollars' worth of sunglasses. And, today, who else but our old friend Zaxxon himself walks into my store— "

"You know Zaxxon?" Carl asked, starting to feel confident

that the Royal Guard in his briefs would not be found.

"Of course," the Chief answered. "Every security guard in Massapequa knows Zaxxon. Now, reach down your pants and pull out that toy so that I won't have to."

Carl slowly reached into his shorts and pulled out the Royal Guard, then handed it to the Chief.

"Ah, look at this," the Chief said, inspecting the figure, moving its arm. "Cool pike, man. Is this guy from a superhero TV show or something?"

"*Return of the Jedi,*" Carl explained.

"*Return of the Jedi*? Is that a Saturday morning cartoon?"

"You never heard of *Star Wars*?"

"*Star Wars*? Is that the show where famous Hollywood actors climb walls and play tug-of-war?"

"You're thinking of *Battle of the Network Stars,*" the Deputy explained. "I think he's referring to a Bruce Lee movie."

"No," Carl said, "it's a movie that takes place in outer space, in a galaxy far, far away. The guy who plays Indiana Jones is in it."

"Who the hell is Indiana Jones?" the Chief asked.

"You never heard of *Raiders of the Lost Ark*?"

"Alright, enough of this, chico, until we figure out what to do about this situation. Do you have any idea what the Genovese family used to do to thieves who stole from them?"

Carl shook his head.

"They would cut off a guy's finger for each time he stole, and then they would make him watch when the dog came in and ate it. I don't even want to mention what they would cut off next after they ran out of fingers."

"Should I call his parents?" the Deputy asked.

"Yeah, sure, why not. I'm sure they will love to hear that their son is a thief. What is your phone number, chico?"

"I don't know."

"What do you mean you don't know? Even the dumbest

kindergartner knows his own phone number! Do you think I'm a fucking moron or something? If you are going to play games with me, chico, I will simply call the police instead, and you will be their problem."

"We just moved here and I don't have it memorized yet. It's 541 something something. Call the operator, we just had the phone hooked up under my stepfather's name."

The Deputy got the number from the operator, then made the call. His mother answered and Carl heard her exclamation after the Deputy explained that he'd been caught shoplifting and that her son was a thief.

After the call, the Chief lined him up against the mugshot wall and took a photo with a Polaroid instant camera.

"This photo," he said as Carl's image began to appear, "will be sent to corporate headquarters and added to the mug book that gets sent to all 77 of the other Genovese drug stores in the Tri-State Area. Every security officer in every store will know your face, so don't even think about going into any one of them or else you will be taken into custody and arrested for criminal trespassing, and your parents will have to hire a lawyer, and lawyers are very expensive."

His mother was there six minutes later, leaving her two youngest children locked in the Buick with the windows rolled up, the cabin fogged with cigarette smoke.

"Your son will be banned from this and every other Genovese drug store for the rest of his natural life," the Chief explained to her.

"The rest of his life?" she asked, trying to light a cigarette, until the Chief coolly produced a Zippo lighter and lit it for her.

"Yes, ma'am," he said. "Your son is a thief, and the Genovese family doesn't like thieves."

"Well, what if I have to run in for something quick like Tylenol or cigarettes? Can he come in if he's with me?"

"No, ma'am. If he comes into the store, he will be trespassing and we will call the police. You are still welcome to come here, but we'll be watching you closely also because your son is a thief."

She had to sign some papers acknowledging his banishment from all Genovese drug stores, and then they finally released him.

"Bye, bye, thief," the Chief said behind them, "and don't come back."

Facing the punishment of his life, Carl followed his mother out of the store and across the parking lot to the car. His brother and sister said nothing as he climbed in, both looking frightened at seeing their big brother, the criminal.

Carl was expecting an eruption from his mother, but instead she spoke in a low, deep tone he'd never heard.

"I'm glad your grandfather isn't around to see this," she said, referring to her own father, a decorated Nassau County cop who'd passed away two years earlier. "His own grandson… my own son… a thief!"

She burst into tears as she started the car. Her brother and sister started crying too.

His punishment was no TV and no Atari for a month.

The next day at school, Zaxxon was absent, which wasn't unusual. He was absent for the next two days and didn't return until the following week, having by then forgotten their brief encounter at Genovese and distracted with his harassment of another classmate, so Carl, not wanting to attract any further unnecessary attention from the scary kid, never said anything.

At some point Zaxxon stopped showing up for school entirely and was never seen again. Nobody knew what happened to him, the most common rumor being that he went crazy and broke all the windows in his house, prompting his parents to send him somewhere far, far away.

Six years later, now a junior in high school, Carl returned to the scene of the crime. He went straight to the toy aisle and pretended to be looking at the crappy merchandise, ready, waiting for anyone to dare lay a hand on him. Who the fuck did that security guard think he was? Zaxxon was a faded memory, but the itch to get back at the Chief and his Deputy for the way they treated him had never gone away, and he was big and strong now and had become a decent fighter over the years.

Trying to look conspicuous, he waited ten minutes, but nobody came. He picked up one of the *Star Wars* action figures, Boba Fett, and looked towards the big mirrors at the back of the store that the security guards used to watch the floor, then slid his fingers beneath the plastic shell, allowing toy and weapon accessory to drop to the mess of fallen toys below, which was the case in many of the aisles, the store in a state of rack and ruin compared to the gleaming fluorescence and neatly stocked shelves he remembered. He dropped the empty package on the floor and, facing the mirrors, stuffed his fist into his front jeans pocket as if the toy were still in hand, then turned and headed towards the front of the store, heart racing, fists clenched, alert for the slightest sign of unusual movement, past the old lady at the cash register who smiled at him as he went by, and into the vestibule, but the man with the hockey stick sideburns did not appear and no one else tried to stop him.

BIG CHIEF LEWIS

May 1968, Massapequa, Long Island, New York

"Do you think it's offensive?" Ethel asked her husband, Charles, both standing in front of the just-delivered two-story fiberglass statue depicting Big Chief Lewis, Native American warrior, adorned with feather headdress and peace pipe ready to be torched, standing on a square of AstroTurfed concrete, flanked by disproportionately smaller statues of a horse and bison, the display intended as an advertisement for the Big Chief Lewis Insurance Company of Massapequa to motorists on busy Sunrise Highway and passengers on the Long Island Rail Road Babylon line beside it.

"Offensive?" responded Charles, newly appointed Executive Vice President of Big Chief Lewis Insurance. "What do you mean?"

"I don't know. It just seems kind of... I don't know... cartoonish?"

"Cartoonish? Just what in the goddamn hell do you mean by that, Ethel?"

"It looks like one of those statues you see at that little amusement park up in Lake George, you know, with the statues of Snow White and the Seven dwarfs, Cinderella, Peter Pan, Captain Hook— "

"What the hell, Ethel? We spend a fortune hiring that Quaker nutjob out in Pennsylvania to build this thing not only as a symbol of our great company, but as a beacon celebrating the culture and heritage of The Greater Massapequas, and you have the nerve to stand here and say it looks like a goddamn Walt Disney cartoon?"

"We've lived here over a decade, Charles, and I've never once seen an Indian at the mall or at the grocery store or at the Club or at church. Everyone here looks exactly like us. And the statue just looks like something designed to humor children. If I was an Indian, I'd be a little offended."

"So, if we built a statue honoring you holding a tray of your famous blueberry muffins, you'd be offended?"

"If it made me look cartoonish, then yes, I would be offended. And my muffins aren't famous, Charles."

"Good God, Ethel, what color is the sky in your world? But I guess I shouldn't expect a woman to understand the way the world works. Women don't even buy insurance, for Chrissakes. Men buy insurance, Ethel, and they will understand the power of this great symbol, and they will equate it to powerful insurance policies that will protect them and their families should disaster strike. I suppose that, if women were the ones buying insurance, I can see how they would be more impressed with a statue of a housewife holding a tray of muffins, or pushing a vacuum, or gossiping on the telephone with friends from the Club... Ethel, are you okay? You look a little flush— "

"I just saw a Negro drive by."

Charles looked around, then back at his wife.

"Well, I didn't see him," he said. "But they are allowed to pass through, Ethel, as long as they don't stop. Probably just on his way back to Amityville. Anyway, he's gone. It's safe now."

"Can we go home now, Charles?"

"Okay, but, hold on, let me get the Kodak out of the car."

Charles went over to the Buick and came back with the camera.

"Well," he said, looking up at Big Chief Lewis, "I for one don't know who in the hell would be offended by such a symbol of power and security. You see, Ethel, that's what insurance is all about: security. If something were to happen to your home, life, or automobile, Big Chief Lewis has you covered. And I'm telling you, Ethel, people are going to drive out of their way to see this thing and snap photographs in front of it. Hell, it's already the greatest tourist attraction this hamlet has ever seen, except maybe for the zoo and the mall. Maybe someday there'll even be a photo of it in the *AAA Travel Guide*. Now, Ethel, I'll stand over here, and you go over there so you can get the whole statue in the photograph. And be careful with the camera, it's a very delicate, expensive instrument. So, okay, go ahead and snap the photo, and then we'll go home and I'll mix some drinks and you can make some houer d'oeuvres and we can relax. And, if you're good, maybe I'll even have sex with you after supper."

"Okay, Charles," Ethel said, carefully taking the camera and walking with it towards the designated shooting spot while her husband posed in front of the statue.

THE HUFFY

Day after Christmas, 1983, fifth grade, in the attached garage at Eric's house—

"They got you a Huffy?" Eric laughed, referring to Carl's new bike. "Huffys are for losers. Did they buy it at Sears?"

"I don't know," Carl said, knowing they probably did. His mother always took them to Sears to buy school clothes. "I asked for a Mongoose."

In Massapequa, Mongoose was the Corvette of BMX bikes, while their "Supergoose" model was like a Ferrari. Huffys were like a *Le Car*.

Last Christmas, Eric's parents—who'd told their children at an early age that there was no Santa or God—had gotten him a Mongoose "Californian" with maraschino red rims, grips, seat, and pads for the handlebar and frame.

This Christmas, "Santa" got Carl a Huffy "Challenger 3000" with dorky black-and-white checkered flag pads.

"I have an idea," Eric said. "It'll be classic."

He started peeling the stickers off the Huffy. Carl did not object. Then, with a Phillips head screwdriver, he removed the bulky plastic chainguard, revealing the freshly greased chain that would stain the inside right cuff of Carl's new Levi's, another Christmas present, Carl finally able to completely phase out his Toughskins.

Afterwards they set out in the cold gray winter afternoon, Carl on his stripped Huffy and Eric on his Mongoose, riding two-and-a-half miles to the Our Redeemer Lutheran Church in neighboring Seaford, where both their families were members—despite their atheism, Eric's parents were members for "appearances, etc.", while Carl's mother felt it was her obligation to force her childhood religion onto her children and new husband, who was raised Catholic but didn't give a damn where he spent his Sunday mornings coming down.

"I knew it," Eric said as they stopped in front of the bike rack just outside the entrance to the "Youth Activity Center"—the "YAC"—at the back of the church building. And there it was, chain-locked next to a flowery white wicker basketed "girl's bike", a supposedly rare "Miami Beach Limited Edition" Mongoose "Supergoose" with teal pads and lower frame bar stickered with the super cool **supergoose** logo in the lowercase black outline with yellow-to-orange sunset gradient fill, and chrome tire caps on both tires.

The bikes belonged to Garry and Jill, twin siblings from Seaford the same age as Eric and Carl, who Eric remembered from his one year of Sunday school back in kindergarten as being serious dorks. They apparently still were, according to Eric's older sister, who attended the confirmation program at the "YAC" and said they were always there doing their homework and then would spend all their free time there, then groan when Pastor Roller started shutting the lights and they had to ride their bikes home, where they were not permitted to watch television, not even PBS, or consume sugar, or play with toys, not even when they were little. Yet, inexplicably, Garry had a seriously cool bike, which Eric would see from the car when his sister was dropped off at the "YAC" every Thursday afternoon—the same bike of which they were now removing the pads and chrome tire caps and, with the aid of a razor blade, carefully peeling the **supergoose** sticker from the lower frame bar, which they would then carefully reapply to the same bar on Carl's bike—

* * *

On the first day back at school after Christmas vacation, Carl's new wheels created a stir at the bike rack. He'd never had a cool bike in his life, and, since moving to Massapequa four months earlier and finding himself utterly lost in her mall culture, it felt good to suddenly be elevated from "loser new kid" to "the kid with the Miami Beach Supergoose". He got nervous, though, when Zack, the dirtbag kid who smoked cigarettes and referred to himself as "Zaxxon" who'd slapped a "KICK ME" sign on Carl's back during his first day at the school, seemed to be looking at the bike suspiciously while smoking his Marlboro, but ultimately said nothing.

Everyone bought it. Carl suddenly found himself on the cusp of being cool, and even a couple of girls looked in his direction—

* * *

On a chilly Sunday in February, Carl's mother asked him to ride up to FoodTown and pick up a gallon of milk. Normally she would have done this herself, but his five-year-old brother was running a temperature of 103, and Rick, his new "stepfather", was in China, or Idaho, or some such faraway place for his job of corporate industrial regional international global sales, so, at the moment, he was the man of the house with an opportunity to play hero with his new bike.

At FoodTown, there were a couple of beat up ten-speeds locked to the bike rack. Carl had a combination lock and chain wrapped around his raised seat post, but it was really cold and hardly anyone was around, so he didn't bother with it and hurried inside. He knew exactly where the milk was and got to the express lane quickly, but the line was slowed down by an old lady writing a check.

Ten minutes later he finally emerged through the slow automatic door. His bike was gone, as was one of the ten speeds. Panicked, he scanned the parking lot but saw only parked cars—

"Fuck!" he said and hurried back inside to the cold foyer with the gumball machines and pay phones and called home—

"Mom, my bike was stolen!"

Ten minutes later her new Polar White Mercedes C-Class that Rick had bought her as a wedding present pulled into the fire lane, with sister and feverish brother in the back seat—

"Why didn't you use the lock?" she screamed.

"I don't know!" Carl cried.

"Get in!"

For the next hour they drove all over the greater Massapequas—Massapequa, Massapequa Park, North Massapequa, East Massapequa—and some of the lesser ones, including Massapequa Heights, North North Massapequa, and Massapequaville, near the sanitarium—but they spied no one riding bicycles in the cold.

Finally, at dusk, Carl's mother pulled back into their driveway.

"We'll call the police," she said, stamping out her Kent in the ashtray full of lipsticked cigarette butts, the cabin fogged from her smoking with the windows rolled up. "What kind of bike was it again?"

"Forget it," Carl said.

"What do you mean, 'forget it'? That bike cost $150!"

"How do you know? I thought it came from 'Santa'."

Carl knew that one stung, and he was glad. "Santa" should have gotten him a Mongoose in the first place. And she never should have cheated on Dad, and never should have moved them to this horrible place where all they cared about was clothes and bikes, and she never should have married Rick "The Dick"—

"I'll call my cousin, Joe," she said. "He's a cop, he can look into it—"

"No!" Carl shouted. "I don't want the stupid bike back! Just leave me alone!"

Carl got out of the car and slammed the door. He heard his mother say, "Hey!" but ignored it, storming into the house and up to his room, slamming the door and cracking it, which "The Dick" would surely notice but he didn't care, it was over anyway—

SATURDAYS

At exactly 10:00 am on Saturday morning, Carl Sr. pulled into the driveway of "The Mansion" belonging to his ex-wife and her new husband, the man who'd cuckolded him, and leaned on the horn of his beige 1982 Datsun—no model, just a Datsun—until the front door opened and The Bitch herself appeared, arms raised as he continued honking.

He lit a Viceroy 100 and waited for his three biological children, whom he now considered chattel belonging to their mother, but corrupt liberal divorce court judges had mandated that he, at his own expense, entertain them on Saturdays between the hours of 10:00 am and 5:00 pm. His lawyers advised him to comply while they continued working on the disownment papers and running up the billable hours.

The oldest of the children, ten-year-old Carl Jr., emerged, followed by the eight-year-old girl and the youngest boy, five, walking slow as possible towards the running Datsun, they as unhappy to see him as he was to see them.

Carl Jr. took the front passenger seat and the other two kids sat in the back.

After backing out of the driveway, he asked none of them in particular, "So, how was your week?"

"Good," they answered, sparing him any details.

After the twenty-minute drive back to West Hempstead,

he pulled into the 7-Eleven on Hempstead Avenue, mere blocks from the house they resided as a family before his whore ex-wife slept with that scumbag playboy and turned his children against him. He bought them piña colada Slurpees, Reese's Peanut Butter Cups, Reese's Pieces, Grape Big League Chew, *Archie and Jughead Double Digest,* quarters for *Dig Dug* and *Zaxxon,* and, for himself, a six-pack of Budweiser tallboys, two packs of Viceroy 100s, two buttered rolls, a 32-ounce coffee, and a bag of Wise barbecue potato chips.

Next, they headed towards his mother's house in Franklin Square, where he'd been living since the divorce, reclaiming the basement bedroom he'd shared with his brother when they were kids. His mother still lived upstairs, widowed over two decades, his father passing when he was ten. Along the way, they pulled up behind an MTA bus with an advertisement on the back for Tom Gulotta, Republican candidate for County Executive, his large, smiling face having been vandalized with a Rollie Fingers-esque handlebar mustache, which, despite being a staunch Republican and Gulotta supporter, he found highly amusing, and even the kids cracked grins.

At the house, his mother emerged from her bedroom to greet whom she still considered her grandchildren. They were even less enthused to see her and escaped to the backyard after saying their obligatory hellos and having their faces scratched by the wiry hair growing from the mole on her chin as she attempted to kiss them.

With an hour to kill before he had to make the grilled cheese for lunch, he took a seat on one of the patio chairs beneath the green-and-red striped canvas awning, sipping a Bud, smoking a Viceroy, watching the boys play Wiffle Ball. The girl, sullen, was seated on the patio chair furthest him, listening to her Walkman, orange foam headphones, she intently not looking in his direction, he trying not to look in hers.

While the kids were eating their grilled cheese, he set up camp in the bathroom with cigarettes, tallboy, and *The New York Post*. After taking a dump and washing up, he sat on the toilet lid reading the sports section, sipping, smoking.

Afterwards, with four long hours left to kill, he wrapped the last tallboy in aluminum foil and they got back in the car and drove to the Nathan's arcade in Oceanside, the cheapest entertainment option save driving around looking for buses with mustaches drawn on Tom Gulotta's face. He gave them each four quarters, killing a good 45 minutes, then, on the way back to the house, they stopped at the Dan's Supreme supermarket, where he purchased three pounds of ground beef, a bag of Kingsford charcoal briquets, a bottle of lighter fluid, frozen store-brand crinkle cut golden fries, a 3-liter bottle of RC Cola, a bottle of store-brand catsup, and a 12-pack of Budweiser cans.

Back at the house, on the black-and-white television in the den, they caught the championship match of the *PBA Professional Bowlers Tour* and cliff diving from Acapulco on *Wide World of Sports*.

Afterwards, he went out to the backyard and started the fire. He was content in the quiet, drinking beers, smoking cigarettes, while the kids stayed inside watching a rerun of *The Love Boat*. He stared at the burning briquets and checked his watch, counting down the minutes until 4:36, when he had to be backing out of the driveway to get them home by exactly 5:00.

The kids ate their burgers quickly and said good-bye to his mother while he wrapped a couple of more Buds in aluminum foil for the road. Right on schedule, unbuckled seatbelt over shoulder, he backed the Datsun out of the driveway and navigated through Franklin Square and

Malverne to the Southern State Parkway, expertly maneuvering the narrow-laned, high-speed twists and turns of the section known as "Blood Alley", followed by the sudden isolation of the Seaford-Oyster Bay Expressway, and finally back to "The Mansion" in Massapequa, where his legal obligation concluded for the day and he could finally go home and relax, but not before a pitstop at 7-Eleven to pick up another six of tallboys and a few more packs of smokes.

ADAM ROAD WEST (PART I)

July 4, 1973

It was a steamy night on the Great South Bay, and Paulie "Pork Chops", just turned 67, was seated in a sagging lawn chair in the driveway of his home at the end of Adam Road West, right next door to Massapequa's legendary Biltmore Beach Club, clad in "wifebeater" tank top, khaki shorts, and black socks with sandals. An extinguished cigar rested in an ashtray on the cracked concrete, next to a metal Coca-Cola cooler containing three more cans of Schlitz.

The Club was crowded tonight to see the annual Grucci fireworks show, which he would be able to see from his driveway. Back in the old days, guys like Sinatra and Bennett and Bobby Rydell used to show up at the Club every so often as a guest of Don Carlo Gambino, who lived in the neighborhood.

Paulie's wife had died of cancer three years earlier, followed by his *gumar* a year later. He wanted to retire to Islamorada down in the Keys and spend all day fishing, but old soldiers who knew a few things didn't get to just up and retire, and were expected to keep earning until they were in the hole.

The fireworks were scheduled to start at 10:00. At around

9:30, a Cadillac rolled by very slowly, then turned up Bayview and parked. A guy got out, and, at first, it was hard to make him in the yellow streetlights, but, hearing the footsteps, he realized who it was—

"John," Paulie said, getting up. On the surface, everything was supposed to be good and it was all hugs and kisses, but John could see that Paulie was nervous. John was holding a t-shirt that he shoved into Paulie's gut.

"What's this?" Paulie asked, unrolling the shirt and recognizing the silkscreened logo of Ted's Auto-Body in Islamorada, "Ted" being legendary Red Sox slugger Ted Williams—

"You know what it is," John said.

"Yeah, I do, John," Paulie said, hanging his head.

"But that's not what I'm here about."

"No?"

"I'm here about that other thing."

"What other thing? That Lynbrook thing?"

"No. That Beach Club thing."

"*This* Beach Club?" Paulie asked, pointing towards next door.

"That's right, Paulie. The *giovenca* in the red dress."

"Fuck," Paulie said, looking away. For all these years, he was, until this moment, never sure if Don Carlo had heard the remark he'd made at the party next door the night Don Rickles was there and had everyone peeing in their pants, and Paulie had a little too much *vino* and got swept up in the moment and asked the guy standing next to him who the *giovenca* in the red dress was, and the guy said back in his ear to shut the fuck up, she was the Don's wife, which is when Paulie noticed Don Carlo himself standing only a few feet away, but who was not looking at him or letting on that he'd been offended—a façade the man would wear for fifteen years, which Paulie now realized was done to keep him worried, because worried guys usually stayed in line. Now, though, Paulie was older and earning less each year, and when word got out that he was thinking of "retiring", it was decided that his services were no longer needed, and now John Gotti was standing in his driveway—

"Is there any way to get me off the hook?" Paulie asked. "For old time's sake?"

"Can't do it, Paulie. But we'll go in the house, down in the basement, so the neighbors won't see, and the kids can still enjoy the fireworks."

"Thanks, John. I appreciate it."

YOU BE ILLIN'

With the money he'd made from his 23-house *Newsday* delivery route, Carl had purchased a TV, a VCR, a $400 Centurion Accordo *Tour de France Limited Edition* twelve-speed road racing bike with tires so thin he got a flat every time he rode it—a purchase encouraged by his friend Eric, whose parents had bought him a Peugeot PZ10—and now, his latest big spend, a Compact Disc player, becoming one of the first in the eighth grade, along with Eric, who'd encouraged this purchase as well, to own this cutting edge audio technology that would put an end to the sorry era of cassette tapes. Carl's stepfather, Rick "The Dick", a corporate sales executive, took him to The Wiz and showed his wares, haggling with the salesman to knock $20 off the $240 tag price. Carl also purchased three CDs that day—Phil Collins' *No Jacket Required*, Bon Jovi's *Slippery When Wet*, and Run DMC's *Raising Hell*. Eric, a rock & roll purist inspired by his older brother's massive record collection, would sharply criticize these choices, particularly the Run DMC, and, from then on, every so often he would say "Sussudio" and laugh derisively, even though he liked Phil in Genesis.

* * *

A few days later, Carl's mother informed him that, a week from this coming Saturday, they would be hosting a "family reunion" with her side of the family—her aunts and cousins and second cousins, relatives they rarely saw, most of the men active or retired Nassau County cops, all the women housewives. Her father, Carl's grandfather, who died of cancer when Carl was six, had also been a Nassau cop.

Carl remembered the last "family reunion" five years ago, when he was eight—

"How could you invite these assholes?" he asked, aware of crossing a line, but feeling justified.

"Watch it, mister," she said, lighting a Kent and exhaling towards the ceiling. "They're family and you'd better be nice and behave."

"Maybe I'll just go to Eric's."

"You'll be here, and you'll be nice. I expect you to say hello to everyone, and not be rude."

The last "reunion" was held at Eisenhower Park, Nassau County's premier inland public recreational facility, with tennis courts, golf courses, hockey rinks, softball diamonds, volleyball nets, picnic tables, iron barbecues cemented into the dust, and Safety Town, where kindergarteners learned to drive. When they arrived at the park on that beautiful summer's morning, they were the first and only kids there, but there was a boy and a girl from another party playing with a beach ball over at the volleyball net about twenty yards away, so Carl and his sister went over. For about a minute, the kids played and laughed together in perfect harmony, until their mother's cousin, Joe—sporting petal-pusher cop mustache, mirrored sunglasses, "Kiss the Cook" apron, freshly lit Pall Mall dangling from lips, and brandishing a spatula high above his head—storm-walked across the dust yelling at the two other kids to go away, using the "N-word", and a few others. The kids sprinted back towards their own party, where their adults were standing and watching, their expressions saying "*not again*"—

Cousin Joe, hands on knees, breathing heavily with cigarette still dangling from lips, looked at Carl and his sister disapprovingly, but said nothing. The last thing Carl remembered from that day was seeing his mother watching from one of the picnic tables, knowing she had seen and heard the whole thing, but she said nothing about it later, or ever. Carl, still believing at the time in his mother's goodness, eventually concluded that she thought it unnecessary to say anything about something so obviously egregious, like the unnecessariness of calling a murderer a "bad man". He also concluded that this was probably why they never saw these people to begin with, but, at least, after that last horror show of a "reunion", there would never be another. Then, after his parents divorced, and they moved to Massapequa, and his mother married Rick, he'd all but forgotten about that day, and these people, until now—

"They're racists," Carl said.

"They're family," his mother said.

"Not my family."

"Well, they're *my* family, and most of them haven't even met Rick yet."

There was no stopping this—not that there was ever stopping one of his mother's parties, which had become more frequent since moving to Massapequa, her and Rick getting more loaded each time with their new friends from the Beach Club, the last one ending with shitfaced Rick running around in a cowgirl outfit. Yet, even that was nowhere near egregious as this—

* * *

"I know what you should do," Eric said. "You should put your speakers up to the window and blast your Run DMC."

"Shut up," Carl said, thinking Eric was still making fun of him for buying the CD.

"Seriously, you should," Eric said. "And you should also buy one of those fat gold chains. And a pair of Adidas so you can stomp over coliseum floors."

"Fuck you."

"No, seriously. Think about it. It'll be classic. You'll be complying by going to the party, but you'll make them uncomfortable. The Dick will hear their racist comments firsthand when they see you, and your point will be proven. Wait, I have another idea—forget about the speakers, just make a tape of the CD and put it in your boom box, and then put it on your shoulder and blast it right when you get out there. You'll be like Rappin' Rodney—"

Carl knew that Eric was trying to get him to make an ass of himself, but he was right, it would be classic. His mother would be pissed, but she totally deserved it. And his mother being pissed would piss Rick off, but he also deserved it. And then his sister would make fun of him endlessly, but who gives a shit. It would all be worth it.

* * *

On Friday afternoon, Carl's mother drove he and Eric in her "Polar White" Mercedes to the Sunrise Mall and pulled to a stop in the fire lane in front of the same entrance they used when going to Carl's orthodontist's office, and Carl, in the front passenger seat, got out of the car, while his mother became distracted by the popping of the car's cigarette lighter, which she then used to light her Kent. When she heard Carl's door close, she did not notice that the back door was still open, and that Eric, who moved slowly, was still getting out, and that his left foot was in the path of the rear tire, and, smoking, she pulled away and ran over his toes—

"Ouch," Eric said, as if struck by a moth.

"Mom!" Carl yelled.

The Mercedes chirped to a halt.

"You ran over Eric's foot!"

"Oh, I thought I felt a bump," she said, taking a drag of her cigarette and exhaling. "Is your friend alright?"

"I'm fine," Eric said, but he was pissed.

"He's fine," Carl said, then slammed the back door as hard as he could, then kicked the tire and spit on the bumper, and said, "Piece of shit."

Their first stop was Spencer Gifts, a favorite for novelties, souvenirs, party tricks, posters, lava lamps, Halloween costumes, and fat plastic gold chains for $2.99 each, of which he bought two. At Herman's Sporting Goods, he purchased a size-13 pair of Adidas Superstars, a bucket-style fishing hat, and, from the clearance rack, a $5 t-shirt with a cartoon depiction of New York Knicks center Patrick Ewing making a slam dunk. Finally, they stopped at the Genovese drug store to pick up a 12-pack of "D" batteries for the boom box.

* * *

On Saturday, Carl, having second thoughts, held out in his room as long as he could, listening for racist comments by the thirty or so people outside on the back deck below his second-floor window, but hearing none. He had on the Patrick Ewing shirt and the Adidas—no laces, tongues high—but not the hat or chains.

Finally, there was a knock on the door. It was The Dick.

He didn't wait for Carl to answer, saying through the door, "Why don't you come down and say hello."

"I'll be down in a minute," Carl said, the intrusion enough to give him back the nerve to go through with it.

Fully clad in his new streetwear, giant boom box in tow—another past purchase with paper route money—Carl went downstairs, but ducked out the front door in order to avoid going through the kitchen, where several guests were mingling. The maneuver also enabled him to sweep around through the large side yard and climb the steps to the back deck without anyone seeing his approach.

At the top step he pressed "PLAY", but the song didn't start right away—he'd queued the tape as close as he could to the beginning of "It's Tricky", but the tape deck on the boom box never stopped the cassette exactly where he wanted it to. Finally the song started, opening with a soft rhythmic high-hat, then the rapping, and finally the crunching "My Sharona" guitar sample and pounding beat, which prompted some woman to yelp. Now everyone was looking at him, and when he finally had the courage to look back, he did not see the anger he'd been expecting, but confusion, and he himself became confused, not recognizing a single one of their faces, Cousin Joe nowhere in sight, and no one sporting a copstache or mirrored sunglasses. In the memory of that day created by his eight-year-old self, their faces in the background were all blurry versions of Cousin Joe, even the women and children, while the people before him now bore no such resemblance.

Out of the corner of his eye, Carl noticed Rick approaching, can of Pabst in hand, Kent dangling from lips, looking angry. He stopped the tape, and, in the sudden silence, heard his sister laughing—

Then his grandmother, who had a really loud voice for such a petite woman, said to the little group she was sitting with, "There he is, still dressing up like Chuck Barris. Did you know when he was little he used to host his own version of *The Gong Show* up in the attic? His mother made him a sliding curtain with a laundry line and everything, and he told jokes with a paper bag over his head." Then, turning to Carl, "Come on, silly, come say hello."

"Hi, everyone," he said sheepishly, then put down the boom box and took off the hat and chains, prompting Rick to halt—

He'd so badly wanted to show them how much he hated them, and how much better he was than they, but, in the end, he went around shaking their hands and hugging them, feeling ill at seeing their confused expressions turn to approving smiles.

ADAM ROAD WEST (PART II)

September 18, 1986

Carl slowed as he approached the house at the end of Adam Road West, the one right next door to the beach club. He'd never done anything this chivalrous, especially for his little sister, but everyone knew this Robbie Rixon kid was a little prick, and the last two days she'd come home from school in tears after he'd picked on her. He just wanted to put a little scare into the kid, so he had brought with him, wrapped in his old "Bob's Auto Body" t-shirt that he hadn't worn since the first day of fifth grade, his Colt 1911 .45 ACP-inspired nickel-plated steel cap gun, unloaded, save one from a previous roll stuck to the hammer.

There were no cars in the driveway, and the house was quiet. He unrolled the gun from the t-shirt and stuck it barrel-down in the back of his Levi's, then walked up the driveway to the front door. He rang the bell, looking nervously at the beach club property next door while he waited.

The little prick himself answered and stepped outside.

"What do you want, asshole?" he asked.

"Stop picking on Audrey."

"She's a cunt!"

"What?"

"She's a cunt!"

The kid was two years younger than Carl, and half his size. As much as he wanted to throttle the little fucker, he knew he'd better not touch him, so he pulled the piece from his rear and said, "Leave Audrey alone, you little—"

That's all he was able to get out before Rixon punched him in the nuts. Carl doubled over, then pointed the gun at Rixon's face and pulled the trigger. The last cap snapped and the kid screamed, covering his right eye with both hands—

At first, Carl thought the kid was acting, and even let out a little laugh, until he saw the blood trickling down his cheek. Then he started crying really loud and ran back into the house, slamming the door behind him—

"Shit," Carl said, smelling gunpowder, a wisp of smoke hovering in front of him. He rolled the gun back into the t-shirt and swiftwalked down the driveway, onto the asphalt of Adam Road West, this being one of those fancy sections of the neighborhood that didn't have sidewalks, and proceeded to the canal on Lagoon Boulevard several blocks away, where once more he unwrapped his piece and tossed it into the brown water coated with rainbow swirls of diesel, in the vicinity of a submerged FoodTown shopping cart half-buried in the muck, its chrome glistening in the late-afternoon sun—

The next day, Audrey reported that Robbie hadn't been at school. The following day she reported the same. Then he didn't show up the entire next week. Carl kept waiting for the hammer to drop, and got nervous whenever he saw a police cruiser or heard a siren, but nothing happened. The kid never went back to school and was never seen or heard from again, and their house was sold.

Every so often, Carl would wake at night in a cold sweat. In public, he would try not to make eye contact with uniformed officers—cops, mall security guards, meter maids—and would sometimes have panic attacks, which he would learn to fend off when around others, but that, when alone, would sometimes debilitate him. Then, years later, at a gas station convenience store in upstate New York, on mescaline, staring at the beef jerky rack, he was approached by a medicine man in full garb—including bone piercings and grass skirt, as well as a "wifebeater" tank top and sandals over black socks—who put a finger to his lips, then proceeded to wrap a blue headband around Carl's head—

"Close eyes," he said with a soft deep voice, then started chanting something in another tongue, while the clerk behind the counter looked on, trying to decide if he should call the cops—

Though his eyes were closed, Carl saw everything. The medicine man then reached through the headband into Carl's mind, plucking out a black-headed dandelion and blowing off the seeds, Carl mesmerized watching the charred blowballs float to the scuffed linoleum. The medicine man crumpled the stem and let it drop, then vanished through the automatic sliding door into the Adirondack night. Never again did Carl think about Robbie Rixon, and the panic attacks stopped.

Carl paid for the Slim Jim with a sweat-soft dollar bill that had been in his pocket all night. Six hours later, still wearing the headband—which, by now, he had no recollection of where it had come from—he watched the sunrise from a mountainside clearing, as an eagle soared high across the sky, towards the west—

"Must be nice and quiet up there," he said, hearing himself as if someone else had said it—

THE SNACK AISLE

At Dan's Supreme supermarket, picking out snacks before the three-hour drive upstate for the weeklong summer vacation with their father, thirteen-year-old Carl was looking at the potato chips when someone tapped him on the shoulder.

Expecting his father, he turned and instead saw a wrinkled, wild-haired old man who smelled of liquor and stale nicotine hovering over him.

"Hey, kid," the man said, speaking softly, leaning in, "you wanna go a couple of rounds?"

"What?"

"I'll make it worth your while. Five bucks. I'll take you to the employee john in the back."

"Uh, no thanks," Carl said, backing into the chips and knocking several bags of BBQ Lay's to the black linoleum floor tiles, but the man kept leaning in closer. "Ten bucks. I'll give you ten bucks."

Carl heard his father say "Hey!" just before seeing him pull the man by his shirt and shove him into the Jiffy-Pop shelves. His father then drew from ankle holster his U.S. Customs-issue Glock and pointed it two-handed at the trembling old man, ordering him through clenched teeth, "Leave now, and if I ever see you in this store again, I'll kill you."

The old man nodded and slithered away.

Since his parents' divorce, Carl had come to see his father as a weak and pathetic man, but, in this moment, of which there would never be another like it, he was looking at him as if at Clint Eastwood.

His father lifted his foot to one of the popcorn shelves and put the gun back in the holster.

"Better not mention this to your mother," he said, concealing the gun with his jeans cuff.

Carl nodded.

"Good," his father said. "Now let's go on vacation."

MAGGIE BENETTON

It started in seventh grade social studies class when Maggie Benetton asked Carl if he would let her copy his answers on a test, then culminated the following week in art when they had a substitute and there was an arm-wrestling tournament in which she was his opponent, her sweaty palm feeling like silk in his as they looked into each other's eyes from across the table and he saw her soul.

The other guys thought she was a plain-Jane, but her soft brown eyes were the most beautiful thing he'd ever seen and there would be no stopping the apocalypse that would give him feverish dreams from which he tried not to wake. He was far from having the nerve to ask her out and didn't know what it would mean if she actually said "yes". As far back as fifth grade he'd heard of classmates "going out", but the logistics of dating were a mystery beyond what he'd seen on TV and in movies, and he didn't want to get his mother involved driving them to the mall the way Daniel's mother did in *The Karate Kid*, Carl envisioning his own mother chain-smoking with the windows rolled up and asking Maggie annoying questions and telling embarrassing stories about him.

With his Bic Cristal pens, he started inking "I ♥ MB" all over the desktops of J. Lewis Ames Jr. High School and, with Sanford King Size Deluxe Marker, adorned the backsides of school bus seats. But asking her out seemed impossible, as it would have to be done at a rare moment when no one else was around. Already this school year a couple of guys had been shot down in flames and everyone heard about both and then no girls wanted anything to do with either of them. Maggie, though, seemed to like him, especially when there was a test coming up in social studies, and he didn't know of her liking someone else who wasn't a member of New Kids on the Block, and she didn't seem out of his league, so he thought he might have a chance, maybe.

The year rolled by seemingly faster than any previous school year since kindergarten. By Memorial day, with only a month left to ask her out before the long summer vacation, he was starting to panic. Then a plan began taking shape to ask her out on the last day, a half-day when there would be shortened periods and a lot of sitting around doing nothing. He'd heard numerous classmates say they weren't even going to bother showing up. At the end of social studies, he could catch her in the hallway and ask her quickly. If she rejected him, at least there wouldn't be too many people around to witness it and he wouldn't have to waste his summer longing for September.

While aware there would likely be a high rate of absenteeism on that last day, Carl hadn't considered the possibility that Maggie would be one of them, and the worst of all possible things happened—nothing.

* * *

The summer was long, hot, excruciating. Her phone number wasn't listed in the White Pages and calls to the operator produced only one other Benetton in the Greater Massapequas, an old woman who claimed no knowledge of anyone named "Maggie", and that her relations were all dead, and to please stop calling, young man.

For the first time in his life, Carl, who'd always hated school more than most, was looking forward to September.

* * *

In seventh grade she'd been in several of his classes, so there was reason to hope she would be in some of them in eighth grade as well, or even just one of the two lunch periods.

By the second lunch period of the first day, having not seen her all morning nor heard her name called during the takings of attendance, he began to panic. He kept looking around the cafeteria but didn't see her among the hundreds of faces. By seventh period English, he hadn't even seen her in the hallway and was worried that she may have moved away. By last period social studies, when she again didn't appear and her name was again not called, two months of anticipation crashed down upon him. He was exhausted. By now all he had to look forward to was playing video games on the Commodore 64 after finishing his paper route.

Then, after class, he saw her in the corridor at locker #324 with one of her friends, a scowling orange-haired girl named Shannon. The locker door was open and a fresh New Kids on the Block bumper sticker had been affixed to the inside. He'd been caught off guard and neither Maggie nor Shannon looked in his direction, so he didn't attempt to say hello.

Hope, though, had returned. He didn't play video games after his paper route.

* * *

Carl was afraid of Shannon, whose locker was only a few over from Maggie's, and they were always there at the same time talking to each other. Shannon didn't really know him and Maggie hadn't yet noticed him pass by, nor had she passed by his locker.

At the close of the first week, after spending the summer swearing it would not yet again be his fate, nothing happened.

* * *

The following Monday during math, he asked to go to the bathroom and passed locker #324 in the empty corridor. Earlier that morning on Z-100, he'd heard that New Kids on the Block were playing six concerts at Nassau Coliseum next month and tickets would go on sale Saturday morning.

He'd already been considering slipping her a note through the louvers on her locker door, but imagine her reaction if the note included a pair of New Kids tickets. Even Shannon would stop scowling for a moment and tell her she'd better not let this guy get away.

Unfortunately, getting the tickets and providing transportation to the Coliseum in Uniondale would both involve his mother.

"You have a girlfriend?" she asked, lighting a cigarette, sipping a mango-raspberry wine cooler.

"Uh, kind of. Not really. She's a girl I like."

"When can I meet her?"

"Uh, well, I was hoping you could give us a ride to the concert, so you can meet her then, maybe."

"What if she says 'no'?"

He shrugged. "I'll sell the tickets, I guess."

"How?"

"I don't know."

On Saturday morning, with his mother's MasterCard at the ready, Carl spent four hours redialing the Ticketron phone number before finally breaking through the busy signal and scoring a pair of tickets for the just-added eleventh show, two obstructed view seats in the second to last row at the back of the arena that, after taxes and fees, cost over fifty bucks, two weeks of paper route earnings.

* * *

The tickets arrived in the mail a few days later. In his room he began composing the note, at first penning a rambling history of his love for her that he quickly scrapped, then writing a simple note asking if she would go to the show with him and, below it, "YES" and "NO" checkboxes, followed by his name, phone number, and locker number. He then folded the note around the tickets and slid them into a letter-sized envelope on which he wrote "Maggie" and sealed it.

The next day during math class, envelope in back pocket of white Lee jeans, he asked to use the bathroom. Moments later, he was in the empty corridor in front of locker #324 sliding the envelope through one of the louvers and heard it land on a pile of papers on the top shelf.

At day's end, corridor crowded, he was sure that, in mere seconds, one way or another, something would finally happen.

But Maggie wasn't at her locker, nor was Shannon, and nothing happened.

* * *

The next morning, he opened his locker and there was no note from her. After every period he checked again, but still, nothing.

At day's end, Maggie was back at her locker and Shannon was there talking to her. He was looking at them as he approached and Shannon looked in his direction, then Maggie looked, but neither seemed to be looking directly at him, and it was only for a moment before they turned back to each other and resumed their conversation.

He'd not anticipated nonreaction. His distracted mind tripped up his feet and he nearly took an embarrassing spill, but he recovered his balance in the traffic flow, which, by then, had already swept him past her.

* * *

In the days that followed, nothing happened. No note, no phone calls, no looks in his direction. For all he knew, the envelope was buried unnoticed in her locker and wouldn't be found until June. Another note seemed laborious, as he would have to explain that he'd left a previous note and two New Kids on the Block tickets, and there was the chance that the new note would also get buried unread.

It seemed a hopeless mess. At this point she'd probably forgotten him, forgotten his allowing her to copy his answers, forgotten their moment in art, hands clasped, looking into each other's eyes. Maybe he should have endured the embarrassment of being beaten by a girl and let her win. Maybe it was only a meaningful moment for him and she felt nothing and had been using him the whole time.

By the end of the week, reality had sunk in. What never was would now never be. Not in this world was there another Maggie Benetton.

In the first game of his Friday afternoon bowling league, formerly the highlight of his week, he threw a 97, the first time he'd failed to break 100 since third grade. Also absent was his usual appetite for Twix bars, French fries, and vanilla egg creams. He spent the rest of the weekend devouring *Archie* comics and *Hardy Boys* books, spending Sunday afternoon reading mystery #78, *Cave-In,* instead of watching football.

Nothing proved a deep enough escape from the nothingness of the days ahead and the rest of his life.

* * *

Weeks went by. The New Kids played the first of what was now a nineteen-show stand at the Coliseum and their t-shirts started appearing everywhere at school, including on Maggie and Shannon after show number three. His mother had asked about Maggie a couple of weeks earlier and he said she already had tickets and that he'd sold his to one of her friends.

By the night of the eleventh show, which would have been *their show*, the ubiquity of New Kids shirts had rendered them hardly noticeable, and, now in the process of healing after the darkness, his eyes were again starting to wander in the direction of other girls who had no idea he was alive.

The next morning, a Friday, he felt a little better that the concert date was behind him. By now he figured envelope and tickets would be found during locker cleanout in June, and that he too would be absent on the last day, and that any embarrassing stories about what he'd done would be lost to the summer breeze.

He was proud to put this girl, who'd given him nothing but grief and heartache, in his rearview mirror and move on. There were so many girls in the corridors of J. Lewis Ames Jr. High, and he was now open to the possibility that, if not in these corridors, that somewhere out there was one better than Maggie. He'd emerged from the dark and was once again looking forward to a weekend of bowling, Twix bars, French fries, vanilla egg creams, and Sunday afternoon football.

Then something happened. A shock of orange hair at locker #324 and green eyes looking directly at him. Shannon said something to Maggie and she turned and they both looked right at him, then looked away and started laughing uncontrollably.

He could still hear them laughing long after he'd passed by. Fortunately, no one else seemed to know what they were laughing at, but that offered little solace.

On the bus there was an "I ♥ MB" on the back of the seat in front of him. He took out his Sanford King Size and X'd it out.

When he got home, he told his mother he didn't feel well and was going to skip bowling that afternoon. This was the first time he'd missed a league match since second grade when he had chicken pox.

Over the weekend, he didn't even feel like reading and lay in bed staring at the ceiling.

On Monday, Maggie and Shannon glanced at him, but didn't laugh and immediately looked away.

On Tuesday, they didn't look at all.

They never looked again.

Nothing else ever happened.

The Wrestler

Uniondale, NY, in a nondescript diner hidden within a weekend-empty industrial zone several blocks from the Nassau Veterans Memorial Coliseum, which would later be packed with over 15,000 World Wrestling Federation fans witnessing the first of the aftermath cards following *WrestleMania 3*, with a huge double main-event featuring the Hart Foundation defending their tag team title against the British Bulldogs, then, in a steel-cage match, the "Macho Man" Randy Savage trying to win back the Intercontinental belt from Ricky "The Dragon" Steamboat—

Carl and his younger brother followed their father into the diner, a large, high-ceilinged space that used to be part of a warehouse now painted Wonka white with red-padded booths, no music, the room very quiet, the only noise the gentle tinkle of silverware from a man and woman seated in a booth in the far corner, the man with long, wet, curly black hair and mirrored sunglasses, the woman with long blond hair and black leather jacket.

The waitress told their father to seat themselves anywhere and said she'd be right with them.

Their father chose a booth far from the man and woman.

The waitress came over with menus. Carl ordered the cheeseburger deluxe with double-mozzarella fries and a Coke.

His younger brother ordered chocolate chip pancakes with chocolate syrup and whipped cream, and, to drink, a hot chocolate topped with triple whipped cream. Their father ordered a "bottomless" cup of coffee, his usual cheapskate move to order no food for himself and pick at their meals. He did spring for the tickets, but they were in the second-to-last row at the very top of the arena.

The longhaired man at the other end of the restaurant slid out of the booth and headed towards the corridor where the restrooms were. He was much larger than he initially appeared, and very muscular, like a professional wrestler.

"I think that's Bret Hart," Carl said, quietly.

"Who?" his father asked, lighting a cigarette.

"Bret 'The Hitman' Hart. He's one of the tag team champs. They're on the card tonight."

His father turned around, then turned back when the man emerged from the corridor.

"It's definitely him," Carl said.

"You should go ask for his autograph."

"Nah. I don't really care about autographs."

"I want his autograph," Carl's brother said. Carl was fourteen, his brother nine.

"Do you want me to go ask for it?" their father asked.

"I'll go ask," Carl said.

"I want to go too," his brother said.

Their father equipped them with a PROPERTY OF U.S. CUSTOMS clic-stic pen and the Ticketron envelope, minus the tickets. The walk across the restaurant seemed eternal. About halfway, the Hitman, over the woman's shoulder, locked eyes with Carl's, warning him not to proceed any further, but Carl looked down and kept going, brother on his heels.

He didn't look up again until they were at the table. He saw the woman first looking at them with an expression of surprise, then looked at the Hitman. Undoubtedly it was him, and he didn't look happy.

"Are you Bret Hart?" Carl heard himself ask.

The Hitman's sunglasses stared him down. Carl's brother hid himself behind Carl. Time slowed. The wrestler was smirking slightly, making him even more terrifying. Perhaps, Carl thought, part of the act, and he would soon break into a smile and happily sign their envelope, especially since there was no one else here and he would not be mobbed.

"No," the man finally said, smirking a little wider.

"Oh," Carl said, turning around to his brother hiding behind him, then back to the table, only now the woman was looking at the man.

Carl turned and said, "Let's go," to his brother, and they started back. After a few steps, Carl stopped and turned around. The Hitman was still looking at them.

"You *are* Bret Hart, and you're a dick," Carl said, seeing the wrestler's eyes widen just before turning back around and hurrying his brother back to their own booth.

"What happened?" Carl's father asked.

"He said he wasn't Bret Hart," Carl said. "And I think we annoyed him. And here he comes."

Carl's father turned and watched the approach of the large, longhaired man in the black tank top and mirrored sunglasses. Carl peeked under the table to see if his father had his gun in the ankle holster. He did.

The wrestler was holding two of the diner's table placemats that had ads for other local businesses on them, each now covered with huge autographs signed in thick black marker, ***"Bret 'The Hitman' Hart, WWF"***.

"You got some balls, kid," said the Hitman to Carl, dropping the placemats on the table, then heading back to his own booth.

THE ENGLISH TEACHER

Carl would catch a whiff of perfume and cigarettes heading into his eighth-grade English classroom, where Ms. Orlando would be seated atop her desk at the front of the room, legs crossed, dark stockings, one of her high heels dangling playfully from her big toe, flipping through a stack of essays, licking her manicured fingertips every few pages. In her forties, with a shapely, petite figure, she had a taste for leather miniskirts, tight body dresses, smoking Parliaments in the teachers' lounge, and driving her red Corvette—a truly classy, sexy woman who knew what she was doing, unlike these silly junior high virgins with their perms, braces, and Benetton—

During class she would assign tasks to the boys she knew had boners under their desks—erasing the chalkboard, handing out papers, going to the A/V room to get the film projector—and whoever was first to be assigned a task, it would be his forever. Her favorite was T.J. Connelly, the class clown, who had the task of sliding under her desk like a mechanic to fix the bottom drawer that got stuck every day. She would sit in her chair while he worked below, which, to the rest of the class, looked as if she were merely sitting behind the desk, but T.J. always claimed she had her legs spread wide enough to tell what color panties she was wearing, and one day claimed she wasn't wearing any at all—

By November, most of the possible tasks had been assigned, but Carl, among Ms. Orlando's more fervent admirers, had not been chosen, until, finally, the Monday before Thanksgiving—

"Carl," she said, standing next to his desk. "Would you be able to stay after school for a few minutes? I have a special favor to ask of you."

"Sure," Carl said, sensing heads turning towards him—

Next period in social studies—

"You sly dog!" T.J. exclaimed, laughing almost maniacally. "She wants it, dude, she wants it!"

"She's not gonna let him do it," Emanuel said. "She can get arrested for that."

"Who's gonna tell?" T.J. said. "Dude, this is the chance of a lifetime! And even if he's right, you're not the one who's gonna get busted. Dude, I'd give a thousand bucks to be in your shoes right now!"

* * *

The corridor was quiet by the time he pushed his locker closed and headed towards Ms. Orlando's classroom, knowing he was going to miss the bus and have to catch the late one with the jocks and detentionites. As much as he'd fantasized of scenarios exactly like this, the realness of it terrified him, he who knew not how to kiss, unhook a bra, or smoke a cigarette afterwards. But he couldn't chicken out—T.J. had been right about this being the chance of a lifetime, and he knew he would regret it forever if he didn't go through with it—

She was waiting for him in a leather overcoat, giant European sunglasses, and an Yves Saint Laurent handbag hanging from her forearm, Carl able to see the pack of Parliaments inside. On the floor next to her desk was a large cardboard box full of green "Phonics" workbooks.

"Would you be a dear and follow me out to my car with that box?" she said. "That's why I wanted you, because I needed a big, strong man for this special favor."

"Sure," he said, throat dry, the word barely coming out.

The box wasn't heavy. She shut the classroom lights and he followed her down the empty corridor, her clacking high heels leading him out of the building to the Corvette parked in a far corner of the lot, apart from the sedans and minivans.

She unlocked the passenger door and opened it.

"Just put it on the seat, darling," she said.

He felt her watching as he gently placed the box on the leather upholstery. There was no back seat, and he wondered how he was going to fit—

"Thank you, love," she said, digging into her handbag for the cigarettes, "and be sure to do your reading tonight. I'll be asking questions in class tomorrow. Be ready, I may call on you... *Ciao!*"

Carl's erection remained firm after the Corvette had disappeared up the street. With aching balls and forty minutes until the late bus, he headed back into the building and up the stairs to the quiet of the second-floor boys' room, where he went into the clean stall and slid the latch shut—

SUMMER NIGHTS

Carl's mother lit her Kent Golden Light 100 cigarette and exhaled.

"You know that girl Nancy? The one you know from school and the Beach Club?"

"Yeah," Carl said. "What about her?"

"Well," she said, twisting off the cap of the Bartles & Jaymes mixed berry wine cooler, "I had lunch down at the Club today and her mother was there, and she told me that Nancy has a bit of a crush on you."

Carl rolled his eyes. Nancy was nice, he'd known her since fifth grade and she was one of the few classmates who was nice to him when he was the new kid, but she still dressed like a fifth grader and looked like one of the Ingalls girls from *Little House on the Prairie*, while most of the other eighth grade girls were trying to show their stuff, a few of them quite successfully.

"You don't like her?" his mother asked exhaling, sipping.

"She's nice, but she's not really my type."

"Why not?"

"I don't know," Carl said, annoyed.

"She was in the car with her mother the other day and they drove by when you were doing your paper route and she ducked down in the seat so you wouldn't see her."

This is the first Carl had ever heard of a girl ducking him for want. Until then, his low self-esteem had prevented him from imagining that any girl, even the least attractive, would actually want him, and that his physical appearance could cause things to happen inside the interesting parts of their bodies. This was Nancy, though, and he'd never hear the end of it from the guys at school if he even hinted at interest in a girl so far down the charts.

"Yeah, well, too bad for her because it isn't going to happen," Carl said, deliberately cold, fending off his mother from interfering in his love life, seeing the nods of approval in his head from his friends, who were ready to resume gawking at the girls with the big boobs and tight neon spandex, especially those rumored to "put out".

* * *

Six months later, in the height of the eighth-grade yearbook signing season at J. Lewis Ames Jr. High School—

She showed up Monday morning donning her new look—hair, clothes, makeup, the works—and, before the fifteen-minute homeroom period was over, Nancy was the talk of the school. Even the crudest of Carl's pal's, Ryan H, vaulted her into his top five "hottest chicks" in school, "maybe even top three material", comparing her transformation to Sandra Dee's at the end of *Grease*, which they'd all seen three dozen times in Mr. C's music class, while the established "hot" eighth grade girls fumed, saying things such as, "Like, who the fuck does she think she is?" and "Like, she'd better not be walking around the mall by herself when I'm around."

Carl, meanwhile, was spinning. This girl liked him. At least she used to. Maybe she still did. But there seemed no possibility of a girl this hot liking him. She'd rocketed right past him on the social ladder into the rarefied air of the cool kids, where she'd have the attention of the few guys their own age who actually knew what to do around girls.

* * *

She hadn't been in any of his classes that year, but the eighth graders all had the same lunch period, and she sat at the far end of the room with some other girls Carl didn't know. It would be ballsy to approach one of the hottest girls in school and ask her to sign his yearbook while the entire eighth grade looked on, but he was banking on the kindness she had previously showed him, a kindness that would overlook his own previous apathy towards her and the shallowness of wanting to be her friend now that she was "hot".

As he calmly made his way across the cafeteria, Carl could peripherally see heads turning towards him, including the one belonging to Mr. Gambaro, the health teacher/failed NFL quarterback/fifth period lunch monitor who notoriously flirted with his female students and was rumored to have slept with over 10,000 women and most of the female faculty and attendance officers. Then Nancy noticed his approach, and the other girls at her table stared in anticipation of a nobody loser making an ass of himself in front of the entire grade.

She looked so different and hot, but she smiled at him with the old friendly smile from fifth grade. When he asked if she would sign his yearbook, she said, "Sure!" in her old friendly Nancy way, then handed him her yearbook for him to sign.

He would spend the entirety of that evening and the next several evenings staring at what she had written very large inside the back cover with her cute chick handwriting:

Carl,
Hey Dude –
Good luck like next year & stuff!
Have a mint *summer.*
I'll see you at the Beach Club this year.
Later,
Nancy

* * *

Since his family had moved to Massapequa and settled into the muck of South Shore Bourgeois, Carl had avoided going to "The Club", as his mother and stepfather referred to it, somehow without even a hint of self-consciousness. This was the legendary Biltmore Beach Club, which Neil Diamond belonged to for a season during the late '60s before he was famous, and a favorite local hangout of suburban mafia sub-bosses who once had the pull to book acts lingering on the outer fringes of the Rat Pack. Carl had wanted nothing to do with this place or the quasi-rich douchebags who hung out here every weekend drinking wine coolers on the beach and gossiping about each other, swearing repeatedly that he'd never become one of "them".

But all that fell away at the prospect of seeing Nancy in a bathing suit. He couldn't go to the Club during the day because he worked in the mess hall of the Merrick Woods Country Day Camp, so, after dinner, he'd put on his red Hawaiian-flowered Ocean Pacific bathing suit and ride his bike down there. She was never there in the evening, though, and he'd take a few dives off the board before heading back home for a night of floppy disk video games on the Commodore 64, *Strip Poker* and *Ultima IV: Quest for the Avatar*, capped off with some tissues and a rerun of "Electric Blue" on *The Playboy Channel* he was able to unscramble with his illegal black market cable box.

* * *

Hater of fireworks, avoider of Independence Day tomfoolery, Carl knew she would be there on the night of the 4th, the big night of the year at the Club when they hired members from the outer limbs of the Grucci family tree to put on their annual "BBC Fireworks Spectacular", the little private beach on the Great South Bay crowded with *ooh*ers and *ahh*ers and the diving board line long with teenagers, including, on this warm Fourth of July, Nancy in a yellow bikini.

Bikini.

Carl was at the end of the line and she was on the board when she noticed him.

"Hi, Carl!" she waved, then dove gracefully into the chlorinated teal, now lit with underwater lights as the last of the daylight faded into crystal-clear night, much murmur amongst the older folk of it being a "perfect" night for fireworks.

Attempting to avoid embarrassment, Carl got off the line and jumped into the regular swimming section and waited to recede, then climbed the ladder and rejoined the diving board line behind Nancy.

"It's funny that I've never seen you here," she said. "I'm here all the time."

"Yeah, well. I've been busy."

"What are you doing this summer?"

She was still so nice, sweet Nancy Ingalls, but oh so hot, budding breasts in yellow bikini top, wet hair, looking like she just stepped out of a David Lee Roth video.

"Well, besides working at the camp, I don't know, really. I was kind of hoping to hang out with you, maybe. On the weekend. If you want. If you're not busy."

She was smiling but didn't say anything. Then he heard

some guy behind him say, "Hey, what the fuck, dude?"

Carl didn't realize the guy was talking to him until he was poked on the shoulder. He turned to see a very large, very muscular, very Coppertoned older-looking guy in a shiny black Speedo and thick gold chain around his neck, pool wet hair slicked back like a 1980s movie asshole.

"I'm talkin' to you, dude. You tryin' to make a move on my girl?"

"He's an old friend and he didn't know about you, Frankie," Nancy said, then turned to Carl. "Carl, this is my boyfriend, Frankie."

"Sorry, Frankie, I didn't know," Carl said, extending his hand, but Frankie didn't offer his and still appeared to be contemplating some form of physical violence. Eventually he backed off but never offered his hand, and, pointing very seriously, warned Carl to "Stay away from my girl, dude."

Nancy looked like she wanted to say something, but Carl didn't give her a chance, leaving the line and steaming towards the entrance gate against the tide of families heading in, not bothering to go back for the towel or Reeboks he'd left behind.

Just beyond the gate, where they were making sure only Club members and their registered guests passed through, Carl exclaimed, "Fuck this place!"

Several people turned their heads and, frowning, watched the angst-ridden, bare-footed, shirtless teenager unlock his bike from the Club rack for the last time and ride away forever.

SHOWDOWN AT THE OLD SAM

He looked in the glass door. His father was at the bar talking to a woman seated next to him. They were the only customers. There was a guy on the dance floor with an amplified acoustic guitar singing "Up Where We Belong". The bartender was wearing a leather vest over a white dress shirt and a bolo tie.

The top glass panel of the door had the Old Sam Dude Ranch logo stickered to it, and, underneath, in a Western font, "SALOON". He pulled it open and went inside.

The woman saw him first, then his father turned around. They both had cigarettes burning in the ashtray.

"Terri," his father said, "this is my oldest son, Carl."

"Nice to meet you, Carl," she said. "You didn't tell me your son was so handsome."

Not acknowledging the woman, Carl asked his father, "Do you know that your other two kids are back in the room crying their eyes out?"

"They are? Why?"

"Because you left them alone. I just got back from the arcade and found them crying."

"They're fine. The door is locked and this is a safe place. They're right down the hall."

"They're not fine. They're crying because they're scared

and said you wouldn't come back to the room."

"Hey, whoa, this is my vacation too. I work pretty damn hard and spend a lot of money to take you kids here every year, and I deserve a chance to relax too."

"Maybe you should go check on them," Terri said to Carl's father.

"No. My son will go check on them, and then he'll come back and let me know how they are."

"No," Carl said. "*You* go check on them."

The guitarist hit a bad chord and stopped playing. The bartender slowed his wiping of a glass.

"It's getting late," Terri said, stamping out her cigarette. She opened her purse and took out some cash. "This should cover the drinks."

"No," his father said to her. "You stay right here. My son is going back to the room."

The guitarist started packing his gear. The bartender stopped wiping.

"It was nice meeting you," she said, then hurried out the door.

His father finished his cigarette.

Carl made a fist of his right hand.

"Go back to the room and stay there," his father finally said, then turned to the bartender and ordered a Bud and a shot of Jack.

Carl waited a beat, then turned and left.

The lodge's main lobby was warmer, but he felt cold after having his sweat chilled by the saloon's air conditioning. Down their wing to the room, he found his brother and sister watching *Miami Vice*, their eyes turning to him as soon as he came in.

"Where's Daddy?" his brother asked.

"He's at the bar," Carl said. "Don't worry about it, everything's fine. I'm here now and I'll stay with you guys. Do you wanna call Mommy?"

Both nodded.

There was a bank of pay phones across the lobby. He led them as far as he could from the saloon. Their father was still sitting in there.

He pressed the "0" button and told the operator he needed to make a collect call and gave her their number. A minute later his mother was on the phone.

"Oh God," she said after he'd explained. "Alright. Just try to go to sleep. He won't hurt you. You guys are coming home tomorrow anyway."

"Can you come get us?"

"No, legally I can't do that. Just put the other kids on the phone and I'll try to calm them down."

She spoke to both of them and afterwards they were calmer, then he got back on with his mother.

"Call me back right away if he does anything," she said.

Passing back through the lobby, Carl saw that their father was no longer at the bar. Several doors down from their room, he stopped his brother and sister.

"I'll do all the talking, and don't be scared," he said. "Even if he's mad, don't worry about it. Everything will be fine. Just try to go to sleep, and then we'll go home tomorrow."

He pushed open the door.

"Where were you?" his father asked, smoking a cigarette in the dark, his voice deep.

"We just went to the phone and called home."

"Why?"

"Because they wanted to say goodnight to Mom."

Their father took a long drag and exhaled.

"How hard I work for you kids," he said, "and how much money I spend on these vacations, and you can't even give me a goddamn break and let me relax for a few minutes."

He went into the bathroom and slammed the door.

Carl turned to his brother and sister, both on the verge of tears.

"Don't worry about it," he whispered. "Just try to be quiet and go to sleep. We're going home tomorrow."

YELLOW

In the southwest corner of the cafeteria at the Alfred G. Berner Ninth Grade School, Carl, sitting across from Eric, dumped the contents of his brown paper bag onto the table, and, as usual, pushed aside the little red box of Sun Maid raisins—

"Why does your mother even pack those if you never eat them?" Eric asked.

"Sometimes I do."

"I've never seen you."

"Do you want them?"

"No."

"Then what do you care?"

"You should throw one at Mark."

Mark sat three tables away. At some point in the distant past, before Carl moved to Massapequa, Eric used to be friends with Mark, but they had some sort of falling out. Mark was in all the smart classes with Eric.

"Why don't you do it?" Carl asked. "He's your friend."

"I have terrible aim. Didn't you used to play baseball or something? You should throw it."

"I don't want to."

"Why? Are you afraid of Mark?"

"No."

"Are you yellow?"

"*Yellow?*"

"Cowardly."

"Are you going to call me 'chicken' next?"

"Your tail, sir, is between your legs."

"Yeah, okay."

"Chicken."

"Fine."

Carl opened the box. Most of the raisins were clumped together, but he shook a couple loose. His first attempt missed badly. His second landed on the table in front of Mark, who looked up and saw Carl and Eric laughing, and gave them back a *ha-ha, very funny* look.

"You still didn't hit him," Eric said.

Carl shook out another raisin and tossed it. The shriveled grape arced high over the two tables between them and Mark, on a trajectory that would take it through the fingernail-sized space between Mark's eyebrow and the top of his glasses frames. As if it had been a hornet and not a Sun Maid that had flown into his eye, he leapt from his seat yelling, "Shit! Motherfucker!", knocking his chair backwards, which landed hard and caught the attention of Mr. Gambaro, the health teacher and former sixth-string backup quarterback of the 1976 Tampa Bay Buccaneers team that went 0-14, who was in charge of the cafeteria during the first lunch period.

A hush fell over the room as Mark put his glasses back on, then steamed towards Carl and Eric's table. Hovering over Carl, he said, "Excuse me, sir, would you care to step outside?"

Eric laughed.

"We're not allowed to step outside for another ten minutes," Carl said.

"Then let's go. Right here. I call you out."

The room gasped.

"Settle down, tough guy," Carl said, hoping Mr. Gambaro would be there any second to put a stop to this, but the failed

QB had been bred in the old school, on the fringes of the National Football League, and down at the marina running errands for Johnnie "Meatball" Panini, so he was willing to allow a quick scrap to get it out of their systems—

"Right now, unless you're yellow."

"That's it," Carl said, pounding his fist on the table and rising swiftly from his seat, prompting a cheer from the cafeteria. He turned to acknowledge the crowd, leaving himself open to be blindsided by a right hook to the side of his jaw. It wasn't a hard punch and Carl shook it off, then cocked his powerful right arm, which had won him two-dozen bowling trophies going back to first grade, and was about to go Bo Burton on his teeth when Mr. Gambaro grabbed his arm from behind—

"Rocky, Drago, fight's over," he said. "Both of you, to the Main Office."

Each received in-school suspensions. Letters signed by the principal were mailed to both households. Carl had his Commodore 64 and television removed from his room for a month. Both served their suspensions in the Attendance Office, with two desks brought in from the study hall/detention room and placed on either side of a tall file cabinet used by the Attendance Officer, Mrs. Lipfvschitz. Their teachers had given them assignments to complete during the day and both worked quietly, seeing only each other's feet.

When Mrs. Lipfvschitz finally stepped away for a moment, Carl could bear the silence no longer—

"Sorry about this," he said.

"You are a loser," Mark said, "and a loser you shall remain for as long as you are friends with Eric."

CANDY'S ROOM

It was less than a ten minute walk from her house on First Avenue to the Massapequa Park train station, yet Candy, to avoid the ridicule she received from neighbors whenever she stepped out of the house, normally called a cab.

But going to the city was expensive and she was tired of wasting what little money she had on their insecurities, as if she were a sign of the coming apocalypse that would destroy their malls and beach clubs. So today, at her bedroom mirror doing her hair and makeup, she decided she was going to walk.

She put on the red dress, the skimpy one that showed more leg and shoulder than even a "regular" girl would be comfortable showing. She chose her brightest shade of red lipstick and went heavy on the eye shadow. With the Aqua Net she teased her curls as high as they would go. She wore her highest black heels.

"You're not calling a taxi?" her mother asked, "especially dressed like, like… *that*?"

"No, mother," Candy said. "I'd tell the neighbors to go to hell, but they're already there."

Purse in hand, she clacked out the door. On the front walk, she encountered the next-door neighbor mowing his lawn, the man who usually said, *Put on some trousers, sissy!* He cut the engine of his Lawn Boy and opened his mouth, but remained silent when she looked him in the eye instead of down at the concrete.

Up the block, she encountered a trio of teenage boys approaching on the sidewalk who bore a resemblance to the ones who'd tried to lynch her in high school. They pointed and laughed when they noticed her. Normally, she would have crossed the street to avoid them, but today she steamed forward. They quieted at her approach, then dove out of her way when she didn't break stride.

She stopped and watched them inspect the grass stains on their slacks.

"Looks like I got a strike," she said, then pouted them a kiss and continued on.

The train was crowded, but there were a few empty seats next to people traveling alone. As she walked down the car, people started shifting over to the aisle seat to block her from sitting. Several ladies put their purses on the empty seat. It was difficult keeping balance in the heels when the train started moving, and she nearly fell a couple of times.

Finally, an elderly woman wearing Coke bottle glasses looked up at her and said, "You can sit here, miss."

Candy accepted the invitation.

The people seated behind them got up and moved to the next car. Others followed. Soon the car was empty, save she and the elderly woman.

As the train slowed at the Freeport station, she saw her friend Lou waiting out on the platform. She got up and hurried to the open door, sticking her head out, calling his name, waving.

MOJITO NIGHTS

Lunch tray in hand, topped with fish & chips, raspberry cobbler surprise, peas, and two little cartons of chocolate milk, Brett, the new kid at the Alfred G. Berner Ninth Grade School in Massapequa, looking a tad too old to be in ninth grade, wandered the cafeteria trying to find a place to sit, but, wherever he went, he was getting dirty looks from most of the guys because they thought he was a narc, while many of the girls were gushing and giggling because he bore a slight resemblance to network television star Kirk Cameron from the hit ABC comedy *Growing Pains*. Eventually, he found himself in the southwest corner of the cafeteria, where the losers were clustered, and spied two empty seats—

Carl and Eric sat directly across from one another at the end of their table, each with a coveted empty seat beside them. They had been laughing and making fun of the new guy having difficulty finding a place to sit, until he started getting closer, then looked in their direction and headed over—

"Do you mind if I sit?" he asked, smiling, looking back-and-forth—

"Sure, have a seat right there," Carl said, pointing to the vacant seat next to Eric, prompting an angry glance—

"Thanks, dude! I'm Brett, by the way."

Neither Carl nor Eric replied.

"And what are your guys' names?"

"He's Eric."

"He's Dickwad."

"Carl."

"So, Eric and—Carl—what are you guys into?"

Before they could answer, two hot girls, who, normally, would not be within 100 feet of this corner of the cafeteria, approached Brett in his seat and took turns whispering in his ear, each handing him a loose-leaf note folded into a puffy perfumed triangle—

"What did they say?" Eric asked.

"The first one said she wanted to give me a blow job," Brett said. "That's actually what the second one said too." He unfolded the first triangle to see the girly handwriting, "Jennifer", with a phone number beneath, then dropped it on the table for Carl and Eric to see. He then unfolded the second note to reveal another "Jennifer" and her phone number, this one dotting the "i" with a little heart—

"Do you guys like to ski?" Brett asked.

"Do you mean like snorting cocaine?" Carl asked.

"No, like snow skiing, in the mountains, with skis and poles. I was up in Killington a few months ago, took a bus up there with a couple of my buddies. On the way home I was asleep in the very back of the bus, you know, where there are three seats in a row, and I don't know how long I was out, but when I woke up, some chick had pulled down my pants and was blowing me. It was great."

* * *

Later, on the school bus—

"He's full of shit," Eric said to Carl. "If he's lying there sideways, is she also sideways on the seats with him? Or is she kneeling in front of him on the floor? Which would mean she was blowing him sideways—"

"A Blow Pop?"

"What?"

"I liked the story."

"Do you believe him?"

"Maybe. You saw those two girls—"

"Maybe it was staged. Have you ever seen those girls before today?"

"Yes."

"Oh."

"But it wasn't just them. They all wanted him."

* * *

During Brett's second day at the lunch table, he said to Carl and Eric, "Dudes, we should hang out at my pad on Friday night. I'll invite a few loose chicks that I know, we'll down some mojitos, we'll have a little orgy—it'll be great! Bring plenty of your favorite condoms."

* * *

On Friday night, they rode their high-performance 12-speed racing bicycles three miles to Brett's apartment near Jerusalem Avenue in North Massapequa, an area known to people in South Massapequa to be rife with drugs, prostitution, and other fare. On the way, they stopped at the Genovese drug store to buy condoms—Eric buying a 12-pack of Trojan lubricated-ribbed, while Carl opted for the Trojan regular lubricated in the apricot-colored packaging, and they split the cost of a travel-sized tub of Vaseline—a tip from Eric's older brother, who attended Brown University, that the lube on a condom is never enough, even the ones that advertise "extra lubrication", so you should always have a tub of "Vaz" within reach—

"I hope they don't smoke," Eric said over the Friday evening traffic as they waited to cross over six lanes of Sunrise Highway to the North, straddling their bikes, Eric on his Peugeot PZ10, Carl on his Centurion Accordo that Eric had recently talked him into spending $400 on, with the ultra-thin tires that got flats every other day—

"Loose chicks usually smoke."

"Not always."

"I hope they do, like Ms. Orlando," Carl said, referencing his eighth-grade English teacher, who smoked Parliaments in the teachers' lounge and had a taste for high-heels and leather miniskirts, and was still a regular in his fantasies.

They arrived fifteen minutes early. The building was a small two-story that looked like a motel, with apartment doors and an outdoor walkway. Brett's apartment was on the second floor. They heard women talking and laughing inside. Brett answered wearing a black silk robe with a little white *Playboy* logo on the breast pocket, holding a mojito—

"Boys!" he said. "Come on in, the party's just getting started."

There were three hot blondes in tight body-dresses and high-heels, definitely not ninth grade or even high school girls, all with leafy mojitos in hand, smoking Marlboro Lights—

"Mojito, boys?" Brett asked. "I pressed some cocaine into the leaves. You guys like to ski, right?"

"Sure!" Carl said, prompting a sharp, concerned look from Eric—

"Great!" Brett said. "Why don't you guys have a seat, I'll bring them right over."

Carl and Eric sat on the couch and watched one of the blondes break free of the pack and approach Brett in the kitchen, then, without a word, sink to her knees, untie his robe, and start blowing him—

"This is the life, eh, boys?" Brett said with a big smile. Then, to the other two blondes, gesturing with his head towards Carl and Eric, "Come on, ladies, jump on in, the water's great!"

The blondes looked at each other and shrugged, then went over to the couch—

"Brett said you guys like to party," one of them said.

"Yeah," Carl said. "We party."

"Cool," said the other one. "I have an idea—why don't you guys stand up and show us how much you like to party—"

Carl and Eric exchanged glances, then rose slowly from the couch—

"You guys look ready," the first blonde said. "Why don't you take your clothes off, then we'll suck your cocks."

"We're really good at it, you know."

"We're the best at it."

Moments later, without having ample opportunity to summon full erections, Carl and Eric stood before the women, who tried to hold in their laughter, but couldn't for more than a few seconds, bursting into a fit so intense they could hardly breathe, until one of them managed to say, "They're so small!", which made them laugh even harder, prompting the woman working on Brett to stop and look, and she too started laughing, and even Brett had to look away to conceal his amusement. Then the doorbell rang—

Carl and Eric's blondes hurried to the door—

"Hey, it's Curt and Eddie from *L.I. 69*!" one of them exclaimed, *L.I. 69 Studios* being Long Island's most prolific adult film studio, cranking out an average of six features per day. Then both blondes started waving imaginary pom-poms and doing a "*Curt-and-Ed-die!*" cheer—

"Boys! What are you doing here?" Brett exclaimed. The

men appeared to be in their late twenties or early thirties, clad in tight polyester button-down prints and khaki slacks, both with muscular physiques and full-on pornstaches—

"Hey, check out their tiny peckers," Eddie laughed.

"Look, they're getting even smaller," Curt said.

Over near the couch, Eric said quietly to Carl, "I know those guys."

"What?"

"They're in a bunch of my father's porno tapes. They have really big dicks."

One of the blondes looked at Brett and whined, "Can we ditch these losers so we can start having some *real* fun with Curt and Eddie?"

Brett, smiling, looked at Carl and Eric and shrugged—

"Sorry, fellas!" he said.

Carl and Eric pulled up their pants, then Brett escorted them to the door and said, "We'll do it again next Friday night. I'll invite some different chicks, more your type. Adios!"

Just after the door had closed, they heard one of the women inside laugh and ask Brett, "Where did you find those losers?"

Carl wondered what he'd meant by "*more your type*"—

* * *

Brett wasn't at the lunch table on Monday. Carl and Eric feared the worst. He wasn't at school on Tuesday either, or the rest of the week.

* * *

On Friday night, backpack stocked with condoms, Vaseline, and a half-full bottle of banana brandy that Eric had swiped from his parents' liquor cabinet, they rode back up to Brett's apartment.

The lights were out. Eric rang the bell, but all was quiet inside. He rang it again and again until one of the windows belonging to the apartment next door slid open and an old lady in hair curlers stuck her head out—

"He's gone," she said. "Moved out Monday past, the no-good, god-damn playboy."

* * *

Six months later—

"What's wrong with you?" Carl asked Eric, never before having seen him so rattled—

"We're in a porno."

"What?"

"At Brett's apartment, the whole thing was filmed. I was going through my father's tapes last night, and there was a new one called *Mojito Nights*—"

"Do you know if he watched it?"

"Yeah, when I put it in, it was up to the part where I said I recognized those guys from one of my father's pornos. But my father probably didn't recognize us."

"He didn't recognize *you*?"

"He hasn't looked at me since I was in kindergarten."

DON'T LOOK AND WALK FASTER.

At the Molly Pitcher service area on the New Jersey Turnpike, late July, as Carl and his younger brother and sister followed their father from the far end of the parking lot towards the building, a woman in the next aisle began screaming that her finger was caught in the car door as her young children looked on helplessly.

Ignoring the woman, their father told them, "Don't look and walk faster."

There was no one else around and the building looked distant through the blur of heat foiling up from the asphalt.

Their father was walking faster and pulling ahead.

"Mister, please help me!" the woman cried.

They were now past her and could not see her without turning around. Their father slowed to allow them to catch up but didn't stop.

"Someone will help her," he said. "They have police and security all over this place. Now, come on, let's get inside."

The blast of air conditioning when they entered gave them a chill. The bathrooms and food court were crowded. Nearby, a janitor was sweeping next to an overfull trash receptacle.

"Stay here," their father said.

They watched him go over to the janitor and start talking

to him. He was an older man and he had to lean in to hear what was being said. The man finally nodded, then resumed sweeping as their father came back.

"I told him about the woman in the parking lot and he said he would let someone know," he explained. "Now, who needs to use the bathroom?"

They used the bathrooms, then went to McDonald's.

The kids picked at their food and sipped their orange drinks, all three staring out the window at the hundreds of cars in the lot and the passing vehicles on the Turnpike.

"Alright, what's wrong?" their father finally asked, eating fries from the two younger kids' trays, as usual, too cheap to order food for himself, only coffee.

Nobody answered.

"Is it about that lady in the parking lot?" he asked, continuing to help himself to the fries, then tearing off a hunk of his youngest son's hamburger. "Because if it is, there's nothing to worry about. Someone will have helped her by now."

"How do you know?" Carl asked.

"Well, I did tell someone who works here, and look at all the people in this place. I'm sure someone was there within seconds, and she's probably already been treated at the First Aid station and is back on the road."

Carl looked out the window. There were people going in and out of the building, but none looking around as if hearing screams for help.

After their father finished their food and smoked a cigarette, they headed back out to the parking lot. There were no cries or screams, no ambulance or police, only oppressive heat and the whir of traffic. The kids looked around in vain for signs of what had happened earlier as they followed their father back to the Datsun, inside of which they would have to continue down to Washington DC and spend the next week "on vacation" with him until the following Saturday at 5:00 pm, when they would finally be released back into their mother's custody.

UNGRATEFUL LITTLE BASTARDS

At the Smithsonian National Air and Space Museum in Washington DC, *The Spirit of St. Louis* hovering above them—

"Can we go now?" Carl Jr., age fifteen, asked his father.

"Go? We haven't been here fifteen minutes. Don't you want to see the Batmobile?"

"No, we wanted to go to Great Adventure, not run around a bunch of free museums and stay at a motel with no pool and bullet holes in the wall and a broken ice machine."

It was the one week every summer when Carl Sr. was mandated by the divorce court to spend a week with his three biological children, whom he'd spent years and tens of thousands of dollars attempting to legally disown.

"We can't spend the whole week at Great Adventure," Carl Sr. said.

"We can also go to Action Park and Hersheypark."

"Do you know how expensive that would be? And you should really get a haircut. You look like a hoodlum."

"I don't think so, guy," said Carl Jr., touching the long part of his mullet, shoulder-length in the back. "Maybe you should talk to Sy Sperling about joining the Hair Club for Men."

"You don't think it's disrespectful to speak to your father that way? My father would have beaten me to a pulp if I ever spoke to him like that."

"He must have been a lovely man. But you disrespected me first. And who are you to comment on my appearance, anyway?"

"I am your father."

"Yeah, some father. I think I'd be better off with Darth Vader as my father, at least he wasn't a cheapskate."

Carl Sr.'s face reddened and he started breathing heavily.

Carl Jr. clenched his fists, then watched his father drop to his knees, crumple into a heap, bury his head in his arms, and sob repeatedly, "I miss my Daddy!"

People started backing away, including Carl Jr. and his siblings, who sidled themselves next to another family.

A security guard hurried over and said into his walkie-talkie, "We have a weeper under the *Spirit of St. Louis*."

Moments later, a dozen armed security guards hurried over and escorted Carl Sr. out of the building, his children watching with their borrowed family, whom they then followed to several other exhibits, including the 1903 Wright Flyer, the Apollo 11 command module, the Batmobile, and Archie Bunker's chair.

* * *

An hour later, on the National Mall—

"Fine," Carl Sr. said. "We'll go to Great Adventure. I only paid for one night at the hotel anyway. We can head up to the Jersey Shore, then zip over to Great Adventure in the morning. I was thinking it might be nice to take a dip in the ocean. I've always wanted to go swimming at the Jersey Shore."

"Didn't you grow up on Long Island?" Carl Jr. asked.

"Yeah. Why?"

"It's the same ocean."

"Yeah, but this is the world-famous Jersey Shore."

"I could see, like, if you were in California and you wanted to take a dip in the Pacific, or if you were in Italy and wanted to take a dip in the Mediterranean, but, if you've been to Jones Beach or Coney Island, it's, like, exactly the same thing all the way down to Florida."

"Well," said Carl Sr., lighting a Viceroy 100, "you'll just have to see for yourself."

* * *

An hour later, the mood in the Datsun cabin improved slightly upon exiting the Beltway and continuing north on I-95 into Maryland, leaving DC behind and heading towards the promise of a better time in the Garden State. There was talk of pizza for dinner as they turned east on I-195 towards Asbury Park, where they checked into another dumpy motel, this one half-mile from the beach but with a clean-looking pool, a Coca-Cola machine, and a functioning ice machine.

"So, who's up for a dip in the Atlantic?" Carl Sr. asked.

"I'd rather just go in the pool," said Carl Jr.

"Yeah, I'd rather go in the pool too," said his sister.

"I don't like the beach," said their brother.

"We're going to the beach," their father responded.

They walked the half-mile past the vacant motels and swam in the Atlantic, then ate at one of the pizza joints on the boardwalk. On the way back to the motel, they stopped at a 7-Eleven, where Carl Sr. let the kids pick out one thing while he purchased two six-packs of Budweiser tallboys and three packs of Viceroy 100s. Back at the motel, he settled into a lounge chair beside the pool while the kids played in the water until dark, then, in the room, they watched the end of a Met game and a rerun of *The Honeymooners* before switching out the light for the night.

* * *

The next morning, without having to make the two-hour drive from Long Island, they arrived at Six Flags Great Adventure right when it opened and the park was still relatively empty, allowing them to go on all the good rides multiple times within two hours.

"Can we go now?" Carl Jr. asked his father.

"What?"

"We've been on all the good rides already, and now the lines are getting long."

Carl Sr.'s face reddened and he started breathing heavily.

"Ungrateful little bastards," he said under his breath.

"Excuse me?" Carl Jr. asked.

"You heard me. I work so hard to pay for all this shit, and all you goddamn kids ever do is complain. You're all just like your whore of a mother."

"Fuck you," Carl Jr. said.

Carl Sr. looked his son in the eye, then backed away and started jogging towards a bank of phone booths, one of which he entered and slid the folding doors shut.

"I miss my Daddy!" he cried into the phone.

A recorded voice instructed him to insert coins and dial or hang up. The now-buzzing receiver fell from his grip and dangled by its metal cord as he slumped to the floor, where he remained sobbing for the next two hours while his kids did another round of rides until they got hungry and came back asking for money.

* * *

The following day, at the Rath Park public swimming pool in Franklin Square, Long Island—

"We're bored," Carl Jr. proclaimed.

"Well, we have four days left, and this is it."

"Can we go to Hersheypark?"

Carl Sr. started to convulse. His kids backed away towards the pool. He'd barely gotten out "I miss my Daddy!" before the white-nosed lifeguards started blowing their whistles and hurried over to the sobbing man. Eventually, the head lifeguard and several of his largest male crew members escorted him to the turnstiles, still sobbing, wearing only his bathing suit, not yet realizing he'd left his clothes, wallet, car keys, and cigarettes behind. Just outside the facility, a Nassau County police cruiser pulled up, its uniformed driver watching through the open window.

After their father was gone, Carl Jr. retrieved his father's wallet, then led his brother and sister to the snack bar, where they ordered all the Good Humor ice cream products they'd always wanted to try, several pounds of candy, French fries, pizza, Coca-Colas, and milkshakes. When there was only a dollar left, Carl Jr. exchanged it for quarters and called their mother from a pay phone.

"He's doing the crying thing again and just got kicked out of Rath Park," Carl Jr. reported. "He left his wallet behind, so we got some food at the snack bar, but now we just want to go home."

After an exasperated sigh, she said, "Okay, I'll be there in half-hour. Just stay inside the pool area."

Beyond the iron bars they could see their father sitting under a tree smoking a cigarette he'd bummed from a passerby, but they ignored him and went back in the pool without waiting the full hour for the food to digest until their mother's white Mercedes pulled up behind the police car.

"Mom's here," Carl Jr. announced.

They got out of the pool and quickly dried off, Carl Jr. dropping the wallet next to the keys and cigarettes, then they all headed for the exit, leaving the towels and the rest of their father's possessions behind.

Their father looked up when they drove by his tree, but their mother kept going and told them not to worry about him or the clothes they had packed for the week, she would buy them new ones, then congratulated them on lasting a day longer than they had the year before.

A MOMENTARY LAPSE OF REASON

"So, let me get this straight," said Carl's mother, raspy voice, seated at the kitchen table, bags under her eyes, wearing an uncomfortably short pink silk robe, lighting a Kent cigarette, sipping a Bartles & Jaymes peach-raspberry wine cooler. "I'm supposed to pick up two fifteen-year-old boys on Hempstead Turnpike in Uniondale at eleven o'clock at night—"

"Eleven-thirtyish, maybe midnight," Carl said.

"After seeing this 'Pink Floyd'—"

"They're from your generation—"

"I'll have to think about it," she said, exhaling, sipping—

"No! It will sell out! We have to call Ticketron *now*!"

"Maybe I should ask Rick—"

"Ask Rick what?" asked Rick—Carl's stepfather, "The Dick"—materializing from behind the short hallway leading from their first-floor bedroom suite, empty rock glass in hand, freshly lit Kent dangling beneath his Burt Reynolds mustache, wearing only a pair of tight white terry cloth shorts, headed towards the cabinet for a refill of Johnnie Walker Red—

"He wants to see this Pink Floyd concert at Nassau Coliseum."

"Pink Floyd? Never heard of him."

Rick listened to country music, his favorites being Kenny Rogers, the Oak Ridge Boys, and Eddie Rabbitt "The Brooklyn

Cowboy", and his all-time favorite song was Shelly West's "Jose Cuervo", a ditty about getting drunk, kissing cowboys, and shooting out lights, which he would sing along to and think he was being funny—

"As long as he's paying for it, then it's fine with me," he said, pouring his Scotch.

"That's it?"

"Yep. As long as he's paying for it."

"I am," Carl said.

"Then it's fine with me," Rick said, taking his refilled glass back towards their bedroom. "Come on, babe."

"I don't really feel comfortable with it, but alright," she said, then followed her husband back into the bedroom with a fresh wine cooler and a pack of Kents from the carton stashed in the kitchen cabinet next to the five-pound bag of peanut M&M's—

* * *

It was a beautiful late-summer's eve. Eric's mother dropped them off in the shoulder of Hempstead Turnpike in front of the Coliseum. The parking lot was alight with tailgaters, many openly passing joints, which irritated Eric. Their old health teacher, Mr. Gambaro, had showed a black & white anti-reefer film reel depicting marijuana as a dangerous, highly addictive narcotic, and that one reefer cigarette did as much damage to your lungs as 40 tobacco cigarettes, and killed as many brain cells as a dozen bottles of whiskey, and that long-term use was a one-way ticket to the sanitarium, or, at the very least, prison. In one part of the film, there was footage showing beatniks being clubbed with nightsticks by police officers outside *Café Wha?* for sparking a jay on MacDougal Street. Eric must have really bought into this film because he was adamantly opposed to marijuana and Greenwich Village—

There were signs everywhere alerting ticketholders that the concert was being filmed and recorded, the contents to be packaged as a double-live LP CD and feature-length concert film titled *Delicate Sound of Thunder*. This was the first time the Floyd had played the Coliseum in eight years, the last time being their famous performances of *The Wall* in 1980, except now they were without bassist and lyricist Roger Waters, who'd left the band in 1982. Guitarist David Gilmour and drummer Nick Mason were now calling the shots and had brought back, as a hired hand, keyboardist Richard Wright, who'd been fired during the recording of *The Wall*. They recorded a new album, *A Momentary Lapse of Reason*, which was still being debated by the different camps as to whether it was a "real" Pink Floyd album, or just a glorified David Gilmour solo project with an army of session players.

After passing through the turnstiles, Eric insisted they first walk the concourse to look at the t-shirts at every different vendor. Carl bought the first one he saw, a black one depicting the signature Pink Floyd circular film screen surrounded by laser beams, and, above the graphic, PINK FLOYD in tall red letters, and the tour dates on the back, which, according to Eric, was a must. Finally, after visiting every t-shirt stand in the arena and finding the same exact merchandise at each one, Eric picked a black one with a giant pink pig on it shooting rainbow prism dispersions from its diamond eyes, one that Carl thought looked kind of gay, but he didn't say anything.

Finally, passing through the tunnel, they entered the arena fogged with marijuana and cigarette smoke, Eric mock-coughing to show his displeasure—

"Don't breathe," he said.

Carl took a deep breath and held it—

"Fucking loser," Eric said.

Their seats were in the very last row of the floor, towards

the back of the hockey rink, in front of the band's control booth. High in the rafters were hung the Islanders' four Stanley Cup banners, and also a banner in the team's orange and blue colors for Billy Joel, the King of Long Island, who'd sold out a thousand concerts here, yet the locals still couldn't get enough.

Shortly after sitting down, Carl saw, in the aisle at the end of the row, a man with long unkempt hair and a long ratty beard, in his 40s or so, wearing soiled jeans with holes and a t-shirt from the 1977 *Animals/In the Flesh* tour, also with holes, spinning in the aisle, and nearly falling several times. Then he stopped, and, quite casually, picked up a nearby folding chair and struck a man in the back of the head with it who did nothing more than walk past him. Carl expected a fight to break out, but the guy who got hit just kept walking and didn't even turn around—

"Holy shit!" Carl exclaimed. "Did you see that?"

"See what?" Eric asked.

"That guy just hit some other guy in the head with a chair!"

"Where?"

"Right there, at the end of the row!"

"What the fuck are you talking about?"

Carl turned back around, but neither the bearded guy, nor his victim, were anywhere in sight. Then he felt lightheaded—

"Never mind," he heard himself say, then wasn't sure if he'd actually said it—

"I told you not to breathe, dumbass," Eric said.

Motionless, they stared at the stage, where dozens of people were working. There was no sign of Gilmour, Mason, or Wright. Neither said a word for fifteen minutes.

Finally, the house lights dimmed, as Richard Wright fingered a prolonged G minor on his organ, the opening to "Shine On You Crazy Diamond". Seated to Carl's left, with an empty seat between, was a group of older people about his parents' age, who lit a joint. Carl heard Eric say, "Assholes," but he sounded far away. Carl, who'd never smoked pot before, observed them inhaling and then holding it for as long as they could before exhaling, then practiced it himself, breathing in slow and deep, holding it, and exhaling slowly, thinking he could probably do it without embarrassing himself, should the opportunity arise—

After the guy nearest him took a hit, he looked at Carl, then offered it across the vacant seat. Carl accepted, pinching it tight, raising it to his lips but not touching them with it, inhaling slowly, gently, canoeing it slightly, but the guy didn't seem to care when he passed it back. He held the smoke in his lungs as long as he could, then exhaled an impressive plume towards the rafters—

"Fucking loser," he heard Eric say, now sounding even further away—

Every couple of minutes the guy passed it again, and eventually Carl abandoned Eric and slid to the seat closer to them. One of the women in their group kept pulling joints from her handbag and lighting them, and soon there were several going at once and Carl couldn't keep up.

After twelve minutes of "Shine On You Crazy Diamond", the rest of the first set was stuff from the new album, closing with "On the Turning Away", a song protesting societal apathy towards the pale and downtrodden, but featuring a signature David Gilmour guitar solo that energized the crowd before intermission—

They broke out the old stuff in the second set, opening with 1971's "One of These Days (I'm going to cut you into little pieces)", followed by "Time", "On the Run", and "The Great Gig in the Sky", from 1973's *Dark Side of the Moon*. Then, from 1975's *Wish You Were Here*, they played "Wish You Were Here" and "Welcome to the Machine", then went back to *Dark Side* with "Us and Them" and "Money"—the latter being both Carl and Eric's least favorite song on that album, prompting Carl to suggest they look for better seats, like he and his father used to do at the end of Met games at Shea after sitting up in the nosebleeds for seven innings.

The main concourse was quiet, the only signs of life being the people working the concession and souvenir stands. They headed in the general direction of the stage, eventually cutting into one of the tunnels and winding up at a spot overlooking the side of it, much closer than they were at the back of the floor. Just below, the sexy backup singers were "oohing" and "aaahing" at the end of the extended "Money" jam, followed by "Another Brick in the Wall (Part II)", then the finale, "Comfortably Numb", featuring Gilmour's majestic guitar solo, accompanied by indoor fireworks, during which, Carl, in the light of the explosions, spied, about ten feet away, the bearded guy from earlier, and he was still spinning, only now he had a syringe with a long needle pointed towards the rafters. He looked at Carl and gave him a big toothless smile, then pressed the plunger just as the lights started strobing. Frame-by-frame, Carl saw a string of fluid arcing towards him against the backdrop of Stanley Cup banners, slowly getting closer, until it struck him in the right eye—

"Argh!" he exclaimed.

"What the hell is wrong with you?" Eric shouted over the music.

"He got me in the eye!"

"Who?"

"That guy with the beard over there!"

"What guy?"

The guy was gone. Carl felt the area around his right eye and there was no sign of moisture, and his vision was normal—

"Never mind," he said.

"What the hell is wrong with you, loser?"

At the end of the song, the house lights came on, and the crowd gave a standing ovation. The band waved and left the stage. Carl was ready to go, but Eric said they had to stay for the encore—

"My mother might be waiting out there," Carl said.

"Who the fuck cares."

They spent the next five minutes not looking at each other. Finally, the house went dark again, and the band came back out. Carl stared at Nick Mason taking a seat behind the drum kit. They played "One Slip" from the new album, then "Run Like Hell" from *The Wall.*

Because they were next to the tunnel, they had a step on the crowd when the house lights were turned back on. Carl established a quick pace across the concourse and out of the building, then over the expanse of the quiet parking lot, well ahead of Eric. Just beyond the fence, a long line of running cars waited for concertgoers on the shoulder of Hempstead Turnpike, while hustlers were selling unlicensed t-shirts for five bucks each, or 3-for-$10, some looking cooler than the official $20 shirts inside, but none having the tour dates on the back, which is what Eric kept checking for—

Carl didn't see his mother's Mercedes and continued walking up the line of cars—

"Hold on," Eric said, looking at the shirts.

"Let's go!" Carl yelled.

"What the hell is your problem, loser?"

"My mother's waiting!"

Finally, Carl spotted her car way down the line and started walking swiftly towards it, not looking back at Eric.

"How was the concert, boys?" she asked when they were climbing in, a Kent between her fingers and the cabin filled with smoke, Eric again fake-coughing to show his displeasure—

"Why do you have to smoke in the car?" Carl barked.

"Sorry," she said. "I know your friend doesn't like it."

"Neither do I!"

As they pulled away, Carl tuned the radio to WBAB, Long Island's rock station, which was playing back the songs that the Floyd had just played at the show. Not a word was spoken, nor Kent smoked, the rest of the way back to Massapequa, until Carl's mother pulled into the driveway at Eric's house and said good-night to him as he was getting out of the car. Eric, though, did not respond, no good-bye, no thank you—

Carl heard the power-window motor, but did not look—

"You're welcome," she called out the open window, her voice echoing against the garage door. Eric flinched, but did not stop or look back on his way into the house—

Neither Carl nor his mother said a word the rest of the way home.

In the kitchen, The Dick, shirtless, sitting at the table smoking a Kent, bottle of Johnnie Walker Red and an empty rock glass in front of him, asked, "How was the concert?"

Carl continued past the table without answering or looking at him—

GIRLFRIEND

In third period health class at the Alfred G. Berner Ninth Grade School—

"Dude, Donna from gym class likes you," Ryan told Carl. Donna was one of the girls who'd been on his team in the co-ed volleyball unit and had not said a single word to him during the entire two weeks.

"Really?" Carl asked. "Wait, who is she again?"

"She's nothin' special, junior, but she's a good start to get your dick wet, you know, so you can get some experience."

"I see you've given this some thought."

"Dude, just roll with it and cover up."

* * *

The next day in health class, Ryan arrived bearing a note written on pink loose-leaf paper folded into a perfect puffy triangle with Carl's name written in girly cursive.

"I've never seen pink loose-leaf paper before," Carl said. "You didn't read this, did you?"

"Never in a million years would I be able to fold it back up like that."

"True. It is impressive."

"Open it."

Carl shrugged and unfolded the note.

Dear Carl,

I had fun playing volleyball on your team and want to go out with you. Call me. 799-XXXX.

Love,
Donna

She had drawn hearts above her name. The paper smelled of perfume.

"Dude, she wants you," Ryan said, slapping him on the shoulder.

* * *

That evening, with the upstairs hallway phone pulled into his room, cord at its maximum, Carl, for nearly an hour, punched in the first six digits until he finally worked the courage to punch the seventh.

The phone rang several times before someone finally picked up.

"Hello?"

"Hi, is Donna home?"

"This is Donna."

"Oh, hi, this is Carl… from school… I got your note."

She didn't respond.

"You said you wanted to go out with me?"

"Uh, yeah."

"Okay. Well, yeah, I'll go out with you."

"Okay. I gotta go."

"Uh, when should we go out?"

"I'll give Ryan a note tomorrow."

She hung up without saying good-bye.

* * *

The next day in health class—

Carl unfolded the pink triangle Ryan had just given him.

Carl,

I can't see you anymore.

Respectfully,
Donna

"Dude, what the fuck happened?" Ryan asked.

"I don't know. I called her last night and we talked. She didn't really say very much, and then she said she had to go and would give you a note."

"Damn, man, that sucks, but at least you got your dick wet."

"What? I don't even know who she is!"

"Well, you're lucky to have at least had a girlfriend and some experience getting dumped like a sack of trash."

"Well, I wish I at least knew what she looked like."

"Don't worry, dude, she'll be in the yearbook."

COLUMBIA HOUSE

"Carl, your friend is on the phone," his mother called from downstairs.

It was Eric, and it was an odd time for him to call, after 7:00 on a school night—

"Come over now," he said.

"Now?" Carl asked.

"Yes. Now. It is extremely urgent."

"Now?"

* * *

Eric was waiting at the door. Up in his room, he handed Carl a postage-paid card torn from a *Rolling Stone* for the Columbia House Compact Disc Club, offering twelve CDs for a penny, with a bunch of small print about buying one CD at full retail price of $18.99 every 90 days for the next decade—

"My mother signed up for this once," Carl said, "except it was with records. She couldn't keep up with the purchases. They repossessed her Volkswagen."

"Not for real," Eric said, in hushed tones. "My brother was just here. He said he fills them out with fake names and sends them to his dorm without putting the room number, so the box is left in this little basket near the mailboxes and he just takes it."

"Whoa," Carl said. "Now I wish I lived in a dorm."

"Not necessary," Eric said.

"No?"

"The people across the street," Eric said, pulling open a space between the blinds. "Nobody home all day. Mail and newspaper sitting there until six o'clock, there for the taking."

"So, a cardboard box full of CDs would be sitting there until six o'clock."

"Yep. The mail comes while we're at school. Then it just sits there for hours, and nobody's paying attention."

"Just walk right up and take it like you know what you're doing."

"Yep. And the homeowner wouldn't be missing anything because they didn't order them, nor would they be responsible for the bill, because it would be under a fake name. But they won't know what the fuck is going on because they never got any CDs in the first place."

"That's fucking brilliant," Carl said.

* * *

They filled out the postage-paid card and mailed it off to Terre Haute, Indiana, using the name "Dole Pineapple", and sent it to a house they walked by every day after disembarking the school bus. The mail was always there, but, after two weeks, there had been no cardboard boxes. Carl was checking on Saturdays as well, risky because people were home, and saw mail in the box, but nothing else.

* * *

After three weeks, it was beginning to look like a bust.

Then, on a chilly, overcast Thursday afternoon in mid-

November, there was a small cardboard box sitting on the step below the mailbox, exactly as they'd pictured it. They slowed, allowing the others who got off at their bus stop to disappear ahead of them, then Carl casually walked up to the house as he did in his newspaper delivery days—he did not fling them like the kid in the *Paperboy* video game, he dropped his bike in the driveway and brought it up to the house and put it in the mailbox hooks—and, as if it had been left there for him by the homeowners, picked up the box with the blue Columbia House logo and Terre Haute return address, and did not attempt to conceal it as he walked back down the driveway and remained staring straight ahead, digging the identity of the smooth criminal—

Minutes later in Eric's room, they tore open the box and a dozen cellophaned jewel cases rained onto the bed, not packaged in the long cardboard sleeves like at the store, where at the Wiz they sold for $14.99 and at Sam Goody for $16.99—

Journey Greatest Hits... Chicago Greatest Hits... The Steve Miller Band Greatest Hits 1974-1978... Best of the Doors double CD... *Money for Nothing: The Best of Dire Straits... Best of the Doobie Brothers... Simon & Garfunkel's Greatest Hits... The Best of Kansas... Eagles Their Greatest 1971-1975... A Decade of Steely Dan...* Foreigner *Agent Provocateur...*

They split the haul, six CDs each. The shipment came with a catalog containing considerably more titles than the magazine ads, though a few things were mysteriously absent, such as the Beatles, Pink Floyd, and the old ABKCO Rolling Stones albums from the '60s.

An hour later they were at the Bar Harbor branch of the Massapequa Public Library tearing out every "*12 CDs for a penny*" card from the "Current Periodicals" section, as well as a few "*6 CDs for a penny*" cards from rival BMG Music Club, also based in Indiana, "*The Music Club Capital of the World*".

The next day they scouted the neighborhood on their bicycles, noting which houses had full mailboxes, and monitored them for the next week. Then, with the new catalog, they filled out the cards and, over the next week, dropped them in various mailboxes, 97 cards in all with different phony names and spread among seventeen different addresses.

* * *

Over the next two weeks, they established routes of checking the houses after school, then would meet back at Eric's, where Carl left his bike in the mornings, riding over there early after slamming a Carnation Instant Breakfast and hanging out for a while before it was time to go to the bus stop, when Eric would play songs and ask Carl if he knew them.

The first shipment had taken three weeks, so it was a surprise when, on a Tuesday afternoon, exactly two weeks and one day after mailing the cards, each returned with a box—

Exile on Main Street... Sticky Fingers... Tattoo You... Who's Next... Who Are You?... Who By Numbers... all three Boston albums... another *Journey Greatest Hits... Darkness on the Edge of Town... Nebraska... The Wild, The Innocent & The E Street Shuffle... Breakfast in America...*

On Wednesday they again each arrived with a box... *The Byrds Greatest Hits... The Association's Greatest Hits... Grand Funk Hits... Foreigner Records... Billy Joel Greatest Hits Volumes I & II... Are You Experienced?... The Best of the Guess Who...* CSNY *So Far... The Best of Three Dog Night... America's Greatest Hits... 1984... 2112... 5150... OU812... The Best of Procol Harum... Workingman's Dead* and *American Beauty...* another *Journey Greatest Hits*, two *Money for Nothings*, and a *Brothers in Arms*—

On Thursday Carl came back with two boxes, Eric with three, each completing their Led Zeppelin collections—

"This is better than any Christmas I ever had," Carl said, as they ripped them open—

* * *

The following Tuesday, Carl collected nine boxes, so many that he kept dropping them on his way back to Eric's house. Eric came back with seven, making a grand total of 192 CDs with a retail value of $2,878.08 at The Wiz, $3,262.08 at Sam Goody, and $3,646.08 at Columbia House full price, before sales tax.

After a few months, during which they had cleaned out the back-issue periodicals in both branches of the Massapequa Public Library, they soon had every rock CD from the catalogs, and a lot of fringe stuff, including Dan Fogelberg, John Denver, Seals & Crofts, Sammy Johns, pre-disco Bee Gees, Edison Lighthouse, Bread, and, former Massapequa resident and member of the legendary Biltmore Beach club, Neil Diamond—

They would hastily track through each new CD looking for songs they recognized in the first two seconds, then toss it aside, many never to be listened to again.

They had 17 copies of *Journey Greatest Hits,* 13 *Money for Nothings*, and a dozen *Best of Kansas.*

* * *

There was a new catalog each month with fresh selections, but it quickly got to where they had everything and were starting to order things for laughs, such as Barry Manilow, Air Supply, Randy VanWarmer, Bill Summers & Summers Heat, and the *Saturday Night Fever* soundtrack, which Carl secretly liked—he liked the movie too, which he would never admit to Eric, who took his hatred of sister disco and its flashing trash lamps seriously. He also never told Eric that he wanted the Foreigner *Agent Provocateur* CD because it had "I Want To Know What Love Is" on it, and the *Heart* album with "These Dreams", tracks that made him think of Colleen, the girl he'd had his first serious crush on in seventh grade, who never returned the note he slipped into her locker, #247, asking her out with "YES" and "NO" checkboxes—

Meanwhile, the Beatles, Floyd, and early Stones CDs not available through Columbia House started to look like gold in the bins of the little CD store next to the bagel shop near the high school, which, in addition to selling new CDs, also bought and sold used ones. Like The Wiz, their new CDs cost $14.99, but here they had more obscure and interesting titles, including some bootlegs.

The store was owned by a short guy who looked like "Oates" from "Hall & Oates" with the black curly hair and mustache. He had a really deep smoker's voice and usually had a Marlboro Light burning in the ashtray on the counter, which really annoyed Eric.

Oates was nice to them the first time they showed up with a backpack containing twenty CDs, including *The Very Best of Hall & Oates*, Carl and Eric having to bite their tongues when he flipped by that one—

"Not a fan of 'greatest hits' albums, but they do sell," Oates said. "I'll give you three bucks cash or five in store credit for each."

They opted for the credit and split it. Carl picked *Beggars Banquet, Let It Bleed, Abbey Road,* and a bootleg of a 1972 Pink Floyd show in Sapporo, Japan. Eric went with the Floyd's *Ummagumma* 2-disc set, and the Stones' *Hot Rocks* 2-disc compilation.

* * *

A week later, Oates wasn't so friendly when they showed up with another backpack of CDs, including some they'd sold him the week before, since greatest hits sold so well—

"Didn't I buy this one last time?" he said, tapping the case for The Police's *Every Breath You Take: The Singles*, then looked at the basket of used CDs on the counter next to the ashtray and found the same one. "Yep, I did."

There was an uncomfortable silence. Oates lit a Marlboro Light even though he already had one burning in the ashtray—

"I don't know where you guys are getting these," he said, "but something doesn't seem cool here."

He declined to buy the CDs. Meanwhile, boxes were coming in daily, so they started scouting the CD store and noted when Oates wasn't there, at which times there was usually a college student behind the counter.

* * *

They would finally return nearly three weeks after their last visit, on a Friday evening after dinner, when some new wave dude with dyed-black hair shaved around the sides and back, clad in German Army surplus shirt, was behind the counter blasting Depeche Mode on the store stereo. This time they brought only ten CDs—

"Fleetwood Mac... REO Speedwagon..." the guy said, flipping through them, "Lynyrd Skynyrd *Gold & Platinum... Toto IV... Asia...* dudes, I wouldn't offer you a nickel for any of this shit. Besides, these aren't even store-bought CDs. See?"

He pointed to the tiny "CRC" stamped at the very bottom corner of the jewel case insert, which was only noticeable if you were looking for it—

"CRC, Columbia Record Club," he said. "I know what you guys are doing. Mail fraud's a pretty serious crime, you know."

They left with their CRC CDs.

"I'm not going back in there," Carl said, while they were

riding home.

"Fuck that freak. We'll just try when someone else is there."

"I don't like the sound of mail fraud."

"What the fuck is he going to do? He doesn't know who we are."

"I think maybe we should stop with the CDs altogether."

"Why?"

"Columbia House must have like hundreds of delinquent accounts from this zip code. They must be trying to figure this out."

"How would they ever know it was us? And what could they even do? Send someone to repo Dole Pineapple's car?"

"I have like over 2,000 CDs in my room stashed in milk crates, and, for the life of me, I don't know how my mother or The Dick haven't said anything. I don't need another copy of *John Williams and the Boston Pops in Space* or *The Very Best of Loggins & Messina.*"

* * *

They did stop for a while. There was no point, until the following August, when the Stones released *Steel Wheels,* which became a featured selection in the new Columbia House magazine ads—

Carl filled out a card and mailed it. Three weeks later nothing had come, so he mailed a few more, two of them to houses he'd never used. Four weeks later, there was still nothing. Eric reported the same.

"It's over," Carl said. "The whole town is blacklisted."

* * *

In a converted basement storage room at Columbia House headquarters in Terre Haute, Senior Collections Supervisor and former Green Beret Randall Bird, on special assignment, unfiltered Camel burning between nicotine-stained fingers, Styrofoam cup of light-and-sweet coffee on his desk, atop which there was an ashtray, a 13-inch stainless surgical steel survival knife with black micarta handle, and a foot-high dot-matrix printout on white-and-sea green continuous form paper of delinquent accounts in zip code 11758—

He picked up the knife and looked at the freshly sharpened blade—

"One of these days," he said, "I'm going to cut you into little pieces," then stabbed the printout with the knife—

42ND STREET

Late Saturday morning at the drive-thru of the Roslyn Savings Bank, straddling the frame of his Centurion Accordo *Tour de France Limited Edition LXE* 12-speed racing bike, savings account passbook and withdrawal slip for $60 in hand, Carl, wiping sweat from his forehead with his t-shirt sleeves, waited for the Ford Aerostar minivan ahead of him to pull away, then pedaled up to the window.

The steel drawer opened and Carl dropped in his paperwork, then watched it slide shut. Seconds later, the teller lady behind the thick glass opened the passbook to the page with the last transaction and inserted it into the little machine that printed the withdrawal transaction in purple ink. She then slid three twenty-dollar bills into a Roslyn Savings Bank envelope and dropped it and the passbook into the drawer, closing it on her side and opening it on his. He took the passbook and envelope and pedaled to a shady spot next to the parking lot, where he slid one of the twenties into his neon green Velcro wallet, then slid the other two bills into his right tube sock and the passbook into his left. Envelope empty, he dropped it in a nearby trash can and began pedaling towards the Massapequa train station.

At the station bike rack, he removed the front tire and chained it with the frame and rear wheel. He then went into the station office and purchased an off-peak, round-trip ticket to Penn Station. The escalator to the platform was slow, but it was too hot to climb the stairs. The platform smelled of melting railroad tar, and passengers were scattered about in the shady spots beneath the overhangs of the empty waiting rooms humid with urine.

A westbound train arrived ten minutes later. At Jamaica he had to change trains, commencing the journey through the graffiti-covered industrial wastelands of Queens, past the Swingline staple factory and the Amtrak yards, and the roaring descent into the ear-popping East River tunnel before the calm arrival in the steamy depths of Penn Station.

He followed the crowd through the terminal, ignoring the homeless people asking for money, and up a series of escalators until he was finally back out in the heat. The air smelled of hot pretzels and cigarettes, and the Madison Square Garden marquee advertised the Ringling Brothers circus. It was even hotter here than back home, and a fresh layer of sweat formed atop the caked layer from earlier as he made his way up Seventh Avenue.

Several blocks later, the 25¢ XXX peep show joints started to appear. At 39th Street, he encountered a small store advertising passport photos and identification cards. The sample laminated IDs in the window looked cheap and unofficial, and it didn't seem like the kind of place that would have the proper equipment to produce an authentic-looking New York State driver's license. Of course, it may have been a front and they were secretly making them in the back, but he was convinced that only on 42nd Street would he find one of these places.

The sidewalks on 42nd were crowded and he passed numerous hustlers offering weed, crack, and sex. He made no eye contact and kept moving. There were plenty of these little photo stores, but they looked no different than the ones he'd already passed. He headed west towards Eighth Avenue, then crossed the street and headed back towards Seventh. After passing several more photo stores, he decided to go into the next one he encountered.

There was a window air conditioner above the front door and the cool air felt good. The store smelled of cigarette smoke. On a stool behind the counter sat a motionless, overweight man.

Carl approached.

The man said nothing and stared at him.

"Excuse me," Carl finally said, annoyed at the uncertainty in his voice, "I was wondering if, you know, you make custom New York State driver's licenses?"

"Identification card," he said.

"Well, yes, but I need one that looks like a real, official New York State driver's license. Know what I mean?"

"Yes. Identification card. See sample."

The man reached under the counter and produced a wicker basket full of various styled "IDENTIFICATION CARDS" no better than the ones he'd already seen. All were photos of the man behind the counter, including several in which he was wearing a wig and makeup.

There was another photo store just next door, but this one proved no different, nor did the one next door to that.

Tired, hungry, sweating, he admitted defeat and decided to head back to Penn. He had just turned the corner at Seventh Avenue when he heard someone behind him say, "Yo, Suburbs!"

He turned to see a man in a green and white "Newport Pleasure" t-shirt looking at him.

"What you looking for, Suburbs?" he asked. "I got green."

"I'm looking for a real-looking New York State Driver's license."

"Yeah, man, I got a guy up the block who can do that. He

got a print shop in the back with a machine that can do that."

"How much?"

"Fifty."

"I don't have fifty."

"He might do forty-five."

"I only have forty."

"Forty? Alright, alright, I can work with that. Follow me."

Carl felt uneasy, but he followed the man across Seventh Avenue to a red-tiled stairwell that led to the downstairs of a Kennedy Fried Chicken establishment.

"My man's shop is down here," he said.

Carl followed him down the stairs to the kitchen, where uniformed workers were prepping and frying the chicken, but none of them paid them any mind.

"I can't take you past this point," the man said to Carl. "I need your money, dude."

"Where's the machine?" Carl asked, looking around.

"It's in the back, just back there," he said, pointing towards a corridor on the other side of the kitchen. "My man doesn't allow just anyone to go back to his print shop. I have to show him the cash before I bring anyone in."

Carl looked towards the corridor, then back at the guy.

"I don't like this."

"You don't like what?"

"I'm not giving you the money until I see the print shop."

"Then you ain't gettin' no fuckin' license, dude. I have to bring him the cash first, then I come back when he's ready for you. But don't worry, Suburbs, you can trust me. Where the fuck am I gonna go? There ain't nowhere else to go from here except to the fuckin' print shop."

After a moment of indecision, Carl reached into his sock and handed over the two sweat-soaked twenty-dollar bills.

"Wait right here and don't move," the man said. "I'll be back in ten minutes, then you'll get your license. Don't move.

Ten minutes."

The man departed, maneuvering through the deep fryers and prep stations before disappearing into the corridor.

After a minute, Carl began to sense the workers discreetly making fun of him.

After two minutes, he knew the man wasn't coming back, but he waited the full ten minutes anyway before crossing the kitchen.

He entered the corridor and encountered a turn that led to another turn that brought him back to the same stairwell he and the man had descended earlier.

He stopped and looked up at the people walking by on the sidewalk, then began to climb.

Wet

Every morning before school, after guzzling a strawberry or vanilla-flavored Carnation Instant Breakfast shake, Carl would ride his high-performance Centurion Accordo road racing bike to Eric's house, where they would listen to CDs before heading to the bus stop.

Carl had never paid much attention to Eric's unattractive older sister, Gretel, the blond-haired black sheep of the family who was getting straight C's at Nassau Community College, while her parents, and, currently, her older brother, attended Brown University, where her younger brother was also likely headed. Eric once referred to her as "The Ugly and Stupid Duckling", but usually just called her "loser". Once, on a rare occasion she wasn't home, he brought Carl into her room to see her original-issue vinyl copy of The Who's *Face Dances*—which he considered a stellar album despite the absence of Keith Moon, the only dud being "Did You Steal My Money?"—then showed him her high school senior yearbook, in which there were numerous signatures and best wishes of graduating classmates, all written in her own hand—

Once upon a morning, Carl had a dream where he was deep in the forest following a trail of popcorn, which eventually led to a giant gingerbread house adorned with candy canes, gum drops, and snow frosting. He rang the peppermint candy doorbell and waited until Gretel pushed open the storm door, as she did every morning while Eric was still in the bathroom struggling to put in his contact lenses, only now she was wearing black high heels, fishnet stockings, Madonna's black bustier with jewel-encrusted-and-tasseled nipples, and big hair and makeup like Sandra Dee at the end of *Grease*, smoking a cigarette—

"Come in," she said, the first time she'd ever spoken to him. "You must be starving. I have just prepared some curds and whey."

"Splendid," Carl said.

She seated him at a hand-cut wooden table and placed in front of him a bowl of lumpy fare that was not too hot, nor too cold, but just right. He'd never had curds or whey—the lumps and liquid found in cottage cheese—and they did not look very appealing, but he took a spoonful anyway, and it turned out to be the tastiest thing he'd ever eaten—

"Golly, these curds and whey are superb!" he exclaimed.

"I'm glad you like them," Greta said. "I also know what else boys like."

"You do?"

She extended her hand and led him to the middle of the room, where she removed his lederhosen and found his morning wood—

"That's the kind of candy I like," she said, then dropped to her knees and put her mouth around it, which was very pleasant for Carl, even more so than humping his mother's old fur coats. He was well on his way to finishing when the clock radio suddenly went off and he found himself humping the mattress like he used to when he was five, stopping just in time before making a mess—

Later that morning, his balls aching and his head in a fog, he couldn't pedal the Accordo fast enough, longing for Gretel at the front door, only to ring the bell and have Eric answer instead—

"Oh," Carl mumbled. "Hey."

"What the hell is your problem?"

"I was just expecting your sister to answer the door."

"Why?"

"She usually does—usually. Except when you do it."

"What the hell is the matter with you?"

"Can I come in?"

The house was a split-level, Eric's room a short trip down the upper floor hall from Gretel's room. Her door was partially open, and Carl slowed to a near stop before finally going into Eric's room.

"What the fuck are you doing?" Eric asked.

"What?"

"Why did you look in my sister's room?"

"Did I?"

"That loser is still adding signatures to her yearbook. There's a new one in there from Gary Herschkowitz—*Hope we can kiss again, and maybe more*—fucking gross."

"She needs it. I need it. You need it."

"Why are you being such a fucking weirdo?"

The next morning, Carl showed up ten minutes earlier than usual, and Gretel answered the door—

"Hi," Carl said, trying to sound studly, this being the first time he'd actually spoken to her—

"Hello," she said, possibly skeptical that her brother had put his friend up to some prank at her expense, but, as she was holding the door open for him, their eyes met, and it was just like the dream, until Eric suddenly started yelling at her from the bathroom for using all of his saline solution—

"I didn't touch your goddamn saline solution!" she yelled back, forgetting about Carl and storming up the stairs with the top of her panties visible above the waistline of her white jeans, a sight that, at this point, proved too much for Carl, who could hold it no longer and ducked into the powder room next to the front door—

DESOLATION DEVILS

1989, another summer in desolate suburbia, another steamy night in the hamlets, the villages, the towns, the census-designated places, all silent save the click of traffic lights changing from green to yellow to red, nobody on Merrick Road, nobody at Tobay Beach, time's a-wastin' and there ain't no gettin' it back, no end in sight, not even Montauk, and still your finger's gonna pick your nose—

Under the yellow streetlights, two male, middle class, and white sixteen-year-olds, Carl and Eric, after a generous helping of blackberry brandy from Eric's parents' liquor cabinet, navigated the Greater Massapequas on their high-end 12-speeds, Carl with his Centurion Accordo *Tour de France Limited Edition*, Eric with his Peugeot PZ10, as if these would impress chicks the way a Corvette would. They were desperate to get laid before summer's end, but, night after dreadful night, the girls would all disappear when the mall closed at 9:00, at which point the only signs of life were the dive bars over near the Massapequa Park train station—the biker bar, the cop bar, and the druggie bar where Candy Darling used to perform in the back room while Irwin Garden recited poems about shopping carts and Jackie Duluoz was passed out on the floor in a pool of his own vanity—

Late in the evening, heading back in the general direction

of majestic Biltmore Shores, Carl slammed on his handbrakes, prompting Eric to do the same, the thin racing tires yelping—

"What the fuck?" Eric snarled.

At the end of an alley leading to a small lot behind the Sunrise Instrumental music store, in the glow of the Exxon sign next door that brought this fair hamlet its only white light, leaning against a dumpster, was an acoustic Mariachi bass with a hole in its big body—

"I'm gonna go Pete Townshend on this thing," Eric said, managing to lift the heavy *guitarrón Mexicano* above his head, but, in the humidity, his sweaty palms lost their grip and he dropped the instrument on his foot—

Carl gave it a go and managed to strike the potholed asphalt, but it was much more difficult than Townshend made it look in the old film clips, and it wasn't worth the effort in this heat with a giant acoustic instrument. They got back on their bikes and resumed their meander upon the main thoroughfares, where there would be the greatest chance of encountering chicks out looking for a good time, but knowing the night would likely end in disappointment, just like every other night had.

As they were approaching the St. Rose of Lima Catholic church on Merrick Road, Carl slammed on his brakes again and said, "Whoa," bringing his aluminum stallion to a skidding stop that surprisingly didn't pop a tire, but nearly caused Eric to crash into him—

"Asshole!" Eric barked.

"Over there," Carl said.

About fifty yards ahead, on the curb of the little driveway in front of the main cathedral entrance where the limos and hearses dropped off the brides and bodies, were seated two chicks around their own age, smoking cigarettes—

"Do you know them?" Carl asked.

"No."

"Me neither. We have to get closer."

"They're smoking."

"Who the fuck cares if they're smoking? What is it with you and the smoking?"

"It's bad for you."

"It means they're loose. They probably put out."

"I don't know."

"What don't you know? We've been riding around this one-horse town all summer looking for chicks, and we finally find some and you don't fucking know?"

Eric said nothing.

"I'm going over," Carl finally said, not waiting to see if Eric would follow, pedaling slowly across the blacktop with its mess of intersecting parking lines, hopscotch boxes, basketball courts, and baseball diamonds used by the church's elementary school. As he got closer he still didn't recognize the girls, one tall and kind of cute, dark hair, big perm, really long bare legs emerging from tight cutoff jeans, and the other short and slightly overweight, dirty blond, zits, loose hot pink tank top and baggy striped Richard Simmons shorts, and she looked mean—

"Nice wheels," the tall one said.

"What's with your friend over there?" the other asked.

"I don't know," Carl said.

"Is he afraid of girls?"

"Maybe."

"Or maybe he likes guys?"

"Uh, I don't think so—"

"Then why won't he come over?"

Carl waved at Eric. After a long pause, Eric finally started pedaling his Peugeot slowly towards them—

"I'm Cara," the tall one said. "And this bundle of joy is Erin."

"I'm Carl. The speedster over there is Eric."

"Yeah, I've seen him at school," Erin said.

"You know him?"

"No. Just seen him."

"She likes him," Cara giggled.

Eric stopped his bike, but ten feet behind Carl—

"Hi Eric," Erin called to him, then took a deep drag and exhaled out of the side of her mouth.

"Hey," Eric mumbled, looking off towards the Bible supply store in the strip mall next door.

Erin and Cara looked at each other and laughed.

"So, I meant to ask," Erin said, "are you two cruising all over town on those sweet road racing bikes looking to get laid?"

"Shut up!" Cara laughed, punching her friend in the arm.

"Well, that's what *she* was doing," Erin said, pointing at Cara with her head.

"Do you guys smoke?" Cara asked.

"He doesn't," Carl said. "I usually don't smoke cigarettes, but I smoke pot sometimes—"

"Got any?" Erin asked.

"No, I'm all out."

After an uncomfortable lull—

"Listen," Erin said, "I'm getting bored and tired, so let's cut to the chase. Cara already called you, blondie on the Accordo, so it's me and Don Juan over there on the Peugeot—"

"Erin!" Cara said and punched her in the arm again, then turned to Carl and calmly asked, "Wanna go for a walk?"

"Sure," he said, trying to sound cool, but his heart was pounding and the erection process had commenced. He hid his bike behind a bush next to the church building then hurried back to Cara, walking beside her into the night shadows of the treelined walk between the blacktop and the east side of the church—

"I saw you at school once," she said.

"Really?"

"I thought you were cute."

"Really?"

"I fantasized about you that night."

"Really?"

"Is that all you say?"

"Uh, no, not really—"

"In my fantasy I kissed you."

"You did?"

"And then I reached into your pants, and then you slid your hand inside my panties—"

"Wow—"

"I want to kiss you now—"

"Yes, yes—"

They stopped and faced each other. She was nearly as tall as his 6'1½", considerably taller counting her perm. They leaned forward and her soft, pink-glossed lips met his, then, into his mouth she slipped her tongue, which tasted of Marlboro Lights. After a minute or so of sloppy making out, she felt his erection through his jean shorts and said, "Let's find somewhere private—"

"I know where," Carl said, thinking of the small bricked-off area next to the school's cafeteria building where they stored the empty plastic milk crates he and Eric used to steal and use for storage of their massive CD collections—

Concealed behind the brick wall they kissed again, only now she more aggressively, backing him into a stack of gray Queensboro Farms crates and guiding his hand up inside her tank top and bra. Her breasts were small and smooth and nice, and she took a deep breath when he found her nipple, which excited him further and emboldened him to bring his free hand up to her other breast. They kissed wildly for a couple of minutes until she stopped and removed his hands, and Carl thought it was over, perfectly content with second base, but then she unzipped and tugged down her shorts, revealing a pair of pink panties with a little white flower, into which she guided his writing hand. They kissed again, now slower, as his fingertips explored the terrain, which was coarser than he'd expected, having always thought it would be soft like his mother's old fur coats he used to hump when he was younger, until they got all crusty. She moaned when he found her clitoris, then he went down a little further to the opening, but she pulled him back and told him to keep rubbing the bump, and he was unsure if this was a triple or if he'd been caught in a rundown between second and third. She reached into his boxer shorts and squeezed his erection, scratching him with her nails, pulling instead of gliding, tugging his short hairs with her sweaty, sticky palms, and it hurt like hell, but he was already close to finishing and did not stop her, rubbing her bump faster until she let out a porno moan, while she yanked furiously until he came in her hand and the juice ran down his leg—

Afterwards, she wiped her hand with his boxers, which he then used to wipe his inner thigh—

"Cigarette?" she asked, taking one out for herself.

"Sure," Carl said.

She lit it for him with her white lighter and he inhaled, prompting a fit of coughing, which made her laugh. He coughed less with each drag and felt pleasantly lightheaded as they were walking back towards Erin and Eric, who were exactly as they'd left them, looking as if they hadn't said a word to each other the whole time—

"Have fun?" Erin asked.

Cara responded with a middle finger.

"That good, huh? And thanks for leaving me with Don Quixote over here. Come on, let's go, I gotta get home."

Carl had been hoping for a good-night kiss, but all Cara gave him was a cold "Bye", concerning him that he'd done something wrong. He wanted to say something, maybe ask for her phone number, or if she wanted to meet at the mall, see a movie and go to Friendly's, but was unable to get any words out. Then, without a word, Eric started pedaling away—

"Dude, wait up!" he called, running to retrieve his bike from behind the bushes, eager to boast of his conquest, pedaling hard out onto Bayview Avenue, where he spotted Eric a block ahead. The Accordo was a faster, lighter, more aerodynamic cycle than the PZ10, and Eric wasn't pedaling hard, so Carl was able to catch him quickly—

"What's your problem?" Carl asked, but Eric did not respond or even look at him and started pedaling harder. At first Carl kept pace, but Eric kept speeding up, and soon they were going too fast and Carl was coming uncomfortably close to the sideview mirrors of parked cars, until he finally gave up the chase, slowing to watch his friend pass through a cone of yellow light and disappear into the black—

THE BOTA BAG

Carl opened his eyes to daylight.

He was in his bed, still fully clothed, including shoes. He had no idea how he'd gotten there, or how he'd even gotten home. He had a terrific headache, and his tongue was stuck to the roof of his mouth. Most of his body was numb, and the parts he could feel hurt like hell. There was a horrible smell, a mixture of urine and vomit. His hair was stiff and clumped together with dead leaves stuck to it.

He began to remember things. Being at Eric's house. Pouring Scotch-whisky, triple-sec, and orange juice into a wineskin bota bag from some long-ago family vacation. They both couldn't believe how all they could taste was the orange juice, despite the concoction consisting mostly of liquor.

Earlier that day, Eric had overheard someone in the hallway at school mention a big party that night on Atwater Place. This was the first time they'd ever heard about a party ahead of time. Normally, they heard about them afterwards, Monday morning in homeroom, when stories would go around of someone getting wasted over the weekend and doing something stupid. Only the cool were in the know of these bashes beforehand, and they kept quiet about them so that every loser at Massapequa High School wouldn't show up. After school, Carl and Eric went to the library and consulted the *Southeast Nassau County Road Atlas*, learning that Atwater Place was in Nassau Shores, down near the water, a small single block that probably only had a few houses on it, so, even though they didn't know the specific address, once they got to Atwater, the party would be easy to find.

He remembered passing the bota bag back and forth while on their high-performance twelve-speed road racing bikes, he on his Centurion Accordo, Eric on his Peugeot PZ10. He remembered starting to wobble, and both laughing about it, then locking their bikes to the rack at the library. He remembered them scream-singing Don McLean's "American Pie" to the passing traffic on Merrick Road as they marched east past John J Burns Park, towards Nassau Shores. He remembered them stealing the flag from the 8th green of the Peninsula Golf Club, then marching it up West Shore Drive and planting it on Judy Pietrowski's front lawn, a girl from one of Eric's smart classes.

After this, his memory was really spotty. He remembered the backyard at the party being bright from a floodlight attached to the house, and there were a lot of people in the yard, but everything was sideways. He struggled to his feet, only to go crashing right back down. Several guys picked him up and threw him over a chain-link fence into the neighbor's yard, then pissed on him while he lay unconscious in the dead leaves.

The next thing he remembered, he was under a yellow streetlight, and it was quiet. Eric and some guy were helping him into the bed of a pickup truck. He remembered none of the ride, but recalled the truck parked in his driveway, engine running, headlights on. They leaned him against the back kitchen door and went away. When the door opened, he fell inside, a barely-conscious heap on the floor. His mother started screaming, and asked Rick "The Dick", his "stepfather", if they should call 9-1-1. He told her to "Calm down, babe," which set Carl off. He pushed himself off the floor and started yelling at him not to tell his mother what to do, and that he'd ruined all of their lives. He took a wild swing at him that missed by five feet and he fell on the floor, while his mother screamed at him to stop. The Dick tried to help him up, but he yelled at him to fuck off. He staggered across the living room and crawled up the stairs, and made it to his bed, where he now still lay—

His mother and The Dick were probably already waiting for him downstairs. They would likely ground him for a month or two and take the TV and Commodore 64 out of his room. By Monday morning, everyone at school would have heard about it. He already knew he wouldn't be able to sleep on Sunday night. Whatever hope of an improved social life he thought the party may bring was gone. His best hope now was that, next weekend, someone else would do something stupid, and everyone would forget him again.

He got up and went into the bathroom. He brushed his teeth, pissed, shit, and showered. He wouldn't deny anything, but he would show no pain. Later that evening, he would go to work as if everything were perfectly normal. Several weeks earlier, he had taken a job as a fry guy at the All-American Burger.

Back in his room, he got dressed, then stood behind the door, listening. They were in the living room talking quietly, but he couldn't hear what they were saying. Already tired of dreading it, he took a deep breath, opened the door, and descended the stairs—

TATTOO YOU

"We already missed The Who," Eric said to Carl. "We can't miss the Stones."

This was the day the Rolling Stones announced their *Steel Wheels 1989 World Tour,* the first time the band would be touring in eight years after Jagger and Richards spent most of the decade sniping at one another.

"I agree," Carl said, "but The Who wasn't our fault. We had no way to get to Giants Stadium from here."

"We could have found a way."

"Get over it already."

"I can't. The Who is never gonna come around again, they're almost dead. I couldn't live with myself if we missed the Stones too. And we better not miss Zeppelin when they finally come around."

"Well, at least the stones are playing at Shea and we can get there by train. All we need now is to get tickets. And if Zeppelin does play Giants Stadium, I would walk to New Jersey if I had to."

* * *

When Carl's mother objected to her sixteen-year-old son taking a Long Island Rail Road train from the safe harbor of

Massapequa to the scary borough of Queens and back at night without parental accompaniment, Carl was ready with his answer.

"I'm sure most of the people at the concert will be your age, so it'll be like having lots of parents around," he said, swallowing his own unpleasant visualization of being surrounded by tens of thousands of Baby Boomers. Yet his own generation had far worse taste in music, most of the other kids at school listening to Paula Abdul and Fine Young Cannibals on Z100 and WPLJ and passing off the Stones as an oldies act, much thanks to Cousin Brucie on WCBS-FM spinning "Satisfaction" ten times a weekend, ignorant of the greatness of such albums as *Sticky Fingers, Exile on Main Street, Goats Head Soup, Tattoo You…*

"I guess it's alright," his mother finally said, lighting a cigarette, sipping her peach wine cooler.

* * *

Tickets went on sale a couple of weeks later. Carl, equipped with his mother's MasterCard, spent that Saturday morning and afternoon hogging the family phone and pressing "REDIAL" to the TicketMaster number until, seven hours later, he finally got through. Somehow there were still a couple of tickets available for the October 28th show, a Saturday night, which meant his mother couldn't object to it being a "school night".

A week later when the TicketMaster envelope arrived in the mail, he carefully opened it and stared at the freshly inked lettering on the ducats:

BUDWEISER PRESENTS
IN ASSOC WITH MTV
THE ROLLING STONES
SHEA STADIUM
SAT OCT 28, 1989 4:30 PM

Carl called Eric and he was there ten minutes later, both staring at the tickets on top of Carl's dresser.

"It's really gonna happen," Carl said. "We're gonna see the fuckin' Stones."

* * *

The day before the concert, Carl rode his Centurion Accordo *Tour de France Limited Edition LXE* 12-speed across the county border to the low-income part of Amityville near the DMV, where there was a liquor store with bars in the windows and thick glass in front of the cashier counter owned by a man who never asked for identification. He purchased a small bottle of Southern Comfort that fit perfectly in the inside pocket of his Levi's denim jacket and, for Eric, a bottle of Hiram Walker blackberry brandy, which, along with flavored schnapps, he'd developed a taste for during raids of his parents' liquor cabinet.

* * *

The next morning, they locked their bikes to the rack at the Massapequa Park train station and boarded the 11:55 am to Jamaica. They would be way early and have plenty of time to walk around the neighborhood looking for loose city girls who couldn't resist white mid-upper-middle-class high school kids from the suburbs with bad haircuts, then go into the stadium for the opening act, Living Colour, whom Carl liked but Eric didn't care for, and have plenty of time to walk the concourses looking at the different t-shirt concessions.

They also thought they would beat the crowds by heading in early, but the train was packed with Boomers drinking Bud Light, wine coolers, canned margaritas, and smoking Marlboro Lights.

"This is fucking gross," Eric said.

Carl didn't agree. These Boomers weren't like his mother and stepfather's cocktail-and-gossip friends from the beach club. They were like old high school kids and they were having fun, unlike the high school kids their own age who drank beer in parking lots and on playgrounds and the bike path woods complaining how much everything sucked and never having any fun.

In the seat ahead of theirs, a gray-haired guy with ponytail and beard turned around to face them.

"Fuckin' Stones, man!" he exclaimed, and people in the surrounding seats cheered. Then he finally noticed how young they were and said, "Whoa, you guys are just fuckin' kids! You like the Stones?"

"Yes," Eric said, annoyed, looking out the window.

"Damn right, man!" Carl yelled, and the guy held up his hand for a high-five and Carl gave it to him. Then the guy held his hand up for Eric to high-five, and he reluctantly obliged.

At Jamaica, they changed trains to one even more crowded with rowdy Boomers. This train was headed to Penn Station but stopped at Woodside, where concertgoers had to change trains to get to Shea Stadium, a facility Robert Moses modeled after the Colosseum in Rome, which, at present, was in better condition than this dump in Flushing, home of the 1969 and 1986 World Champion New York Mets.

There were NYPD officers around the outside of the stadium and the show wasn't going to start for hours, so they walked along Roosevelt Avenue sipping their bottles under the tracks of the elevated 7 subway line. After seeing no girls for two blocks, they headed back towards the stadium, at least they thought, but it seemed to be getting further away, until they were in a neighborhood of unpaved roads and third world auto-repair joints—Willets Point, the "Iron Triangle", where most of the stolen cars in the New York City metropolitan area wound up.

"What the fuck?" Carl asked.

"I don't like this," Eric said and stopped walking.

"Dude, this is what Tijuana must be like."

"And that would be a good reason to turn around and head back to the stadium."

"Where all the fuckin' cops are? Dude, don't you know the kinds of shit you can get in Tijuana? And for fuckin' cheap! I'll bet there's a bar around here somewhere that won't even check for I.D."

"Yeah, well, if it's around here, that's not a bar I want to go to."

A block ahead, parked facing them next to the side of the road where a curb would normally be, was a teal and white '57 Chevy with big fins on the back, the interior adorned with amber tassels along the tops of the windows.

The lights flashed and a musical horn started playing "Babalu".

"This feels like something from *The Warriors*," Carl said.

"Let's get the fuck out of here," Eric said.

The horn went on for another ten seconds or so, then the driver-side door opened and out stepped a woman about in her thirties with dark curly hair squeezed into a teal minidress the same color as the car, spiked red heels, and fishnet stockings.

"You boys looking for fun?" she asked, Cuban accent.

"Yes!" Carl said, enjoying his daylight buzz. Eric was shaking his head, but Carl ignored him and approached the car.

"What you mean 'maybe', Chachi? And what is his problem? He doesn't look like someone looking for fun."

"He doesn't know how to have fun," Carl said. "But I do."

"Ha! I can tell already. But I can take you both. What is

your name, Chachi? I am Flora Maria."

"Eric," Carl answered. "And that back there is 'Dick'."

"Are you here for the Rolling Stones?"

"Yep, but we're a little early and have some time to kill."

"I can help you kill time, Chachi. But your friend Dick is making me nervous."

"He makes me nervous too."

Flora Maria laughed.

"You are funny, Chachi. I like you."

"I like you too, Flora Maria. Want some Southern Comfort?"

"Sure. We can have it in the car if you like. And you can invite Dick too."

Carl looked back at Eric.

"Oh, Dickie Boy, would you like to have a drink in the car with Flora Maria?"

"Uh, I think we should go."

"Go where?"

"To the stadium."

"We still have like two hours before they'll even let us in. And the stadium is right there."

"And Flora Maria is right here, Dickie," said Flora Maria, pouting at Eric. "She will show you how to have a good time."

"No thanks."

"Suit yourself," Carl said, then turned to Flora Maria.

"Get in, Chachi," she said.

He climbed into the back seat and she climbed in behind him and closed the door.

"Let's see that *Comodidad Sureña*," she said, "then we talk *pavo*."

Carl reached into his jean jacket and pulled out the bottle, then uncapped it and handed it to Flora Maria. She took a big swig, far more than the nips he'd been taking, then handed it back. He took as large a swig as he could, but it was too much, and he started coughing.

Flora Maria laughed.

"I like you, Chachi," she said. "But Flora Maria needs money. How much you have?"

"Twenty bucks," Carl said, which is what he had in his neon green Body Glove wallet, not counting the sweaty bills stuffed inside his Hanes tube socks and beneath the tongues of his white Nike Air high-tops with orange swoosh. "But I was gonna use that to buy a t-shirt."

"T-shirt? What size are you?"

"Extra large."

"Extra large? Hold on, Chachi."

She got out of the car and opened the trunk, then came back with an XL black t-shirt that had the *Tattoo You* album cover on the front, the Stones' last great album and Carl's favorite of the Ronnie Wood era, and, on the back, the Stones tongue logo licking Shea Stadium and the concert dates in blue and orange New York Mets lettering—by far the coolest Stones shirt he'd ever seen.

"You like?" she asked, holding it up for him, then turning it around to show him the back.

"It's fuckin' awesome," Carl said.

"We sell them after the show, but it can be yours now with a Cuban blow job for twenty bucks."

"Whoa," Carl said. "What's a Cuban blow job again?"

"I cannot describe, but it is the best blow job you will ever have, and you will also be the owner of the coolest Rolling Stones t-shirt ever, all for twenty dollars. It is the best deal you will be offered all day."

There was no track record to speak of, but the Cuban blow job would remain the best ever for years to come. His guess as to what distinguished it from a "regular" blow job was a sweet-spicy tingle he felt just before it was over.

Eric was waiting where the pavement began again. Carl

emerged from the Chevy wearing his new t-shirt over the old one and holding his denim jacket.

"I hope you didn't pay more than two dollars for that fake fuckin' shirt," he said.

"I paid twenty."

"Twenty? You fucking idiot! You probably could have bought one of those for five bucks after the show. Now you can't even get a real one inside."

"I like this one, and I don't give a shit about the so-called 'real ones'."

Carl didn't tell him about the blow job and Eric didn't ask any more questions. They walked in silence towards the stadium and stopped to finish their bottles before heading into the security zone.

Despite most of the seats being empty, Living Colour rocked the massive stage under the golden October sun tinting amber the Flushing Meadows and Unisphere. During "Cult of Personality" and "Open Letter (To a Landlord)", Carl danced in the aisle of the empty section high in the red seats of the upper deck, prompting Eric to move two sections over.

After the set, they headed into the concourse so Eric could buy his t-shirt. After visiting twenty different concession stands on all the different stadium levels only to find that every one of them had the exact same merchandise, he finally settled for the official *Steel Wheels 1989 World Tour* t-shirt that so many other people were already wearing.

Meanwhile, Carl successfully purchased a Budweiser from one of the concession stands using the "STUDENT IDENTIFICATION CARD" he ordered for five bucks from an ad in the back of *Rolling Stone* stating that he was born in 1967 and a student at the College of Aeronautics at LaGuardia Airport, which was right next door to the stadium and where a cousin of the girl selling the beer happened to be attending, which made her happy and Carl was hooked up with Buds for the rest of the night.

As the pleasant autumn evening settled upon the city, the World's Greatest Rock & Roll Band took the stage and fired into "Start Me Up". The show was as great as one would expect the Rolling Stones, now in their forties, to be on a beautiful night in New York City. Hits, rarities, tunes from the new album, others they never played live from albums released during their hiatus, old deep cuts like "Little Red Rooster" and "2000 Light Years from Home", giant blow-up dolls flanking the stage for "Honky Tonk Women", massive pyrotechnics during the "Jumpin' Jack Flash" encore, the stadium upper deck shaking so violently against the shimmering Queens night it appeared about to crack off and topple onto everyone below—maybe it was only rock & roll, but it was the greatest thing ever.

After the show, on the train platform crowded with drunk, sweaty Boomers buzzing about the show and set list, they wound up waiting next to the gray-haired ponytail guy who high-fived them earlier.

"Whoa, cool fuckin' shirt, dude!" the guy said to Carl. "*Tattoo You,* man, their last great album! I didn't see that one anywhere in the stadium, and I looked all over, man. Where the fuck did you get it?"

"Outside the stadium," Carl said. "Kind of way outside the stadium."

"I had to settle for this one," he said, wearing the same officially licensed *Steel Wheels 1989 World Tour* shirt as Eric. "Honestly, I haven't even listened to this album yet. Damn, your shirt is way fuckin' cooler!"

"Hey, you guys could be twins," Carl said, showing the guy Eric's shirt.

"Yeah, baby!" the guy exclaimed, holding up his hand for Eric to high-five, which he did, even more reluctantly than he had earlier.

YANKEE DAD

Under the tree in the corner of their grandmother's small backyard, sixteen-year-old Carl Jr. and his younger sister and brother, fourteen and eleven, watched their new "stepbrothers" and "stepsisters" from Texas—six in all, ages two through six, the youngest a set of triplets—gleefully run back and forth with the clothesline roller as if it were the greatest thing ever.

"This is messed up," Carl Jr. said.

"Yeah," said his sister.

"Yeah," agreed their younger brother.

Their father, Carl Sr., a U.S. Customs Inspector, divorced by their mother after her hot affair with the man who was now her husband, had, for the past six years, been living in his mother's house rent-free in the basement bedroom he and his brother shared as children in the 1950s and 60s. He'd just returned to New York after a three-month work assignment in San Antonio, and, when he picked them up earlier that morning to resume their court-mandated Saturday visits between the hours of 10:00 am and 5:00 pm, he informed them that, while in Texas, he had gotten married, and that they now had a new "stepmother", "Alice", a former Dallas Cowboy cheerleader from the sad end of the Tex Schramm/Tom Landry era, and six new "stepbrothers" and "stepsisters", all waiting to meet them at Grandma's house.

The Texas children had apparently been excited about meeting their new "step-siblings", up until the moment it actually happened, when they huddled around their mama as if being stared down by a pack of frothing Yankee wolves. Carl Sr. had no idea what to do and said he was going into the kitchen to get started on the grilled cheese.

All nine children lunched at the picnic table on the patio shaded by a 1940s-era green-and-red-striped canvas awning, their triangle-cut sandwiches oozing American cheese onto paper plates, their RC Cola flattening by the second in plastic cups. Nobody said a word. Then, several minutes into the meal, they began hearing noises from inside that were getting louder and faster by the second, Alice's unbridled moans, Carl Sr.'s staccato grunts in 4/4 time, prompting all to hurriedly finish their sandwiches and resume backyard activities.

In the corner, Carl Jr. offered his sister a Marlboro and they each smoked one behind the tree while the Texas children played with the clothesline.

The screen door opened and their father, can of Budweiser and freshly lit Viceroy 100 in hand, emerged from the house, prompting the Texas children to scream with delight.

"Come play with us, Yankee Dad!" exclaimed the oldest boy.

"Yeah, come play with us, Yankee Dad!" echoed the oldest girl.

The door opened again and his wife stuck her head out.

"Bubba," she said to her husband, "if your mama keeps carryin' on like this, you're gonna have to make another run to the package store."

Carl Sr. went back inside.

The Texas children started playing with an inflatable rubber ball, and it wasn't long before it rolled into the corner under the tree.

The backyard fell silent. The Texas children kept still until one of the triplets started crying, then the other two joined in.

Then the screen door flew open and Carl Sr. emerged.

"What happened?" he asked, looking towards the tree in the corner.

His biological children shrugged.

"The Yankee Kids took our ball and won't give it back!" cried the oldest Texas boy, then all of them began to cry.

"Is this true?" Carl Sr. asked, seething, storming towards the corner.

"No," Carl Jr. said. "The ball rolled over here. We didn't touch it or say anything to them."

"Liar!" the oldest Texas girl exclaimed, pointing.

"What the fuck?" Carl Jr. asked. "They're the liars. They're fucking deranged."

Carl Sr.'s face turned crimson and he stepped closer, but stopped when Carl Jr. stepped towards him with clenched fists.

"You be nice to these kids," Carl Sr. said, under his breath. "They're your family now."

"No they're not," Carl Jr. said.

Face now maroon, Carl Sr. didn't respond.

Carl Jr., ready to start swinging, stood down when his father dropped to his knees before him and crumpled into a sobbing heap on the overgrown lawn, head buried in arms crying, "I miss my Daddy!"

"Oh no, Yankee Dad's down!" cried the oldest Texas boy. He and his siblings hurried to their stepfather, crying, asking if he was okay, until, suddenly, the boy became quiet and rose with a look on his face that silenced the others. Calmly, he went over to the garage and began picking up rocks from the flowerless flowerbed, and, as if under his power, his siblings joined him, gathering as many rocks as they could hold, then following him towards the tree, where he halted them three paces out.

"What are you going to do, stone us?" Carl Jr. snickered.

"Fire!" the oldest boy ordered his siblings.

"Shit!" Carl Jr. exclaimed, jumping over the rusty chain link fence into the neighbor's backyard, then helping his sister and brother over as the rocks landed all around them. They ran up the driveway until they were at the sidewalk out front, each scratched and bruised but not seriously injured.

"We're not going back there," Carl Jr. said. "We're calling Mom."

He led them to the shopping center down the block and was about to go into the Dan's Supreme supermarket, but stopped as the automatic door began to open.

"No, he might find us here," he said, then led them to the Great Wall Buffet, where they'd never eaten because their father didn't like Chinese food and was too cheap to eat in a restaurant that wasn't a diner, a pizza place, or a fast-food joint. There was a pay phone in the lobby, but he didn't have any change, so, as he'd done numerous times over the years when they were with their father, he called his home number collect.

His mother accepted the charges immediately.

"I'll be there in half-hour," she said. "Just stay where you are, and don't worry about your father. I'll call the lawyer first thing Monday morning."

SWEET LITTLE SIXTEEN

The invitation for Colleen O'Halleran's "Sweet 16" party—thick stock, gold wedding script, tissue paper, RSVP card, stamped return envelope, and map with directions to the Ancient Order of Hibernians banquet hall—had lain in his wastepaper basket for days, half-buried in tissues, balls of wastepaper, and Jolly Rancher wrappers, Carl having dropped it in there promptly after opening it.

He used to love her, the curly redheaded beauty who worked at the All-American Burger, but that was months ago. The first time he saw her, she'd taken his order for a quarter pounder with cheese, fries, and a vanilla milkshake, and he thought she looked cute in her uniform of red-and-white-striped polo shirt and blue pants. The next afternoon he went back and answered their faded ***HELP WANTED*** sign that was always in the window, and they hired him as a "fry station trainee". She was a year younger than he and went to an all-girls Catholic school, so she didn't know what a loser he was at Massapequa High School, and that his only friend, Eric, was an even bigger loser. He worked his way up from peeling and dicing the potatoes in the back to working the deep fryers up front, where he dropped baskets of raw cuts into the boiling oil for three minutes, then dumped them onto the brushed-stainless-steel surface beneath the amber heat lamps, where he would shake some salt on them and scoop them into the "large" size boxes and the "small" size bags. He worked with her on Saturday afternoons/evenings, and, when it was slow, she would come over to the fry station and talk to him, and they would eat cheeseburgers together during their breaks. She wasn't just cute, she was funny, and nice, and he was really starting to like her, and he thought she was starting to like him. Feeling confident, he decided to ask her out the next time they would work together, on Saturday, during their cheeseburger break.

On the Thursday evening two days ahead of the big event, Carl was working the fry station when one of the other cashiers, Monica, came over—

"Guess who Colleen likes," she said.

"Who?" Carl asked, playing it cool because he knew it was he, and was now about to hear confirmation—

"You!" she said.

Trying to contain his glee, he tried to think of a witty response, but was interrupted by Monica—

"Just kidding," she said. "She likes Seth."

"Wait, what—Seth? Now you're really kidding— "

Seth was a former fry guy, now promoted to cashier. He was a total dork, tall, skinny, no sense of humor, barely said a word—

"*Ohhh*," Monica said. "*You* like her— "

"Yeah, well, maybe— "

"Don't worry, I won't say anything. It'll be our little secret."

"Uh, that's okay, you can tell her— "

"Don't worry, I won't say a word, I promise!"

For the rest of the night, Monica put a finger to her lips every time she looked at him. At the end of the shift, he quit, and hadn't been back since. But he couldn't stop looking at the invitation in the wastepaper basket, and, finally, he picked it up and caught a whiff of her on the stationery, awakening something—

"Sure, I'll attend," he said, grinning. He checked the "WILL ATTEND" box and stuffed it into the return envelope, then jumped on his Centurion Accordo high-performance 12-speed road racing bike and dropped it in the mailbox up the block. He then continued on to Sunrise Mall, where he went to *Jackman's Leather Apparel for Men,* a narrow shop with black walls, green neon lighting, mirrors everywhere, Pete Townshend's "Rough Boys" on the store stereo, and, behind the counter, a man in a gladiator outfit—

"Hey, sailor," the guy said.

"I'm looking for a leather jacket," Carl said.

"I would love to put you in leather."

Carl liked the ones worn by bikers and heavy metal guys, and not so much the red-and-black Michael Jackson/Eddie Murphy/crotch-rocket style.

"Is this for a special occasion?"

"Sweet sixteen party. Actually, I'm kind of crashing it."

"Funny crashing or scary crashing?"

"Mostly to show her what she's missing out on—"

"That would be scary crashing. Girls that age like guys who scare their parents. Assuming that other family will be there, including children and old people, and you with that sweet blond hair of yours, if you want to scare the piss out of them *and* walk out of there with a piece of ass, you'll want to go with the Rob Halford."

"The what?"

"Lead singer of Judas Priest. I met him once backstage at the Coliseum back in '86. Hellbent for leather, and lots of other things. Lovely man..."

He spent nearly $200 on a studded leather jacket with zippers all over it, tight leather slacks with an extra-snug crotch, and a pair of extremely uncomfortable size-13 ankle-high boots with a raised heel that he was concerned looked a little too feminine, but the guy was insistent and said to trust him, so he did. Afterwards, he went to the Genovese drug store and purchased a pair of mirrored sunglasses, a birthday card for Colleen into which he would put a $10 bill, and a pack of Marlboros. On the way home, one of the Accordo's skinny racing tires got a flat, which happened every other day on this piece-of-shit that Eric had talked him into spending $400 on, and he had to walk it the remaining two miles back to the house.

* * *

On the Saturday morning of the party, Carl patched the tube on the Accordo tire in preparation for the ride up to the banquet hall, which was up near the mall, and stashed his new purchases and several condoms in the shed, planning to change in there just before leaving so that none of his family would see him in the leather.

Later, dressed in his noisy new outfit, he put the condoms, birthday card, and cigarettes into their own zippered jacket pockets, and nearly fell when he took his first step in the heeled boots. Ready to head out, he discovered that the other tire on the Accordo was now flat, even though that one had been fine this morning and he hadn't touched the bike the rest of the day—

He wasn't about to try patching it in the dark, so he shoved the 12-speed back into the shed and pulled out the beat-up BMX dirt bike with plastic Queensboro Farms milk crate bungee-corded to the handlebars, which he had used for his old *Newsday* paper route. He pumped up the tires and set out under the yellow streetlights, but, halfway there, the right pedal broke off and went clunking onto the shoulder of Unqua Road. He managed to keep pedaling, though, using the inside of his boot to push the right crank forward, eventually making it across Sunrise Highway and the last few blocks to the banquet hall.

A light snow was falling. The parking lot was full and the party had already started—which was part of the plan, to make a grand entrance when it was underway. There was a van from the caterers, and another from *DJ Mikey Mike and His Fresh Posse*. He heard the muffled beat of Young MC's "Bust a Move" playing inside. Colleen liked that song. He hid the bike behind some bushes around the side of the building, then pulled out the Marlboros, lighting one and having a coughing fit that prompted him to toss it onto the snowy grass. After recovering, he put on the mirrored shades and went inside, just as the music silenced and DJ Mikey Mike was saying, "Yo yo yo, everyone clear the dance floor so the birthday girl can share a dance with her special man, Seth..." The song was "At This Moment" by Billy Vera, the melancholy love ballad from the NBC television sitcom *Family Ties*, an extremely slow number in which the dance partners hardly move at all and feel an overwhelming urge to cry, as do the spectators—

He navigated a short corridor with dark green carpeting on the walls, floors, and ceiling, then entered the main hall, which was dark except for the dancers alone in the spotlight. Colleen was wearing a blue gown, her hair done up in a fancy way that Carl, having fallen in love with the girl in the All-American Burger uniform, did not care for. Seth was wearing a dark blue suit a couple of sizes too small.

No one noticed him until he emerged from the shadows onto the dance floor.

A woman screamed.

A man called out, "*Hey!*"

Through the giant speakers, DJ Mikey Mike exclaimed, "*Yo yo yo!*"

Carl approached Seth from behind and tapped him on the

shoulder—

"Excuse me, sir, may I cut in?"

"What?" Seth said, confused.

"Carl, you're here!" Colleen exclaimed. "Why are you dressed like Andrew 'Dice' Clay?"

Colleen's father grabbed his arm from behind and said, "Hey, laddie, this is a private party!"

"Don't touch the leather!" Carl exclaimed, shaking free—

"Dad, he's invited! He's my friend from All-American!"

"Well, girlie, I'm personally uninvitin' him! Take a walk, ya horse's arse!"

The children and elderly were terrified. His former All-American Burger co-workers were aghast, except Monica, who had a finger to her lips. Seth was crying.

Arms raised, Carl said, "I'm goin', I'm goin'." As he was walking away, he pulled the birthday card out of his jacket and flung it towards the gift table, landing it perfectly on top of the other cards—

He heard Colleen call after him, but he kept going, out of the main hall, down the carpeted corridor, to the parking lot—

It was snowing harder now. He lit a cigarette and this time didn't cough. He hoped Colleen would come out and see him smoking and looking cool, but the music started up again inside and no one came out. After he'd flicked the butt away and was about to leave, the banquet hall door opened and out stepped a gorgeous woman with fiery red hair, wearing red high-heels and wrapped in a mink coat—

"You're still here," she said.

"Jessica Hahn— "

"Well, tonight I'm Colleen's godmother," said the *Playboy* centerfold and Massapequa High School Alumni, Class of '77. "Colleen really wanted me to be here, so I flew in from L.A. at the last minute. Anyway, that was some show you put on in there—I like your style, kid, and those boots are adorable!"

"Uh, thanks—"

"God it's cold out here. Do you need a lift somewhere? I'm just going back to my hotel. I don't have anywhere I need to be."

"Sure."

He followed her to a red Mercedes. She unlocked the passenger-side door for him. The inside smelled like perfume. The rental contract was on the dashboard.

She climbed in and turned the ignition, then looked at him—

"Do you want to know a secret?" she asked, running her red-painted fingernail the length of his leathered thigh—

"Yes," Carl said, parched, barely able to get the word out, his budding erection fighting the extra-snug crotch—

"I can't resist a man in leather," she said, pouting her lips. She then backed out of the spot, pulled onto the street, and gunned it, the Benz fishtailing in the wintry mix. Moments later, they were racing east on Sunrise Highway, then made the slight right at the bend onto Old Sunrise, and, finally, turned into the small lot of the Carman Mill Motel, parking next to a white Trans Am. Though it was the closest lodging to the banquet hall, Carl was surprised she was staying at this dump, popular with mall hookers for their hourly rates—

"Shoot," she said.

"What's wrong?"

"Don't worry about it. Come inside."

He followed her to a room down at the end of the building. She slipped in the key and opened the door. He heard a man inside say, "There you are..."

"Sam!" she exclaimed. "What are you doing here?"

Carl followed her in and found himself staring into the crazed, bloodshot eyes of comedian/actor Sam Kinison, who was sitting on the bed with a large wall mirror laid out in front of him like a table, on top of which was a mountain of cocaine and several tightly rolled hundred-dollar bills—

"Well, what do we have here," he said, looking at Carl, sliding off the bed. "Jessica, why did you bring this gay kid here?"

"Sam, I didn't know you would be here—"

Kinison erupted—

"Why did you bring the sissy here?" he screamed. "Answer me! Say it! Say it! Oh! Oh! Ohhhhhh!!!!!! "

Jessica turned to Carl—

"I'm sorry, darling—what was your name again?"

"Eric," Carl said, backing towards the door—

"Eric, I'm afraid I can't leave him alone when he's like this. We'll have to do it another time. Hey, maybe we'll see each other at Colleen and Seth's wedding!"

He didn't bother to retrieve the bike from the banquet hall bushes, instead walking the three miles home in the falling snow, the boot prints disappearing in his wake nearly as quickly as he'd made them—

THE SODA JERK

The '80s were over, and the end of eleventh grade was approaching for Carl and Eric. The two had been friends since fifth grade, 1983, the year Carl's parents divorced and his mother would marry the man she'd been having an affair with, Rick "The Dick", and they would buy a house together in Massapequa, exiling Carl from his friends and former life in West Hempstead.

Eric had been Carl's only real friend during these past six-and-a-half years. They had always sat across from one another at the same lunch table, which would go without saying on the first day of school each September when they chose their seats for the year. When they got to high school, which, in Massapequa, started in tenth grade, and were allowed to leave campus for lunch, they would eat every day at the bagel shop next door to the high school parking lot, the one with the giant "MHS: HOME OF THE CHIEFS" mural with the war bonnet and Batman symbol painted on its side wall.

Carl was sick of the bagel shop. Eric always insisted on going there because it was the cheapest place to eat, and every day it was the same thing—the "School Special", bacon-egg-and-cheese-on-a-salted-bagel and a can of Coca-Cola Classic for $1.99—

"Let's eat at Neighbors," Carl said. Neighbors Soda

Fountain was the 1950s-themed place in the shopping center across the street that served burgers and had an old-fashioned soda-fountain in which they used their own syrup to make really bright red cherry cola—

"No," Eric said, which is what he always said whenever Carl suggested it.

"We've eaten at the same place for almost two years. I want a burger. And fries. And a cherry cola."

"No."

"Just today."

"No."

"Alright, I'll go by myself."

"Have fun, soda jerk," Eric said, chuckling as if getting the last laugh. Carl, though, knew that one of Eric's greatest fears was eating lunch by himself, and that he wouldn't go into the bagel shop alone and would instead go to the school cafeteria, not a place one wanted to be seen, where he could sit with "Blind Barbara", the legally blind girl whose glasses were fitted with telescope lenses, which, from a distance, looked like peach-colored blurs, but, if you got close enough, you could see Jupiter and some of the moons transiting across—Ganymede, Europa, Io, Titan, Enceladus—each disappearing briefly as they passed from one lens to another. Or he could sit with Ethan, the kid with the phone modem on his home computer who knew how to call $1.99-a-minute sex lines for free—

"I will, asshole."

The last part just slipped out, but it felt good, and he didn't take it back. He turned and walked away, towards the shopping center. Eric did not follow.

Neighbors was not a full-sized restaurant, but there was room enough for four tables that would usually get taken quickly by high school students at lunchtime, and a long counter with round spinning stools bolted to the floor. Going in, Carl did not fear, but welcomed, the notion of dining alone. He wasn't worried about anyone saying things like, "Hey, check out the loser eating lunch by himself." These people didn't mean anything to him, and this place was not his home. In a little more than a year would come the day he finally got out of here, away to college upstate. What happened between now and that day didn't mean a thing. All he had to do was bide his time, and not do anything stupid that would jeopardize his departure. He didn't need a friend now. He would have more time to practice his guitar, so that, by the time he got to college, maybe he would be good enough to start a band. This place didn't matter. It never mattered. This was not his home. It was a place he resided. He didn't have a home, not since leaving West Hempstead, that home being long gone now. Home was out there somewhere, and he alone would have to find it, or her.

He walked past the *PLEASE SEAT YOURSELF* sign, and the four tables of high school students. He heard no significant break in their murmur as he went by, or derisive laughter, nor did any heads whip in his direction. Most didn't even notice him, and the ones who did looked away once they saw it was someone they didn't know.

Why, he wondered, *hadn't I ditched this loser sooner? Like in sixth grade?*

He seated himself at the counter and ordered a bacon cheeseburger, mozzarella fries, and a cherry cola. He read the *Newsday* sports section while he ate. It was the best lunch he ever had.

He never spoke to Eric again.

MORE THAN A WOMAN

Charles Humphrey was the big dopey kid in Carl's gym class, only he wasn't really a kid anymore, having been left back a couple of times on the way to eleventh grade. He was 6'4" and well over 300 lbs, drove his parents' old Chevy Caprice Classic, and talked real slow like he was from Kansas, even though he grew up right here in Massapequa.

"Whatcha doin' for prom?" he asked Carl, both waiting their turn at bat in the area designated as the "dugout" of the gym class "softball field", which was not at all a proper diamond but just some old bases on an expanse of intramural field dust—

"Prom?" Carl asked.

"Sure. Junior Prom. I should have been more specific."

"I'm not going."

"Why not?"

"I don't have a girlfriend."

"Neither do I."

"No?"

"Nope."

After a brief lull—

"Aren't you gonna ask me what I'm doing for prom?" Charles asked.

"What are you doing for prom, Charles?"

"Going to a party in the Hamptons."

"Really."

"Yep. A lot of people are skipping prom and going right to the Hamptons, where everybody's going after prom for parties anyway."

"And there's more than one party?"

"Well, yeah, but I'm going to one specific party. A bunch of us put in money to get a suite at one of the hotels out there."

"Who put in money?"

"Me. Some other guys. My brother, who's 32. Probably a couple of girls, maybe."

"And where in the Hamptons is this?"

"Just out in the Hamptons, is all I know."

"And which hotel is this at?"

"I forgot. I have it written down at home."

"And in which one of the Hamptons is this hotel? East Hampton, Westhampton, Hampton Bays—"

"I forgot. But I have that written down too, I think."

"Good."

"Hey, I have an idea."

"What's that, Charles?"

"Since you're not going to prom, why don't you ride out to the Hamptons with me and my brother? It'll be a blast. You can just give us a few dollars for gas, and a few dollars for the suite. I'll pick you up at FoodTown at nine o'clock on Saturday night."

Carl knew better than to trust Charles Humphrey—not that he was a liar or a bad dude, but he was like a little kid in a grown man's body—yet, if he was telling the truth, and there really was a party at a hotel somewhere in the Hamptons where there would be girls who didn't go to the prom—

"Sure, Charles," Carl said.

"Don't be late. My older brother will be with me, and he might get mad if we have to wait for you."

* * *

By that afternoon, Carl had forgotten his conversation with Charles until overhearing two girls in math class talking about how the junior prom was lame. Then they asked each other which party they were going to out in the Hamptons, which, apparently, was a difficult decision, as there were "so many good ones to choose from". As much as Carl wanted to find out the location of even just one of these parties, these were A-list popular girls, both very cute, and he knew that everyone, including the teacher, Mr. Klein, would laugh at him for even attempting to talk to girls so far out of his league, let alone ask them where the after-prom parties were, which, supposedly, everyone but he already knew, so he kept his mouth shut.

* * *

Friday morning in gym class, in the softball "dugout"—

"So, are you still going out to the Hamptons tomorrow night?" Carl asked Charles.

"Yep. And so are you, right? I'm picking you up at nine o'clock at FoodTown."

"Yeah, I'll be there. Where in the Hamptons are we going again?"

"All's I know is that we're going to the Hamptons."

"Which one?"

"I don't know. One of them, I guess."

* * *

Knowing it would be far easier to sneak out all night and sneak back in the next morning than trying to convince his mother for permission to get in a car with some guy from school and his 32-year-old brother and go to a hotel out in the Hamptons, where there would quite obviously be alcohol present, Carl devised a plan to make it appear that he was following his usual Saturday night routine of late, which was to stay in his room all night watching TV and speaking to no one, then have light timers shut off the lights and TV at 3:00 am. Then, when he got back the next morning, he would casually stroll back into the house under the premise that he'd just gone out for a minute to drop something in the mailbox at the corner, and they would have no clue that he'd been gone all night.

On Saturday morning, he rode his Centurion Accordo 12-speed up to the Pergament hardware store and purchased two light timers, then went next door to the Genovese drug store and purchased a three-pack of Trojan lubricated condoms, a pack of Marlboros, and an orange Bic lighter. Then he rode up toward the Carman Mill Motel, to the one-aisle liquor store with the steel cage in front of the counter, owned by the old Asian guy who never asked for ID, and bought a four-fifths pint of Southern Comfort.

* * *

The first part of the plan worked to perfection. His mother and "stepfather", Rick "The Dick", went out at 8:00 and saw him in the kitchen just before they left, and he appeared to be going nowhere. He waited until they were gone before getting in the shower, then, at 8:30, leaving the television and lamp on in his room that the timers would shut off at 3:00, he jumped on the Accordo and rode up to the FoodTown shopping center.

After locking his bike on the rack, he went through the automatic door into the foyer with the gumball and vending machines and bought a can of Coca-Cola Classic, which he cracked open and took a long swig, then refilled with SoCo. Back outside, he sat on the curb, feet in the FIRE LANE, sipping his canned cocktail and smoking Marlboros. By 9:20, he hadn't seen a single Caprice, and by then he knew that Charles wasn't going to show.

It had crossed his mind to take the two-hour train ride out there, where the land was narrow and the stations and hotels probably right in town—but there were lots of Hamptons on the L.I.R.R. Montauk branch—Westhampton, Hampton Bays, Southampton, Bridgehampton, East Hampton—and he had not heard where any of these supposed parties were taking place.

After tossing his empty Coke can and buying another from the machine, he rode up to the Massapequa Park train station and locked his bike on the rack. He took the escalator up to the platform, mixing some SoCo into the second can of Coke during the slow ride up, and sat on a bench facing the eastbound tracks that ran all the way out to Montauk.

The headlights of an eastbound train soon appeared in the western darkness. Minutes later it pulled into the station, but, by then, he had already given up the idea of going out east and was content to sit and watch the trains go by with his SoCo, Coke, and Marlboros, imagining the better places these vessels traveled in either direction without having to spend much time here—

The doors slid open. He didn't look directly at the disembarking passengers, but he saw their shoes pass by on their way to the escalator, until one pair caught his attention—pointy, shiny, black high-heels with a pair of dark-stockinged legs and a leather miniskirt very much like his eighth-grade English teacher used to wear—

"Carl? Is that you?"

"Ms. Orlando?"

She still looked good for a woman in her forties, and sexy

as ever. Carl was surprised she even remembered him. He once carried a box of phonics workbooks out to her Corvette after school, an event that fueled a thousand fantasies—

"Why, Carl, it's so good to see you. How are things? You're in, what, eleventh grade now?"

"Yeah, just about done with it," he said.

"Isn't tonight the junior prom? Why aren't you there?"

"I didn't have anyone to ask."

"Oh, Carl, I'm so sorry."

"That's okay, I'm used to it."

"How old are you now?"

"Seventeen."

"Are you waiting for a train?"

"No. I was supposed to get a ride out to the Hamptons for a party, but they didn't show. Then I was thinking about taking a train out there, but at this point it doesn't seem worth it."

"Do you mind if I sit?" she asked, the two now alone on the platform—

"Sure," he said.

She sat close next to him on the bench and retrieved a pack of Parliaments from her Yves Saint Laurent handbag—

"Also," she said, "if you don't mind, I'm going to have a cigarette. Would you like one?"

"No, thanks, I've got my own."

They both lit up.

"I didn't go to my junior prom either," she said, exhaling, red lipstick on recessed filter—

"Really?"

"No."

"Why not?"

"None of the boys asked me."

"I thought you would be the first girl they asked."

"Well, I was a bit of a nerdy bookworm back then. I

changed my style after that."

"Did you wear glasses?"

"Big, thick ones, like Coke bottles. Thank God for contact lenses. By the way, I also know that you used to daydream about me in class."

"How do you know?"

"How do you think I knew?"

"Oh— "

"I always thought you were a handsome young man."

"Really?"

"Of course."

"I thought you liked T.J. best."

"He was cute, but you were handsome, and more of a gentleman. And now you are a fully-grown, handsome man."

"Thanks," he mumbled—

"I have an idea—why don't we have our own junior prom back at my place? That is, if there's nowhere else you have to be— "

* * *

She still had the red Corvette, which was parked down in the station lot with a ticket on the windshield that she shoved into her handbag. The vehicle's interior smelled like stale cigarettes and perfume. She stomped the pedals with her high-heels as the Corvette roared to life—

"Buckle up," she said, then stick-shifted out of the parking lot and across Sunrise Highway, then down desolate Park Boulevard glowing amber under the yellow streetlights, Phil Collins' "In the Air Tonight" on the stereo—

"Are you a virgin, Carl?"

"Uh, I got a hand job once, if that counts for anything— "

"You are no longer a virgin when you have made love to someone. Have you ever made love to someone, Carl?"

"No, I guess not, Ms. Or—"

"Carl, you are a man now and my date for the junior prom, so please call me 'Susan'."

"Yes, Susan."

She drove swiftly and skillfully, heading east on Merrick Road towards Nassau Shores, both smoking cigarettes, exhaling into the salty June breeze blowing in through the open windows as they passed John J. Burns Park—

"Don't you just love smoking?" she asked.

"Yeah," Carl said, exhaling.

* * *

She lived in a bungalow on the Great South Bay with a pool in the yard. The interior was classy, clearly not a house inhabited by children, decorated with big Picasso-like paintings and abstract wood sculptures. The bedroom door was open, and, inside, was a bed large enough to fill with her and several men, covered with sheets of black satin.

"We are going to do this right," she said, foregoing the tour and instead directing him to move the furniture in the living room out of the way to create a dance floor, offering no assistance with the heavy lifting. He liked her directness, it was so much easier than trying to figure out what was going through the heads of girls his own age. After the leather couch and the teak coffee table were out of the way, she led him to the garage for a folding ladder, then up to the attic for a genuine disco-used mirror ball, which he hung from a hook already on the middle of the living room ceiling. She then dimmed the lights, and the room, with the nice hardwood, had become a dance hall for two—

"Now, let's get you dressed," she said. "Into the bedroom and strip down to your underwear. I have some old tuxes in the closet, one of them should fit."

There was no hiding his boner when he was down to his boxer shorts.

"So adorable," she laughed. "Now, into the closet."

The walk-in closet was enormous. There was a small section of men's suits, tuxedos, jeans, t-shirts, Hawaiian shirts, khaki shorts, leather slacks, and a pair of nunchucks.

"You're not married, right?" Carl asked.

"Dear God, no," she laughed. "I was once, when I was nineteen. I had become pregnant, but then I lost the baby. The whole thing didn't even last a year. Afterwards, I swore I'd never do that again and went to college. But that was all a very long time ago, so you can relax knowing that I am now completely unattached in every way, which is the way I like it, and the way it shall stay."

She fingered through the tuxes on the rack until picking one—

"Try this one," she said. "It's for tall and large."

"Whose clothes are these?"

"Honestly, I don't remember who they belong to. They are just things that men have left here over the years and never came back for. I must have scared them away. It sometimes comes in handy to have some extra men's apparel lying around, this being one such occasion. Now, go out to the bedroom and change. I'll stay in here and get dressed."

Staring at himself in the mirror, tux baggy and clip-on bowtie askew, he felt ridiculous and began to worry that this was some sort of gag. He then sat on the black satin sheets and waited until she finally presented herself, looking magnificent like Elizabeth Taylor in her red ball gown, elbow-length gloves, big diamond earrings, dark stockings, and red high heels. She twirled for him, then handed him a box containing a fake corsage—

"Pin me," she said, holding the box open. He didn't know how to do this and became nervous—

"Like this," she said, showing him how, then having him practice it three more times until he had it down.

"These things are important," she said. "Next year, at the senior prom, your beautiful date will appreciate that her man knows how to pin her corsage. Women appreciate men who know what they're doing. Confidence, Carl, is the key to unlocking doors. Now, take me to the junior prom."

Arm-in-arm they proceeded to the living room, where she went over to the turntable and selected the soundtrack to *Saturday Night Fever*, dropping the needle on the Bee Gees' "More Than a Woman", then heading out to the dance floor and waiting—

"Well, aren't you going to ask me to dance?"

"Sure," he said, walking up to her and asking, "Would you like to dance?"

"Dear God," she said, hand on hip. "Is that how you ask a woman to dance? Try it again, but this time look me in the eye. Tell me I look pretty this evening. Then ask me to dance. And say my name. Women like it when men say their name."

Carl looked up and met her eyes, then started feeling lightheaded. He held out his hand and said, "Susan, you look wonderful tonight. Can I have this dance?"

"*May* I have this dance. Ask again."

"Susan, you look wonderful tonight. May I have this dance?"

"Why, thank you, Carl. I'd love to."

Carl, though, held up his hands and said, "I don't know how to dance."

"Don't worry about dancing. Just let go of your inhibitions and let the music flow through your soul."

"I don't know how to do that either."

She took his hands and said, "You are here with me, and your life starts tonight. Hold on to me, Carl, and let go of everything else."

She leaned backward and he did the same, but not too far since he outweighed her by sixty or so pounds, and together they started spinning to the sweet falsetto harmonies of the brothers Gibb, looking up at the mirror ball, then back at each other, laughing, spinning faster—

"That was wonderful, Carl," she said as the song faded out. "Let's take a break, I need a cigarette."

They smoked overlooking the slow reflections of the mirror ball on the dance floor, Yvonne Elliman's "If I Can't Have You" on the hi-fi—

"Pay attention to your date," she said. "Don't start drifting away like you used to in class. Talk to her. Let her know you're having a good time. Show her you're interested."

"I'm having a wonderful time, Susan. Are you enjoying yourself, Susan?"

"Don't overdo it with the name thing. Just relax, look into her eyes, and let your heart speak for you."

He looked into her eyes and, again, felt lightheaded—

"Susan," he said, "tonight is very special to me, and I'm honored that you're my prom date. I'll never forget this night for the rest of my life."

"Good, but drop 'for the rest of my life'. Clear and concise. Economy of words. 'Susan, this is special to me. I'll never forget tonight.' Something like that. Anyway, now it's time for our special dance, so let me change the record."

She put on Bob Seger & The Silver Bullet Band's "We've Got Tonite"—

"This is my song," she said, then turned towards him and waited, and he offered his hand without saying anything—

"Good, Carl," she said, allowing him to lead her out to the dance floor, where she positioned his hands on her waist and draped her bare arms around his neck. They swayed to the slow piano chords, butterflies aflutter in Carl's stomach as he looked into her eyes, and the way she was looking back made him feel like he was about to start crying, which is when she whispered, "Kiss me, Carl—"

He leaned in slowly and met her lips, tasting her lipstick as he slid in his tongue—

"Don't jab," she said. "Slide slowly, gently—"

He tried again, and, this time, she didn't stop him. Slow and passionate they kissed through the song's building crescendo, and, towards the end, she started kissing more aggressively, positioning his hands on her bottom, leaning into his erection—

"Do you want me, Carl?" she whispered.

"Yes," he whispered back.

"Tell me you want me."

"I want you, Susan."

"Again."

"I want you, Susan."

"Again."

"Susan—I need you—"

"Come with me," she said as the song ended, leading him to the bedroom, where she ordered him to remove his clothes—

"All of them?" he asked.

"Yes," she said, then went into the closet and closed the door.

Carl unbuckled and removed the tuxedo pants, then jacket and shirt, and, finally, boxer shorts and socks. Fully erect, he stood at the foot of the bed staring at the doorknob for what seemed an eternity before it finally turned and she emerged wearing a Playboy bunny suit, including puffy white tail, big rabbit ears, collared bowtie, fishnet stockings, and high-heels—

"I used to waitress at the Playboy Club on 59th Street," she said. "That's how I paid for my first year at NYU. I only worked there a year, but they let me keep the outfit, and I'm proud to say it still fits."

"Wow—I mean, you look stunning, Susan."

"Thank you, Carl," she said, twirling, then inviting him to sit on the bed, while she remained standing—

"Before we go any further," she said, "you must understand that when a woman gives a man oral sex, she is doing it to enhance his stimulation prior to intercourse, and not as a finishing act. So, I am going to do this briefly, which is all a man needs, but it is imperative that you do not finish. Is this understood, Carl?"

"Yes, Ms.—Susan—"

"Now, lie back and close your eyes—"

It felt warm, soft, and moist, and made him harder than he'd ever been. It was only a minute before he opened his eyes again—

"Good, Carl," she said. "Did you bring condoms?"

"Yes."

"Good. A man should always be prepared. And be sure to always wear one, at least until you find that special woman you are going to stay with, if you're into that sort of thing." She winked. "Where are they?"

"In my pants."

"Get them."

He showed her the strip of Trojans in the apricot-colored wrapping, still connected at the perforations—

"A woman can tell if a man knows what he's doing by the way he puts on a condom," she said.

This made him nervous, but he was able to tear one from the strip and get it open without much difficulty, then started rolling it on—

"What are you doing?" she asked.

"Uh, putting the condom on?"

"You didn't stretch the tip first. You have to make room at the tip or else the fluid has nowhere to go and will spill out the back. And do you have any lubricant?"

"Like Vaseline?"

"No. Like KY jelly. Vaseline, yuck. Really, Carl, you must be prepared at all times. The lubricant on lubricated condoms is never sufficient, especially if it's been in a guy's wallet for a while. Buy a small tube. Nothing to worry about this time, though, I have a wide assortment of oils and jellies."

She showed him how to stretch the tip, then, after rolling it on, he chose a cinnamon oil, some of which rubbed onto his scrotum, making it warm and tingly—

"The man should proceed slowly from here," she said. "He should kiss her again, tenderly, and allow her the opportunity to insert it for you. If she doesn't, look into her eyes and tell her you want to make love to her—at this point, we are beyond subtlety and will want to be explicit about our intentions. A more experienced woman will know exactly what she wants; however, many of the young, inexperienced girls you will be with, especially in high school and early college, will not know what they want. They will be confused and conflicted. They will want to, but they won't want to. Some will change their mind at the last moment. If you hear the word 'no', immediately stop whatever it is you are doing. Show concern, ask her if everything is okay. Do not try to convince her to proceed or change her mind if she says 'no'. Respect her. Now, if you are with a woman who gives consent, look into her eyes one last time, then move slowly to insert. If properly lubricated, it should slide right in. Slowly and gently, go as deep as you can, then, start motioning back and forth—slowly at first, but gradually increasing speed until you establish a comfortable pace for both of you. Don't go too fast like you're trying to catch a train. Motion and location have more to do with it than size, as long as it isn't *too* small and can't reach said location. *Your* penis, Carl, is more than adequate in size, and would make most women happy if used properly. Keep motioning; you will be able to tell from her sounds whether or not you are pleasing her. You should also be able to tell when she is approaching climax, and you should try not to climax until she gets there. Are you ready, Carl?"

"Yes."

"Say my name, Carl."

"Yes, Susan."

Gently she lay him down on top of her, the black satin sheets feeling nice against his nudity. She was about to unsnap her bunny suit, but stopped—

"This," she said, "has come to be known as the 'missionary position', which is how some Christian ministries believe is the only proper way to copulate under the eyes of the Lord. Do not buy into this nonsense, Carl. It is a wonderful, classic position, perfect for your first sexual encounter, but there are many great ones, so do not be afraid to experiment, and keep an open mind for things she may suggest that you had never thought about trying."

He looked into her eyes and she nodded. Slowly he put it in, she not offering assistance but nodding him on, moaning when he was inside her, then whispering, "Make love to me, Carl."

And he did. She said "slower", "faster", "not yet", and "a little longer", then, finally, between moans, "Now, Carl, release me, let me go…"

They climaxed together. When both had finished, she nudged him away and reached into the nightstand drawer, retrieving a pack of Parliaments and taking one out for each—

"We'll spoon after this," she said, exhaling, both now sitting up, an ashtray on the bed between them—

"I don't know what that is," Carl said, examining the recessed filter of his Parliament—

"Most men don't. We're just going to kiss and cuddle and

touch each other's bodies, without having sex. Carl, it is important to note that being someone's lover is more than the main sexual act. There is the before, there is the during, and there is the after. And, Carl, when you do make love to a woman, you stay the night and have breakfast with her in the morning. Do not be one of those jerks who gets dressed and runs out the door as soon as it's over, even if it is with someone you don't particularly care for. Don't ever leave unless she tells you to. Always be a gentleman. Is this understood, Carl?"

"Yes, Susan."

* * *

She awoke at first light and put on a pink satin robe with fuzzy white trim, then went into the bathroom. She was in there for a while, taking a shower and blow-drying her hair, which she set in big hot curlers. She emerged in a pink satin robe with fuzzy white trim, then went into the sitting room just inside the closet, and noticed in the makeup mirror her lover watching through the open door—

"You may enter, Carl," she said without looking.

He stood in the doorway, naked and erect—

"Some men are turned on watching a woman do her hair and makeup," she said, penciling her eyebrows. "I see that you are one of these men."

"Yes," Carl said.

She stood and turned like she was going to kiss him, but stopped short of his lips—

"Take me, Carl," she said, "but no kissing or oral, I don't want to smudge my makeup."

Carl put on a condom, tip properly stretched, and lubricated himself with a mentholated oil that was cold and tingly, which he liked even better than the warming cinnamon. She lubricated herself with coconut oil, then, still in robe and curlers, bent over in front of the makeup mirror, looking back at him over her shoulder—

* * *

A short time later they were back in the Corvette, roaring east on Sunrise Highway, past the shopping mall and the sanitarium into Suffolk County, to the South Bay Diner in Lindenhurst, her favorite breakfast establishment—

"Why is it your favorite?" Carl asked.

"Because I don't know anyone in Lindenhurst," she said.

* * *

She ordered hard boiled eggs, toast, bacon, and coffee. He ordered the "Full House"—pancakes, waffles, French toast, bacon, hash browns, toast, eggs sunny side up, orange juice, and bottomless coffee. Afterward they lit cigarettes and ashed them on their plates, Carl, not a fan of the recessed Parliament filters, smoking one of his Marlboros—

"So, Carl, what are you going to do with your life?"

"Go to college upstate. Then, I don't know."

"After college, I highly recommend experiencing a different part of the world. London. Paris. Bangkok. Seattle. And don't waste your four years of college dating some sweetheart who still sleeps with stuffed animals. Party hard with your male friends and get it out of your system. Then, after college, see as much of the world as you can. If you are planning on getting married, wait at least until you're thirty. People who get married in their early twenties usually wind up divorced."

"Like my parents," Carl said.

"I am sorry to hear that, Carl."

"It's okay, Susan."

"I have one last reading assignment for you—"

She reached into her handbag and retrieved a pink notepad and a red pen, writing in sexy cursive:

"On the Road"
by Jack Kerouac

"Read it," she said. "It will change your life."

* * *

With the Montauk sun rising behind them and the Bee Gees' "How Deep is Your Love" on the stereo, the Corvette roared west on Sunrise Highway, back towards the Greater Massapequas. Both smoked cigarettes, but neither spoke. Carl could feel her and the night drifting away. In a few minutes they would say good-bye, and then he would never see her again. He was in tears by the time she pulled up to the curb at the train station, where the Accordo was still locked to the rack—

"Don't be sad," she said. "Your life has just begun."

LESSONS

In the cab of the Carson Home Improvement dump truck rumbling through Farmingdale, behind the wheel, 38-year-old Carmine, foreman of the cleanup crew, and, on the passenger side, his summer hire, a strapping sixteen-year-old named Carl.

"Hey, I know where we are," Carmine said. "The Crystal Café, the strip joint, is over here. I used to go there in my drinking days."

"Oh yeah?"

"Yeah, yeah, yeah. This was back in '81, '82, '83. Lots of hot broads there back then. I can't believe it's still open. Ever been to a strip joint?"

"Nah. I wouldn't even try it with my shitty fake ID."

"Wanna try right now?"

"What?"

"We don't have any more jobs today. All we gotta do is go to the dump and then go back to the shed, so we have a little time to kill."

"I don't even have ID on me except my real license."

"I bet they don't even card you."

"Really?"

"It's three in the afternoon. The place will be dead, and there probably won't even be a bouncer at the door. During the day they're usually sleeping in the back and they only get bothered if there's trouble, so whoever's bartending will decide whether to card you. And both of us are covered with dust and plaster. They ain't gonna card me, and you look way older than sixteen, especially all dirty like that. Hey, I know what we can do. We can go to the dump and get you a little dirtier so you'll look even older. We'll walk in there like real working men."

"Are you okay going to a bar?"

"Sure. I'll just get a club soda and lemon, and I'll buy you a beer. And if they ask for your ID, we'll say you left it in the truck and we'll just get out of there."

At the dump, Carmine instructed Carl to stand near the spot where the load would be dumped, then went into the cab and pressed the button. The bed rose and the plaster and broken wood and sheetrock and old sinks and toilets they'd collected during the day slid out, creating a sizable dust cloud that enveloped the lad.

"Now spit on your hands and rub your face and hair and arms," Carmine said.

Carl did so, smearing the gray dust on his exposed skin, then wiping his hands on his jeans and Led Zeppelin "Swan Song" t-shirt.

"Now you look like you're at least thirty," Carmine said. "Thirty and dirty. Fuckin' filthy. Now let's go to the strip bar."

The dump truck had large Carson Home Improvement signs on both sides, so Carmine parked behind the building, out of sight from the traffic on Conklin Street.

Caked with debris, Carl, butterflies fluttering, followed his boss around the building and through the front door into the secret world of adult lust, an experience that, until now, had been limited to magazines, videos, and sneak-peaks behind the curtain of the XXX section at the video store. But no images of women he'd seen on VHS box covers, nor in film, nor on the pages of *Playboy, Penthouse,* and *Hustler* could compare to seeing the real thing mere feet away, a woman bearing some resemblance to Susanna Hoffs, lead singer of The Bangles, wearing only a neon orange bikini bottom, her long, teased-up, curly brown hair hanging down the front to her large bare breasts, dancing for the only customer in the place seated at the bar, her big brown eyes turning towards the newcomers before turning back to the man.

Dazed, Carl followed Carmine to the bar, behind which awaited an attractive woman with blond hair also with an amazing body covered only by neon green tube top and bikini bottom. He thought for sure she would ask for his ID, but Carmine had pulled from his front pocket the large wad of cash he always carried around and peeled off a hundred-dollar bill, greeting her with a friendly, "How we doin'?" and slapping the bill on the bar. Before she could respond, he was ordering a club soda and lemon and a bottle of Bud and telling her, "Don't mind my buddy here. I told him I'd buy him a beer if he put in a hard day, and, as you can probably tell, he did a hell of a job today."

The woman smiled and picked up the hundred and brought it to the cash register and Carmine subtly nudged Carl's ribs with his elbow. Moments later she was back with their beverages and Carmine's change, all singles and fives.

"Thank you, sweetheart," Carmine said, taking a five from the pile and sliding it towards her, a generous tip for a three-dollar beer and two-dollar club soda. She smiled and thanked him, then he took two more fives from the pile and quietly said something to her that Carl couldn't hear over the music and she nodded, then took those bills and dropped them on the stage with the several singles that were already there.

The Aerosmith song ended and the place became uncomfortably quiet. The bartender said something to the dancer and they both looked in his direction, then the bartender put in a new CD. Seconds later, a John Bonham drumbeat/cymbal crash exploded into the room, followed by the chromatic progression of Led Zeppelin's exotic masterpiece, the trancelike "Kashmir".

The dancer slid off the stage and went around the bar, smiling at Carl.

Carmine leaned over and said in his ear, "You know the rules, no touching."

Carl was aware of this rule and remained stone still as she swayed to the music, her bare breasts dangerously close.

"What's your name?" she asked.

"Carl," he mumbled.

"Hi, Carl. I'm Angel."

"Hi."

She swayed before him, her Susanna Hoffs eyes encouraging him to look at her breasts, then turned around so he could admire her perfectly curved bottom. Carmine kept sliding over bills for him to add to the tip pile, which, by the time the near ten-minute song started fading to silence, was up to twenty-seven dollars.

When it was over, Carmine applauded and whistled and Carl clapped too but stopped because of the construction dust clouding from his hands.

"It was nice meeting you, Carl," Angel said, allowing him one last closeup of her breasts before gathering the pile of cash from the bar and collecting the money and her other belongings from the stage.

The bartender put on at a lower volume Mötley Crüe's "Girls, Girls, Girls".

"You alright in there, kid?" Carmine asked.

"That was the greatest thing ever," Carl said. "My loser father would never do anything like this for me."

"Well, most fathers wouldn't take their sixteen-year-old sons to strip joints and buy them beers. I'm more of a lesson of what not to be."

"My father's already a lesson like that."

"It doesn't hurt to have more than one. Ultimately, you're gonna have to make your own mistakes and learn your own lessons the hard way, but, along the way, just keep me and your old man in mind. Trust me, kid, you don't wanna turn out like us."

THE RABBIT

"There you go, kid," Carmine said, behind the wheel of the Carson Home Improvement dump truck he'd been driving for fifteen years, roaring through quiet suburban East Meadow, to Carl, working with him for the summer before his senior year of high school.

Carmine slowed the truck to a stop next to the rusted brick-red Volkswagen Rabbit with the "FOR SALE" sign taped to the hatchback window:

'78 VW RABBIT
199,000 MILES
RUNS GREAT!
$300

Carmine pulled the truck ahead of the Rabbit and parked next to the curb. He and Carl got out and slowly circled the Volkswagen, looking at it from all angles. The car, twelve years old, had rust around the windshield and a softball-sized hole in the floor of the back passenger side through which asphalt could be seen. Yet it wasn't nearly as bad as the Camaro that Carl had looked at several nights earlier, in which there was no floor at all in the back, and they were asking "$500 or best offer".

"So, whaddaya think?" Carmine asked, wiping the sweat

from his receding hairline with a red paisley bandana, then lighting a Marlboro and offering one to Carl.

"It doesn't look too bad," Carl said, reaching for the cigarette and lighting it.

"You can probably talk down the price. Offer two-hundred."

"I don't know. I still want a Camaro."

"Fuck the Camaro. At this point you need wheels, any wheels. I'm tired of going all the way out to Massapequa to pick your ass up every morning. Go knock on the fucking door and ask for a test drive. I'll be in the truck if he tries anything."

Carl looked at the split-level house, then back at Carmine, again wiping sweat with the bandana.

"Let's go! It's fucking hot out here!" Carmine barked, heading back to the idling truck.

Carl started up the walk and climbed the steps. He rang the bell and a small dog started barking inside. He looked back at the truck.

Eventually, an elderly woman in a baby-blue nightgown answered. It was four in the afternoon.

"Hello, young man," she said through the door slightly ajar. "Can I help you?"

"I'm here about the Rabbit," he said.

"The what?"

"The Rabbit. The car." He pointed at the Volkswagen.

"Oh. Then you'll want to talk to my husband, Larry."

She let the door close and started calling for Larry, who asked what the hell she wanted, then became friendlier when she said there was a handsome young man here asking about the car.

Carl heard the floor creaking until a chubby, white-haired, white-mustached, pink-faced man in his sixties wearing too-tight white tennis shirt and even more disturbingly tight white shorts appeared at the second-floor landing. The man looked at him, then descended the stairs to the front door.

"You can go back upstairs now, Millie, and close the door," he said, and she obliged.

The man waited until she was gone before opening the door.

"Hi there," he said, cheerfully. "I'm Larry. And you are?"

"Here about the car," Carl said.

"My, it's a scorcher out here," Larry said, pushing the door open a little wider. "Care to come in? We have Central Air, and I can make us drinks. I mix a mean Rob Roy."

Carl looked back at the truck.

"Is that your truck?" Larry asked.

"My boss's truck."

"Oh, there are two of you. Do you think your boss would care to come inside?"

"I just wanna take the car for a test drive."

"You don't think he'd like a cold drink?"

"No. He's a recovering alcoholic."

The passenger-side window of the truck rolled down and Carmine stuck his head out.

"Let's go, we're on the clock!" he yelled, then rolled the window back up.

Carl looked at Larry.

"I'll get the key," Larry said.

Carl went back to the truck, around to the driver's side.

"I think this guy's spent the last forty years in the closet," he said to Carmine.

"You want my piece?"

"Nah, man. I can take him if he tries anything."

"Here," Carmine said, handing him the switchblade from the glove box.

Carl took the knife and slipped it into his tube sock, then went over to the Rabbit and waited for Larry.

"Will your boss be joining us?" Larry asked.

"No," Carl said.

Larry handed Carl a key with a black rubber top and cutout of the Volkswagen logo. He then went around to the passenger side and got in.

Carl opened the driver door and slid into the bucket seat. The car was so small it felt like a go-kart. Larry was uncomfortably close.

"Anything I should know?" Carl asked before putting the key in the ignition.

"Nope," Larry said, smiling. "It's an automatic, so all you have to do is slip in the key and turn it on. The wheel's all yours, tiger."

Carl inserted the key and turned the ignition. The car started right up.

He shifted into "D", then looked in the sideview mirror and pulled around the dump truck.

"We can go around the block," Larry said. "Or, there's also a nice little park a few blocks from here with a nice shady parking lot."

"Around the block," Carl said, speeding up.

"Your boss seems like a scary man," Larry said.

"He's only scary when he's not your friend."

"It must be exciting riding around with him in that big truck all day," Larry was saying as Carl pressed harder on the accelerator, despite the STOP sign at the oncoming intersection.

"Stop sign!" Larry yelped, but Carl kept accelerating until he felt the old man's hand on his thigh. He hit the brake pedal hard and the little car screeched and swerved to a halt in the vacant intersection, a trail of wavy black lines on the asphalt behind them.

Carl pulled the knife from his sock and switched it open in front of Larry's fat pink face.

"Touch me again and I'll kill you," he said, echoing the threat his father had made years earlier to another creepy old predator who'd approached Carl in the supermarket. His father had pulled his U.S. Customs-issue Glock on that old perv. It was the only cool thing he'd ever seen his father do.

Larry, sweating, crying, nodding, refusing to look at Carl, blubbered, "I'm sick, I know. I'm sick, I'm sick, and I'm sorry!"

"I'll give you two hundred for the car," Carl said.

"Yes, yes, you can have it!" Larry blubbered.

Carl looked around the intersection, then made a slow U-turn and stopped. With his left foot on the brake, he floored the gas pedal with his right, revving the little engine to the max, the car shaking violently, Larry pleading for Carl to stop. When the engine could give no more, Carl took his foot off the brake and the tires chirped, the Rabbit racing towards the dump truck until Carl slammed on the brake pedal, the car screeching to a halt in front of the truck's huge grill.

Carl got out of the Rabbit as Carmine descended the truck cab. Larry remained inside blubbering.

"Do you have two-hundred bucks and a pen?" Carl asked. "I'll pay you back tomorrow."

Carmine reached into his pocket and pulled out a large wad of cash from which he peeled off ten twenty-dollar bills, then climbed back into the truck and removed a Carson Home Improvement clic-stic pen from the glove box. They waited as the old man removed himself from his old Rabbit, then unfolded the vehicle title and signed it on the roof. Carmine inspected the title, then showed Carl where to sign and told him to give the guy the cash.

Larry, without looking at either of them, accepted the cash and turned up the walk. Carmine climbed back into the truck as Carl slid into his new ride, both watching the old man climb the steps to his waiting, nightgowned wife, before starting their engines and roaring away.

SPIT LOT

Moments before the start of fourth period English class—

"I like your Rabbit," Jacqui said to Carl, referring to his rusted, brick-red 1978 Volkswagen.

"Really?"

"Yeah. I want you to take me for a ride in it."

"Yeah. Sure."

"Are you gonna cruise Spit Lot Friday night?" she asked, referring to the parking lot of the Spit nightclub in Levittown, where Nassau County high school students did their cruising.

"Uh, maybe?"

"I'm gonna be there Friday night. You better be there with the Rabbit."

* * *

Spit, a nightclub and music venue also known as *Uncle Sam's,* was best known for hosting Madonna's early gigs before she became famous. In 1985, when the drinking age changed from 19 to 21, the parking lot became more popular than the club itself, a veritable "meat market" attracting cheeseballs from all over with their bass-thumping Monte Carlos, Cougars, Olds 98s, Camaros, and Grands Prix—1990 Nassau County's version of *American Graffiti,* one of Long Island's crown jewels of cruising alongside Suffolk's Deer Park Avenue, Brooklyn's 86th Street, and Queens' Francis Lewis Boulevard.

* * *

Friday afternoon—

Carl parked the Rabbit in front of his friend Pete's house. His parents were still at work, and their friend, Jim, was seated on the couch flipping through the channels.

Both laughed when Carl suggested they take the Rabbit up to Spit Lot.

"You'll *scare* the chicks away in that piece of shit," Pete laughed.

"Well, Jacqui wants a ride in it and said I'd better bring it tonight," Carl bragged.

"She said that?" Jim asked.

"Yep. I even stopped at Auto Barn on the way over here and bought Turtle Wax and pine air fresheners—"

Pete and Jim laughed, but neither had cars of their own, and none of them had ever been to Spit Lot. So, after the laughter subsided, they headed outside and waxed the Rabbit, bringing back some of the faded brick red, but also highlighting the scars of rust, particularly around the windshield. They also vacuumed the interior, including the mat that was covering the large, rust-eaten hole in the floor on the rear passenger side, and hung the Forest Pine air freshener tree from the rearview mirror.

When the Rabbit was ready, Carl and Jim went home to take showers and eat dinner, then reconvened at Pete's.

* * *

It was late September, still summer warm, teenage lust swirling over Hempstead Turnpike. The lot was crowded and many weren't even trying to get into the loop, instead parking on a side street and walking over to hang out in "The Middle"—the two long rows of parking spaces that the cruisers drove around, where, like at a racetrack, the serious partying was going on, people swigging from cans and bottles, smoking joints and cigarettes, and a few lucky ones engaged in back seat sex.

Two blocks away, Carl pulled the Rabbit into the line of cars waiting to get into the lot, Public Enemy's *Fear of a Black Planet*—"Welcome to the Terrordome"—pumping through a sound system worth three times the vehicle, subwoofer in the hatchback, the little car vibrating as if about to blow off the doors and shatter the glass.

Pete was wearing his usual purple Los Angeles Lakers cap with yellow lettering. Jim had on his usual black Chicago Bulls cap with red lettering. Carl, though, before his stop at Auto Barn, had swung by the mall and purchased a phresh red Philadelphia Phillies cap and a light blue Maui and Sons t-shirt to top off his black Levi's and black Nike Airs with white Swoosh.

They mostly idled for ten minutes and had only moved two car-lengths.

"Let's just go fuckin' park," Pete said for the third time.

"No," Carl said. "Jacqui wants a ride in the Rabbit."

"She still can," Jim said. "You can meet her in The Middle, then take her out to the parked car and drive her around the block."

"Not the same," Carl said.

"He's got pussy on the brain," Pete said. "I'm getting out."

"Me too," Jim said.

They got out and walked towards the lot.

Twenty minutes later, Carl finally made it into the lot and was next in line to join the loop. He switched tapes in the deck to *It Takes a Nation of Millions to Hold Us Back*—"Bring the

Noise"—then waited for an opening and eventually squeezed in ahead of a black Monte Carlo.

The Rabbit's windows were rolled down and he started hearing comments and laughter from The Middle, but he paid them no mind as he rolled slowly passed, scanning the crowd, until finally spotting Jacqui with a couple of her friends.

"Oh my God, it's Carl!" she exclaimed, hurrying over to the Rabbit, leaving one of her friends to wonder aloud, "Like, oh my God, does she, like, know that loser in the toy car?"

Jacqui paid them no mind and got in on the passenger side.

"Cool stereo," she said, snapping her wild strawberry Bubblicious. "Can I put on Hot 97?"

"Sure," Carl said, eyes wide. She looked hotter than ever and more scantily dressed than at school, showing some serious cleavage.

The Monte Carlo behind him honked. Carl took his foot off the brake and the Rabbit moved a few inches, then stalled. Every red and orange light on the dashboard illuminated.

"What happened?" Jacqui asked.

"It stalled. Don't worry, this happened before. We just need to wait a couple of minutes for the starter to cool off."

The Monte Carlo honked again. Carl turned the ignition a couple of times, but there was only a clicking noise, and the engine didn't turn.

"Maybe I should get out," Jacqui said.

"Wait, hold on," Carl said, turning the ignition again.

"I gotta get back to my friends," she said.

Before he could say anything else, she was out of the car and had left the door open.

"Why did you, like, get in the little car with that loser?" he heard one of her friends ask.

Behind him, more cars were honking. Carl turned the ignition, but, again, only clicking.

Then he heard someone say to put it into neutral. In the rearview mirror, he saw Pete and Jim getting ready to push.

He shifted and they pushed the car out of the loop and off to the side.

Carl turned the ignition. Clicking.

"When this happened before," he said, "I usually just had to wait a little while, and then it would start again."

"How long did you wait last time?"

"I don't know. About two hours, maybe."

"Two fuckin' hours?"

"Maybe it'll be sooner."

An hour went by and it still wouldn't start. Nobody wanted to call their parents, but they probably didn't have enough money for a cab that would get them all the way back to Massapequa.

Finally, just before midnight, Carl turned the ignition, and this time it started. The crowds had thinned by now and he managed to maneuver out of the lot to Hempstead Turnpike, then to Sunrise Highway and the desolate, amber-lit thoroughfares of Massapequa, where there were a few good parking lots, but nowhere to cruise.

SAUSAGE AND PEPPERS

Autumn 1990, heading west on the Belt Parkway, Carl navigating the '78 Volkswagen Rabbit into the Brooklyn sun, Pete riding shotgun, Jim in the back squeezed behind the driver seat to avoid the softball-sized hole in the passenger-side floor. The Friday afternoon traffic was heavy in the eastbound lanes back to Long Island, but the westbound lanes were light and the potholes were shaking the rusted little car to where it seemed about to break apart, driver and passengers clenching teeth and squeezing hand straps as they continued forward towards the promised land.

Pete's cousin, Tommy, lived in Marine Park, and Pete had suggested they hang out with him in Brooklyn because it was boring spending Friday and Saturday nights in Massapequa drinking beer in the same old parking lots or cruising Spit lot with the cheeseballs, but, most important, Tommy knew a lot of girls, and, supposedly, unlike prudish suburbia, Brooklyn girls put out.

Tommy was also a senior in high school and his family lived in a townhouse. His mother used one of the rooms for her hairdressing business and his father worked in a lumber yard. His older brother was away at college and there were a pair of twin beds where Carl and Jim would sleep, while Pete would sleep in the extra bed in Tommy's room.

Tommy's mother made sausage and pepper subs for dinner. It was a family favorite and Pete and Jim had grown up in Italian households where it was a fixture, but Carl hated peppers, and the smell from downstairs was making him nauseous. Unlike home or at one of his own relatives' houses where he could refuse what he didn't like without concern of offending anyone, the gravity of being a stranger in someone's home was weighing on him, and Tommy's mother, despite meeting he and Jim for the first time, was treating them all like they were hers and that the four of them were brothers. Tommy was excited that they'd all get to experience the very favorite of his mother's meals and he playfully hugged and kissed her on the cheek, and Carl knew he couldn't dare refuse or even pick or nibble at it. He was going to have to take big bites and make it look like he was enjoying it as much as everyone else and eat the whole thing without throwing up.

The sausage and bread weren't bad, but there were a lot of peppers, and onions, which he hated even more than peppers. Their smells had become so overpowering that he couldn't even taste them, but their soft crunch was a reminder they were there. He sipped his frosted glass of Coke after every bite and emulated the others' nods and *Mmmm*s and grunts as they chewed until there were only crumbs and grease on his plate.

"So, what do you Long Island clowns think of Ma's sausage and peppers?" Tommy asked.

"Better than my mother's," Jim said.

"Delicious as always," Pete said.

"Good," Carl nodded.

"Come on, they're better than good," Tommy said.

"I thought you didn't like peppers," Pete said to Carl.

"Well, I've never had any as good as these," Carl said.

Tommy's mother smiled and Tommy laughed.

"Thanks for making this delicious food for us, Aunt Marie," Pete said. Jim and Carl also thanked her.

"Yeah, thanks, Ma," Tommy said, sliding out of his chair. "We're gonna go out for a while now. Don't wait up."

"Don't stay out late and no drinking," she said, and Tommy kissed her on the cheek, then kissed his father's bald forehead and said, "Night, Pop, don't drink too much wine," and his father, chewing, mumbled something back in Italian and sipped his Chianti, then the Long Islanders followed Tommy outside.

The Rabbit was parked up the street and Tommy said to leave it because they wouldn't be driving anywhere.

"Did you take the stereo out?" he asked Carl.

"Yeah, I left it in your brother's room."

"Good, because it would be gone in the morning if you left it in the car. And make sure there's nothing else valuable in there and leave the doors unlocked so nobody breaks your windows. And don't worry about the car getting stolen, the chop shops won't want this thing."

Their first stop was the Carvel over on Flatbush Avenue, where Carl got a cup of orange sherbet to try to get the pepper taste out of his mouth, then a large vanilla soft-serve cone with colored sprinkles.

It was dark by the time they finished, Carl taking in the headlights and honking on Flatbush Avenue as he attempted to wipe his sticky fingers with a small, thin napkin. Tommy's pager started beeping and vibrating and he pulled it from his belt clip and looked at the number. Pete had also recently bought a pager, but out in Massapequa it was still pointless since so few people had them, while in Brooklyn everyone seemed to.

"Gimme a quarter," Tommy ordered his cousin. Pete reached into his pocket and pulled out some change and handed one over. Tommy then went to one of the graffiti-markered pay phones at the side of the Carvel and dialed the number on the pager, which turned out to be a pay phone around the block, where his friend Mikey picked up the receiver the instant it started ringing.

"Tommy, where the fuck are you?"

"Carvel. Where the fuck are you?"

"Around the fuckin' block."

"What the fuck is everybody doing?"

"Just fuckin' around, but everyone's going to Freddie's Playground. I'll be there in about an hour."

"Alright, but beep me if you're doin' somethin' else. I got my cousin and his Long Island friends and we gotta show them a good fuckin' time."

"Don't worry about it, they'll have a fuckin' blast."

There was a bodega up the street. They followed Tommy inside and he led them down a narrow aisle to the beer cooler in the back and watched as he selected a 40-ounce bottle of Olde English "800".

"This stuff has more alcohol than regular beer," he said, "and they're only a buck fifty."

They each selected a bottle, Carl going with Colt 45, Pete with King Cobra, and Jim with a green bottle of Mickey's. They followed Tommy to the counter and he said to the cashier, "Gimme a nickel and some papers." The guy put down a small stamp bag overstuffed with weed and a package of E-Z Wider rolling papers and Tommy paid with exact change, then the others paid for their forties and Carl splurged an extra $1.75 on a pack of Marlboros.

A few blocks away was "Freddie's Playground", as the park was known in the neighborhood, named after a beloved high school kid who was beaten to death there by members of a local gang, and where a large graffiti mural in his honor depicting him as Fred Flintstone now spanned the walls of several handball courts. A bunch of Tommy's friends were already hanging out at one end of the basketball court, including some girls. Everyone had forties.

The Colt 45 was gross, especially when it got warm. For a

while the Long Islanders talked among themselves, then Tommy rolled a joint out of the nickel bag and everyone formed a circle beneath one of the netless basketball hoops and passed it around. Carl started feeling it right away, a little dizzy at first, lightheaded, then, after the second hit, paranoid, and, after the third, pretty fucked up.

There was a bodega across the street and several of them went and bought forties. This time Carl bought a quart of Budweiser and chipped in for another nickel bag.

Back at the playground someone suggested playing spin the bottle. Everyone was into it and more people were there now and another circle formed. Tommy volunteered to go first and spun the empty Colt 45 bottle, the capped top coming to a stop pointed at a tall, blond-haired girl named Stephanie, prompting everyone to laugh and go *Whoaaaa!* Carl was expecting to see some awkward gesturing like kids at a school dance, but Tommy went right up to her and they made out for a few seconds as everyone cheered, then they raised their arms and took a bow.

There were no volunteers for the next spin, so Tommy spun to determine the next contestant and it landed on a pretty girl with short brown hair named Nina. She was shy compared to the others and looked a little embarrassed.

Her first spin landed on one of the other girls, resulting in a do-over.

The next spin landed on Carl.

Everyone went *Whoaaaa!* and Tommy laughed, "Long Island boy!"

A short girl with dark curly hair named Betty, the loudest of the girls and a true Brooklyn chick, eyeing Carl, said to the girl next to her, "I was hoping to kiss the one with the hair."

Carl, stoned, a bit drunk now, watched as Nina, businesslike, approached, then gave him a quick peck on the lips and immediately returned to her spot.

"Oh, come on, Nina!" Betty exclaimed, leaving her spot and crossing the circle to Carl, who was nearly a head taller than she. "You have to put a little effort into it, like this—"

She reached up and put her hands on his cheeks and, for a moment, in the soft brown of her eyes, he was floating above the Brooklyn night and going higher, over the five boroughs, Nassau, Suffolk, the Tri-State area—and then he was back on the basketball court with her tongue all over the inside of his mouth and her thigh leaning into his crotch and everyone cheering in the background sounding a million miles away. He did his best to kiss her back, but her aggression had caused him to lose his balance backwards, then it was over and she was heading back to her spot.

"And that's how you do it!" she declared, everyone cheering.

Then a guy named Billy showed up with a bottle of Jack Daniel's and the game broke up. Billy was a friend of the group who had already enlisted in the Navy and would be leaving for boot camp the day after high school graduation. He passed the bottle around and Carl took a small swig of the whiskey expecting to gag like he usually did when drinking straight liquor, but this stuff was smooth and went down easier than expected, and he took a bigger swig each time around.

The night became a blur and Carl laughed and clowned with everyone else and enjoyed Betty telling everyone, "Look at Long Island over there, he wants me to kiss him again," then she'd pout her lips at him and look away.

Then one of the guys turned serious and said the same car had been driving by the playground for the past ten minutes. The basketball courts were surrounded by twenty-foot high chain-link fences with only one way in and out and they were worried about being rolled up on by one of the local gangs. Freddie's Playground was turf belonging to the Avenue T

Furies, which was okay to traverse if you were a civilian, but, if they thought you were somehow affiliated with another gang, even by distant relation, they wouldn't hesitate to give you a serious beating, and a large crowd hanging out on their turf always drew their attention.

"I think it's time to call it a night," Betty said, then looked at Carl. "Good night, Long Island."

"No goodnight kiss?"

"I'll kiss you again next time you come to Brooklyn, so you better fuckin' come back soon."

"Come on, let's get the fuck out of here," Tommy said to the Long Islanders, and everyone streamed out of the court and went their separate ways.

It was after midnight and little was said during the walk back to Tommy's house. He told them to be quiet so they wouldn't wake his parents, and, drunk as they were, they managed to get into their beds without making much noise, Carl passing out blissfully with thoughts of kissing Betty again.

At some point in the night, though, he woke up and the room was spinning. It was slow at first and he tried to will it to a halt, but that only made it go faster. Upon realizing that puking was inevitable, it was too late.

He puked in the bed, on the floor, in the hallway, and all over the pink-tiled bathroom across the hall, before finally managing to direct the flow into the pink porcelain, bits of sausage, pepper, onion, and colored sprinkles floating in the bowl. Then he dry-heaved for a while, bursting blood vessels in the whites of his eyes and leaving Satanic-looking red spots that would last nearly a week. He waited until the spinning slowed and he could no longer hold himself up before heading back to bed. Cleaning the mess was not a consideration and making it back across the hall was far from guaranteed, but he somehow made it without waking anyone, then fell onto the bed and passed back out.

He was awakened at first light by a scrub brush outside the door and Tommy's mother mumbling in Italian.

Across the room, Jim made a sound from his bed.

"What's that smell?" he groaned.

Carl opened his eyes. He didn't know where he was. The room was hot and smelled of vomit. It was on the pillowcase, the sheets, the floor, his t-shirt, his jeans, his socks, caked to his face, stiff in his hair.

The bedroom door flew open. It was Pete.

"Oh, man, it reeks in here!" he exclaimed, holding his nose, turning away.

Tommy came in and exclaimed, "Dude!" and laughed.

"I'm so sorry," Carl moaned, pushing himself up, head pounding, mouth dry.

"Go apologize to my aunt," Pete ordered him like a big brother, really pissed, but Tommy was laughing.

"I'm usually the one who pukes around here," he laughed, then turned and said to his mother, on her knees scrubbing the bathroom floor with her feet sticking out of the doorway and into the hall, "Hey, Ma, Carl is sorry and he feels really bad."

She mumbled something in Italian.

"Go!" Pete said to Carl.

Carl rose from the bed, looked down at the mess, then, feeling the dried vomit on his face, went out to the hall. He stopped at the bathroom, standing above Tommy's mother as she scrubbed the floor around the toilet.

"I'm really sorry about the mess," he said. "I can help clean it up."

"No, it is okay," she said without looking up. "I am finished in here, so you shower now and I will get you some of Tommy's clothes to borrow."

She gave him a washcloth and an amber bar of Dial soap

and came back with a white tank top and white sweatpants and, for his soiled clothes, a plastic shopping bag that said *Have a nice day!* on it and had a big yellow smiley face. His boxer shorts were clean, if not a little crusty in the middle. He turned on the water and waited for it to get warm, then got in and washed himself as fast as he could and shampooed with the Head & Shoulders on the shelf. She hadn't brought socks and he went without them. He stuffed his soiled clothes into the plastic bag and tied it closed at the handles.

She was waiting outside the door.

"Now go downstairs with the others and eat breakfast," she said.

They laughed when they saw him wearing Tommy's clothes. Tommy's father had prepared a feast and the table was covered with scrambled eggs, sausage, prosciutto, bacon, toast, orange juice.

The food helped, but Carl still felt like he'd been hit by a bus.

"Thank you for the food and I'm so sorry about the mess," he said to Tommy's parents across the table.

"Don't feel bad," Tommy's father said. "We've all been there. This one," he said, pointing his fork at Tommy, "he's been sick three times in this house. And me too, every now and then, one too many glasses of *vino*, and then I am making friends with the same *toilette* you did. I call her '*Rosa*'."

* * *

Heading east on the Belt Parkway, Carl navigated the Rabbit towards the rising Long Island sun, still early enough on a Saturday morning for the traffic to be light.

"How are you going to explain your new clothes to your parents?" Pete asked.

"And your eyes," Jim added.

"I'm gonna park around the block and go through the old lady's yard behind us, then sneak in the back kitchen door, go up to my room, change and put on some shades, then sneak back out and get the car and drive up front to my usual spot, then stroll through the front door cool as a pool cue."

"Jeez," Pete laughed.

"What are you gonna do with the puky clothes?" Jim asked. "The smell is gonna give you away."

Rabbit in the left lane, Carl rolled down the window, grabbed the knotted plastic bag from the passenger-side floor, and made a no-look pass out of the car to the parkway shoulder barrier. He watched in the rearview mirror as it bounced along the broken asphalt, then his eyes shifted to a nearby cluster of buildings.

She was back there somewhere, and she was gonna kiss him again when he came back.

COWARD OF KINGS COUNTY

Carl had been looking forward to the party because Betty would be there, the girl who kissed him a month ago. That was the first and only time he and his friend Pete had come to Brooklyn from Massapequa, Long Island. Pete's cousin, Tommy, lived in a townhouse in Marine Park, and, on this night, his parents would be away.

They arrived while some of Tommy's friends were in the kitchen tapping a keg of Budweiser. In the living room there was an ounce of weed and a torn-open carton of Marlboros on the coffee table. People started showing up, but not Betty, which was good because for the past month all he'd been thinking about was her promise to kiss him again, and hopefully more, when he came back to Brooklyn, but he'd thought about it too much and was now paralyzed by fear. Then the blunts started going around and he got paranoid and hid in the kitchen next to the keg trying to get the beer buzz going, but the blunts followed him in and the shit was good.

"Dude, your eyes are so fuckin' red!" Tommy laughed, leaning in to get a closer look at Carl's bloodshot peepers.

Then he heard her in the living room. She was a Brooklyn girl and her voice was loud and she was tough and seemed a little crazy, a girl the likes of which he had not encountered in Massapequa.

Then the voice started getting closer to the kitchen and would be there any second. His mind went blank.

"There you are, Long Island," she said, smiling, holding out her red plastic cup. "Wanna fill me up?"

"Sure," Carl said, taking the cup. He picked up the tap and it started squirting foam.

"I was beginning to think you were hiding from me," she said, watching her cup fill with tiny bubbles.

"No, I got stuck in here and everyone started handing me blunts."

She leaned in and looked into his eyes.

"Jesus Christ, you *are* fuckin' high," she said. "If you manage to get any beer into that cup, why don't you bring it into the living room and sit next to me on the couch."

He spent the next several minutes filling both of their cups, scooping out the foam with his fingers then filling a little more, until the layer of beer was finally visible from the top. He then rinsed his hands and brought the beers into the living room.

Betty was on the couch with a vacant spot next to her.

"What took you so long to come back?" she asked, then sipped her beer.

"I tried to get the foam out, but I was having some trouble with the tap."

"No, I meant back to Brooklyn."

"Oh. Well, this is the first time since then that Pete wanted to come out—"

"You could have told Pete that you wanted to come out here to see me."

"Oh. Yeah, I didn't think to—"

"Or you could have just got my phone number through Tommy and called me."

"Oh. I didn't think of that."

"I thought you liked when I kissed you, Long Island."

"I did! That's all I've been thinking about! But I didn't know it would be okay to just call you."

"You didn't know. Well, now you're going to have to work for that next kiss."

"What do I need to do? I'll do anything."

"Sit here and say nice things about me and tell me how beautiful I am and how much you want me."

There was a commotion in the kitchen. Some of the guys were talking about a car that kept driving by out front that they thought belonged to the Avenue T Furies, the local gang that had no tolerance for other gang members passing through their turf. A girl across the room started telling someone how Tommy had walked down Avenue T the other day and one of them thought he was with another gang and the next thing he knew he was running for his life. He got away, but they were still after him.

Moments later, one of Tommy's friends passed through the living room with a metal Easton baseball bat, then another guy with a piece of iron pipe. Then Pete came in with a thick piece of chain.

"You stay here," he said to Carl. "This doesn't involve you."

Upstairs a couple of Tommy's friends were hoisting him up to the attic crawl space, while the rest of the guys, except Carl, went outside and formed a wall in front of the house with weapons in full view.

"Aren't you gonna go out there?" Betty asked Carl, serious now.

"Pete said to stay in here."

"*Pete said*... Don't you have any fuckin' balls of your own? Are you just gonna sit in here like a coward and hide with the girls? Do you listen to everything Pete says? Is he your fuckin' father?"

The room became silent as Betty and the twenty or so

other girls in there awaited his answer, but he was stymied.

"What's the matter, sweetie? Do you need Pete to answer for you?"

"Shut up, Betty," said Stephanie, another girl Carl had met last time. "He's a fuckin' guest."

"Tell me to 'shut up' again and I'll knock your fuckin' teeth out," Betty warned her.

A siren chirped outside. The guys started streaming back in with their bats and chains and hammers. There were about fifty people squeezed into the living room and kitchen, but it was quiet and tense, and several of the guys were peeking through the curtains.

The cop drove by several more times, then didn't come back, nor did the Furies' car. Eventually it was deemed safe to retrieve Tommy from the attic.

"I'm outta here," Betty said, getting up from the couch and hugging Tommy, telling him to be careful. On her way out she gave Carl a sharp glance, then looked away.

After everyone was gone, Tommy, Pete, and Carl were in the kitchen cleaning up.

"I should have gone out there," Carl said to Pete.

"No," Pete said. "I *had* to go out there. If he wasn't my cousin, I'd have been in here with you."

"Yeah, the T-Furies are fuckin' animals," Tommy said. "You don't want to get mixed up with them. You might wind up dead like Freddie."

"Betty called me a 'coward' in front of the rest of the girls."

"Don't listen to her shit," Tommy said. "She's got a big fuckin' mouth. Half my friends can't stand her. You're better off stayin' the fuck away from her anyway. Dude, for your own sake, just stay the fuck away from her."

NO SLEEP TILL BROOKLYN

They'd been driving around South Brooklyn all night, Carl visiting from Long Island and alone in the back seat of Tommy's Olds 98 sipping quarts of Budweiser and packing his little brass pipe with some fine green they'd bought at a red light somewhere near Coney Island. Big Scott "Buddha" was riding shotgun, pager in one hand and roll of quarters in the other, the pager beeping every few minutes and he would tell Tommy to pull over at the next pay phone.

For hours everyone had been calling each other from pay phones trying to figure out where to meet. Carl had some serious munchies and they stopped at Roll-N-Roaster for a dripping Roast Beef-N-Cheez sandwich and Fries-n-Cheez, which was fine with Buddha because he was always up for food and there was a bank of clean pay phones there. An hour later they stopped at Lenny & John's for pepperoni slices and Grape Crush, and Buddha gave Carl one of his quarters to play *Super Punch Out* but was knocked out in the second bout by Dragon Chan and his flying leg kick.

At midnight they were back in the car and still without a place to meet up with everyone else.

"Yo, this is fuckin' boring!" Carl suddenly blurted out from the back. "Just pick a fuckin' place and tell everyone to go there!"

Tommy hit the brakes and the tires chirped. He and Buddha turned around and stared at Carl, making him paranoid.

"The silent stoner speaks!" Buddha finally laughed.

"He's right, though, Bood," Tommy said. "This is fuckin' boring."

"Alright, let's forget about trying to meet up with everyone. I know exactly what we need to do. We need to turn this boat around and drive into Manhattan and find some fuckin' hookers!"

"Fuckin' Jesus, Bood, we're not goin' into fuckin' Manhattan."

"Let's ask Cheech & Chong back there. Whadda ya say we feast on some whores?"

"I only have a few bucks left and I need another quart," Carl said. "And I have to piss again."

"Jesus fuckin' Christ," Tommy said.

Buddha's beeper started beeping and they pulled over again. Buddha made his call, then Carl pretended to be making a call but was pissing on the pay phone pole.

It had finally been decided that everyone meet at Brighton Beach, a good thing because Buddha was nearly out of quarters. Carl knew that Betty would probably be there, the girl he liked who now thought he was a coward. A couple of months earlier, Tommy had a party at his house that was interrupted when the Avenue T Furies started driving by, a local gang who'd mistaken Tommy for a rival gang member trespassing on their turf. A couple of Tommy's friends hoisted him into the attic crawl space and the rest of the guys went outside with bats and chains and metal pipes, except Carl, who was told by Tommy's cousin to stay inside because it didn't involve him. So he stayed inside, which is when Betty called him out in front of the twenty or so other girls in the living room, one of whom stepped in to defend speechless

Carl, which didn't help.

At the next bodega, Carl switched it up, going with a quart of Miller Genuine Draft and another nickel bag. After a quick hop on the Belt Parkway, they drove around some neighborhood for twenty minutes until Tommy finally found a parking spot.

Everyone else was already on the beach drinking and smoking. Carl was dragging in the sand twenty yards behind Tommy and Buddha, then went right by everyone, ignoring their calls inquiring where he was going. He continued on to the lifeguard chair and climbed it, then packed his pipe, but it was breezy and he couldn't get it lit. Then the chair began to shake.

Carl looked down. Betty was on the ladder looking up at him.

"Can I come up?" she asked, softer than her usual tough-Italian-girl-from-Brooklyn tone.

"I brought my balls this time and I'm not in a good mood."

She climbed the rest of the way and sat next to him and slid her arm into his and leaned her head against his shoulder.

"I'm really sorry," she said. "Tommy got so mad at me for how I treated you and I was drunk at the party and I'm sorry."

"I'm not a coward."

"I know. You want me to help you get that thing lit?"

Carl stopped trying to light the pipe.

"Here," she said, unzipping her hoodie sweatjacket, revealing tank top cleavage. "Go ahead."

He leaned in and she wrapped the hoodie around his head and flicked the lighter. It was like he was in a small tent with a pair of candlelit breasts. He took a hit, then pulled out and exhaled. He offered her a hit, but she declined and told him to finish it. He went back in and took another, then pulled out and exhaled into the wind.

"Got a condom on you?" she asked.

"In my wallet."

"How long has it been in there?"

"A while."

"Well, if it's still any good, I wanna fuck your brains out right here."

The wrapper was wrinkled, but the condom was still lubricated. He was already hard and she put the condom on him, then unzipped her own pants and rolled her petite body on top of him. She was nimble and knew what she was doing and slid him inside her and fucked his brains out in the same wild manner she had kissed him that first night.

Condom in the sand, she leaned her head against his breast. Carl wanted to say something, but he didn't know what and she started falling asleep.

When the sky started getting light, Tommy came over and said they were going.

"What does this mean?" Carl asked Betty.

"It means it's time to go home," she said, sleepy. "And I know that's not what you meant, but I don't wanna fuckin' talk about it right now."

They held hands walking across the sand. Tommy was ahead of them and nobody said anything. At the car they kissed like teenage lovers, then she walked away without a word.

Carl climbed into the back of Tommy's car and packed his pipe. Tommy didn't say anything. Buddha was snoring, then woke with a start and asked if they were going for breakfast.

They stopped at the Oasis Diner on Flatbush. On the way in, Carl bought a pack of Marlboros from the cigarette machine next to the gumball machines.

Within minutes their table was covered with pancakes, bacon, sausage, ham, eggs, toast, hash browns, orange juice, coffee, and an assortment of Smuckers jellies.

Carl put out his cigarette and took a bite of sausage.

"Forget about her," Tommy said, then bit his toast.

Buddha, chewing, nodded and said, "He's right. You better fuckin' forget about her."

"Why?"

"She kind of has a boyfriend," Tommy said.

"*Kind of?*"

"They're broken up, but she thinks they're more broken up than he does."

"Shit."

"And he's kind of psycho," Buddha said.

"Fuck."

"Don't worry," Tommy said. "He doesn't know your face, and no one around here really knows you."

Carl stopped eating and lit a cigarette.

"Just forget about her," Tommy said.

"Yeah," Buddha said, chewing, "and maybe don't come back around here for a while. A few months or so. Maybe more."

"And you better fuckin' forget about her," Tommy repeated, then gave Carl a light slap on the cheek and laughed.

He never did forget about Betty, not a chance of that. But he never went back to Marine Park and he never saw her again.

THE FLAP

Jerry pulled the '79 Ferrari 308 GTS—the *Magnum P.I.* model used in the original 1979 season, and also Christie Brinkley's ride in National Lampoon's *Vacation*—into the only available space in the "guest" section of the Massapequa High School parking lot, facing the giant mural on the wall of the bagel shop next door painted by students in the art club that featured a giant war bonnet and "MHS: HOME OF THE CHIEFS", and also the Batman symbol, which had been there on his own class' mural back in '72—each year, shortly after it was finished, someone in the night would spray-paint the Batman symbol on the mural, not over the main artwork but in a blank space off to the side that would make it look like it was part of the piece, and it was a mysteriously cool thing that continued through the decades, though now it looked sloppily done, the paint having run and left long black and yellow streaks down the wall, and the bat inside the oval totally crooked—

Inside the building, he navigated the familiar old corridors to the Little Theater, where he met his old "Public Speaking" teacher, Mr. Herrmann, who'd always reminded him of Gilligan—hyper-flustered, skinny, shirt untucked, mop of hair. The class featured a different guest speaker each day, from people who'd succeeded greatly, to others who'd failed miserably, including a recovering alcoholic who said he used to check the front of his car every morning for blood to see if he'd hit anybody the night before, and WBAB disc jockey Roger Luce, who said ZZ Top was the coolest band he'd ever met, and after leaving the radio station they walked off into the sunset with a beautiful woman on each arm and fade-vanished like they did in their videos. The students didn't have to take any tests or quizzes for the class, but they were required to sit up and listen.

Since Jerry was a "special" guest, they would have class down in the Little Theater so more people could see him than up in the classroom—despite having his own prime-time sitcom on NBC, school administrators did not consider him big enough for the Main Auditorium, which was reserved for those of a certain ilk, such as pop stars Debbie Gibson and Tiffany, Nassau County Executive Tom Gulotta, and astronauts. It did make him feel better that, six weeks earlier, TV weatherman Storm Field had been relegated to the Little Theater, as was local novelist William Gaddis—who lit a cigarette on stage, then cursed at the first student who asked him a question and stormed out, which, Mr. Herrmann realized, was for the best, because he'd been a total pain in the ass to deal with, and not one student, even the smart ones, had ever heard of the guy, nor had any of the English teachers—while actor William Baldwin was relegated to the cafeteria—

There was a smattering of applause after Mr. Herrmann introduced the comedian. The students already looked bored.

"He will not be telling jokes today," Mr. Herrmann explained. "He will be speaking about his time here at M.H.S., and answering your questions."

"Hi, everyone," Jerry said. "How is everybody today?"

No one responded.

"So," Mr. Herrmann jumped in, "why don't you tell us

about your time here at Massapequa High School."

"Sure. Let's see, I graduated in '72, I liked it here, it seemed like a good education—yes, uh, it looks like someone has a question—"

"Yes, Bridgette," Mr. Herrmann said.

"Are you going to, like, tell any jokes?"

"No, Bridgette," Mr. Herrmann said, throwing his arms in the air. "I just explained that he will not be telling jokes today. Please pay attention, everyone. No sleeping. Yes, Robert has a question—"

"Why not?" Robert asked, clad in Megadeth t-shirt that had a big hole under the right armpit.

"He's not telling jokes, Robert," Mr. Herrmann said, face turning red. "I apologize, Jerry. Please continue."

"Well, as I was saying, I enjoyed my time here, and actually performed in this theater once—"

"Hold on, Jerry," Mr. Herrmann jumped in. "Carl has a question, this is the first time he's raised his hand all year. Yes, Carl—"

"Are you friends with Howard Stern in real life?" Carl asked.

"Uh, sure. I know Howard."

"Any other questions before Jerry continues?" Mr. Herrmann asked.

No one raised their hand.

"So," Mr. Herrmann said, "why don't you tell us about your television program. Thursday nights on NBC."

"Okay, sure," Jerry said. "We do a sitcom on NBC, which is in its third season—"

"Yes, Robert has a question," Mr. Herrmann interrupted.

"Your TV show sucks," Robert said, getting a good laugh.

"That wasn't necessary, Robert," Mr. Herrmann said. "Does anyone else have any questions?"

Jennifer C. raised her hand.

"Yes, Jennifer C.," Mr. Herrmann said.

"Can we hear the band now?"

The students cheered.

"You booked a musical act?" Jerry asked Mr. Herrmann.

The band, Bambi and the Forest Friends, led by student guitar hero Ian Rummer, plugged in their amps and set up the drum kit, then ripped into Led Zeppelin's "Black Dog", the audience leaping from their seats—

"Thanks for coming, Jerry," Mr. Herrmann shouted in his ear, offering his hand—

Back out in the Ferrari, Jerry noticed he was low on fuel—

"308GTS, horrible MPG," he said out loud to himself, annoyed, stomach in knots, even worse than the ones he used to get after subpar Carson appearances. He roared out of the lot and onto Merrick Road, then pulled into the Mobil station across the street in the corner of the FoodTown shopping center. It was an old station with two garage bays and an office cluttered with engine belts and soiled car manuals, and a metal cash box for the gas customers, who were required to come in and pay before they pumped. The office also doubled as a waiting area for customers having their cars fixed, with a stained Mr. Coffee machine and a tower of Styrofoam cups on top of a small table, and, next to it, a metal folding chair, presently occupied by Dee Snider of Twisted Sister—

"Hey, Dee Snider," Jerry said.

"Hello, Jerry," Dee said.

"Do you live around here?"

"Nah, my parents do. That's actually why I'm here, I brought my mother's car in to get fixed."

"You're a good son. Where'd you go to high school?"

"Baldwin. You're from here, right?"

"Yep. I was just over at the high school."

"Oh yeah? Were you there to see Bambi and the Forest Friends?"

"Uh, no. Just dropped in to say hello to someone. Listen, it was good to see you, and good luck with the band, I'm just gonna pay for my gas and go—"

"Sweet ride. Is that the *Magnum P.I.* car?"

Back in the Ferrari, his stomach now further unsettled, he decided to remedy it with a chocolate egg cream at Krisch's Ice Cream Parlor.

He parked out front and plugged the meter for two hours. Inside, he found his sitcom castmate, Jason Alexander, seated at a booth with Massapequa native Alec Baldwin—

"What are you doing here?" Jerry asked Jason. "Hi Alec."

"Hello, Jerry," Alec said.

"I heard about the flap," Jason said.

"Flap? What flap? I left there like ten minutes ago. Oh yeah, I saw Dee Snider at the Mobil station over near the high school. He was getting his mother's car fixed."

"He's a good son," Alec said.

"We should do an episode about it," Jason said.

"About seeing Dee Snider at a gas station?" Jerry asked.

"No, about the flap."

"What flap?"

"The one at the high school."

"I heard about it too," Alec said. "Sounded ugly, but I heard the band was good."

"Where are your brothers?" Jerry asked Alec. "Don't you have like fifteen brothers?"

"Do I look like their keeper, Jerry?"

"No, not really."

"Then damned if I know where those maniacs are."

"Hey," Jason said, "at that table in the corner, the guy in the wheelchair—isn't that Ron Kovic?"

"Oh yeah, it is," Jerry said.

"Should we go over and say hello?" Alec asked.

"Wouldn't that be complicated for him, you know, with

the wheelchair?" Jerry asked.

"Perhaps," Alec said.

"Leave the man alone, he's been through enough," Jason said.

GIRLFRIEND II

Sunday night, in his bedroom, moments after spending some time with himself, a knock on the locked door—

"What?" Carl asked, annoyed, stuffing the wad of toilet paper between mattress and boxspring.

"There's a girl here to see you," his mother said through the door.

There were no girls he knew of who would just drop in at 9:30 on a Sunday night, except, possibly, Sherry from next door, but that was doubtful, and his mother would have said so if it was her.

"I'll be right down," he said.

He put on the neon yellow jogging shorts and white Vuarnet t-shirt he'd been wearing all weekend, then thumped down the stairs to the front door.

At first, he didn't recognize her. She was taller, slenderer, her hair was longer—Colleen O'Halleran, whom he used to work with at the All-American Burger a year-and-a-half ago when he was in eleventh grade and she was in tenth, whom he used to like, whom he thought liked him back until she ripped out his heart and tossed it in the deep fryer when she began dating another of their co-workers, a loser named Seth.

The last time Carl had seen her was the night he crashed her sweet sixteen party dressed in the fashion of Rob Halford, leather-clad lead singer of Judas Priest.

"What happened to Seth?" he asked.

"He's a loser," she said, looking as if she'd been crying and was about to start again. "Can you come out so we can talk?"

His Nike Airs were near the door and his mother was lingering. He grabbed the high tops and brought them outside, closing the door behind him. Colleen, hands in jacket pockets, watched him slide them on. He didn't tie them.

Across the street, in a cone of amber streetlight, on the hood of an old gray Chevy Caprice, sat a girl with dirty blond hair and metal-framed glasses smoking a Parliament.

"I'm not involved in this," the smoking girl said, hands in the air. "I'm just the driver. She's been drinking and she insisted on seeing you and I'm only driving because I was afraid she was gonna get behind the wheel herself."

Colleen was looking down at the asphalt.

"Well, here he is," the smoking girl said to her. "Now say what ya gotta say so we can all go home."

She didn't respond or look up.

"Colleen!" the smoking girl exclaimed.

Colleen shushed her, then looked at Carl.

"You're the one I liked," she said, then looked down again. "I didn't really like Seth that much. He liked me, and he was the same age as me, and he also goes to Catholic school, and you're a year older and go to public school, and that intimidated me. I didn't think you would take me seriously."

"Well, I did like you. That's why I quit. I wasn't going to hang around watching you two play kissy-face."

"I'm so stupid."

"So, you invited me to your party because you still liked me?"

"Yes. I wanted you to be there. I thought something special might happen."

"Like what? Me getting into a fight with Seth?"

"That would have been *sooo* awesome," the smoking girl said. "Especially in your hot leather outfit. Do you still have that?"

"Shut up, Karen!" Colleen exclaimed.

"Why are you telling me this now?" Carl asked Colleen.

"Because she still likes you," Karen said, lighting another Parliament.

"Karen!"

"I'm sorry, Colleen," Karen responded, "but it's Sunday night and we have school tomorrow and I'm tired and need to go to sleep. So, let's wrap this up. In fact, I have a suggestion. Why don't you guys get in the car for ten minutes and talk things out, and, if all goes well, you can kiss, and, who knows, maybe even more— "

"Karen!"

"Colleen!"

Karen opened the back door.

"Both of you, get in," she ordered.

Carl got in first, then Colleen.

"You've got ten minutes, starting now," Karen said, then closed the door.

The cabin was utterly silent and smelled of stale cigarette smoke.

"Sorry about her," Colleen said. "She's actually being nice right now. I'm the one being an idiot."

"Your timing is pretty bad," Carl said. "I wasn't really with anyone this whole time, but now I'm going away to college in a couple of months."

"I knew it might be my last chance. I couldn't hold it in anymore."

"But why were you so intimidated? Couldn't you tell I was flirting with you? I was, like, on the verge of working up the courage to ask you out when the bomb dropped."

"I didn't think it was real. I didn't think I had a chance

with you. You're a hot public school guy. You probably have hot girls crawling over you all day."

"You think I'm hot?"

"Of course. Especially your hair."

"Wow. Well, the public school girls don't seem to think so, but thank you. And I thought you were hot too, and you still are. Even hotter now."

"Thanks."

There was a lull of about twenty seconds.

"So, what now?" Carl asked.

"I don't know," Colleen said, starting to cry.

"Colleen, no, please don't—"

"I want you to be my boyfriend."

"Really? Now?"

She nodded.

"I mean, when I go up to college, I wasn't planning on, like, having… I don't know… I want to be, you know, free when I get up there, if you know what I mean."

"That's okay. I just want you to be my boyfriend right now. This second."

"This second?"

"This second."

"Oh. Uh, okay."

Another lull.

"I want you to kiss me," Colleen finally said.

"Okay."

She looked at him, then closed her eyes and leaned in. His lips met hers, which felt soft and nice. At first, they kissed hesitantly, then she slipped her tongue into his mouth. She was a good kisser, and he liked the way she put her hands on his cheeks. He kissed her back with a passion she could not have known with that loser Seth. The world fell away. The windows fogged.

They were interrupted by a pounding on the glass.

"Time's up, lovers!" Karen said from outside.

Colleen looked away, then started crying.

"Are you okay?" Carl asked.

"I'm so sorry," she said.

"About what?"

"It's over."

"What?"

The door opened and she got out.

"Wait, what's going on?" Carl asked, following her out.

"It's over, Carl," she said, then started crying harder.

"What do you mean, 'It's over'? It's been like, five minutes!"

"You heard the girl, Romeo," Karen said. "It's over."

Karen shut the door while Colleen went around the front of the car and got in on the passenger side.

"Sorry," Karen said. "I know it's tough being dumped. Cigarette?"

She held open the flip-top box. He pondered the recessed filters, then took one and she lit it for him.

"Thanks," he said.

"Don't take it so hard. If Colleen wasn't my best friend, I'd go out with you."

She got into the car and the engine started. Carl watched the taillights turn the corner and disappear, then listened to the engine fade into the static of the night. He smoked the Parliament down to the filter, then flicked it to the curb before heading back across the street and into the house, where his mother was still lingering.

THE PRETTY GIRL NEXT DOOR

At the side of the house where the trash receptacles were kept, Carl, who had, the night before, pilfered several cans of Budweiser from the fridge and consumed them in his room, was now quietly disposing of the empties when he thought he heard a girl call his name.

He looked around but didn't see anyone, then resumed his task until he heard it again. This time it was closer and came from the other side of the rotting stockade fence surrounding their next-door neighbor's backyard, a rusty grave of car parts, oil drums, bench presses, alcohol stills, and lawnmowers surrounding an above-ground pool full of primordial green water.

"Oh," Carl said. "Hey, Sherry."

Sherry was a year younger than Carl. She wasn't that pretty and had a bad home perm that didn't help, but her body had blossomed and she was wearing a neon pink tank top, cutoff jeans, and a little bit of makeup. She'd always just been another of the kids on the block, but now she looked like sex.

"You're getting good at guitar," she said.

"Thanks," Carl said, surprised. He had recently purchased a used white Phantom electric guitar and 12-watt Peavy Audition amp and had been practicing riffs from *Led Zeppelin II*.

"I was watching you play the other night when you had your shirt off," she said. "You had on the yellow bandana and you were sweating."

"Uh, yeah, I was just working out in the basement and then I went upstairs and started jamming."

"Yeah, and you were really pumped up. It made me touch myself."

"Oh. Wow."

"I finished really quickly, then I did it again."

"Jeez, Sherry. Why are you telling me this?"

"Because I see you touching yourself all the time, and I thought that— "

"Wait, what? How?"

"When your window is open like that, I can see your reflection on the glass when you're on your bed."

Carl looked up at his bedroom windows. They were Andersen casement windows, the kind that swing out by turning a handle, and, sure enough, on one of the panes, he saw the reflection of his unmade bed.

"You do it a lot," she said.

"No I don't! What the hell?"

"It's okay. I do it way more than you. But it gets kind of boring after a while, and, you know, I was thinking that you probably get bored of it too."

"Uh, yeah, I guess."

"Do you wanna come over? Nobody's home, and I'll let you go all the way. I want you to."

Carl looked at one of the "NO TRESPASSING" signs posted all over their yard, then back at Sherry.

"For real?"

"Sure. It's no big deal."

He looked around again, then said, "Uh, okay, but I have to run into the house for a minute."

His mother was out food shopping, his stepfather at work.

His younger brother and sister were in their rooms with the doors closed. He stopped in the living room and listened for a moment, then proceeded into his mother and stepfather's bedroom, where, from his stepfather's travel bag, he retrieved from inside the lining of the Remington electric razor case a Trojan ribbed and lubricated condom, which he slid into his tube sock.

Sherry was waiting at the gate and unlatched it. He followed her through the yard and into the house, a ranch with early-1960s décor that smelled of stale cigarette smoke and Lysol, but tidy.

Her room was at the end of the hall, the walls covered with posters and magazine photos of Michael J. Fox, Ralph Macchio, Kirk Cameron, Jon Bon Jovi, and New Kids on the Block.

She closed the door.

"I can't believe you're really here," she said. "I've never done this before for real, but I think I know what to do. And I'm a good kisser. I've kissed two boys. Do you wanna make out?"

Carl shrugged and said, "Sure."

Like shy dancers, they positioned themselves in the middle of the room and tried to figure out what to do with their hands, until she had hers around his neck and his on the small of her back. Carl was taller and had to lower his head to kiss her. Their lips met. A tentative peck. Another peck.

She slipped her tongue into his mouth. Her kisses became aggressive and he fell backwards, landing on the stuffed animals, she on top of him, still kissing.

She sat up and removed her tank-top, then unhooked her bra and tossed it aside.

"You can touch them," she said.

Her nipples were firm and sensitive. She closed her eyes and shivered at his touch. He leaned forward and put his mouth on one of them, prompting her to moan. She touched him through his shorts.

"Do you think I'm pretty?" she asked.

Hesitating very slightly, Carl answered, "Yes." He knew she had noticed.

"I know that I'm not," she said. "But that's okay."

"You are. It's just a little weird because you were always just the kid next door. But I think you're pretty hot now. I really do. I mean it."

She smiled, then leaned in to kiss him. Eyes closed, mouth parted, she did look pretty.

Just as their lips met, there was a noise from somewhere else in the house.

"Oh no, it's my father," she whispered. "He's home early, which means he's probably drunk and will kill you if he finds you here. Just wait here a minute and I'll go distract him, then sneak out the back the same way we came in."

She put on her tank top and left the room, running down the hall exclaiming, "Daddy! Daddy! I just saw the mouse again in the kitchen!"

"What? Where is he?" he growled. "I'm gonna kill that motherfucker!" Then there was a crash of pots and pans and more cursing.

Carl slipped out the back door unnoticed.

Moments later, in his own bedroom, he closed the windows and lowered the blinds.

CHRISTMAS LIGHTS

Carmine had been sober eight years. He met Judy after he'd stopped drinking for good. She'd never once seen him take a drink, and she didn't drink or ever bring up the subject, yet he knew not to take too long when he went to the store, or to come home even a minute late from work.

It was their oldest son's sixth birthday party. Two-dozen first graders running around the house making a horrible racket. Judy hadn't noticed her husband disappear until ten minutes after he'd been gone. She waited another five before checking the upstairs rooms, but all were empty. She found him in the basement, sitting on the tool room floor, back against the wall, legs splayed, swigging a whiskey bottle.

He didn't look at her. She said nothing.

"Get out," he finally growled, still not looking.

"Let me get you help," she said. "I'll call your sponsor— "

"Get out!" he roared, then threw the bottle, missing her head by inches, hitting the pegboard, hammers and hooks and screw bins crashing down, party noise upstairs silenced.

"No," she said, angry-calm, stepping towards him, pointing, "you get out. Use the back door. Do this and I won't call the police, but I will if you show your face here again."

The sun was about to set. He breathed the cold air deep into his lungs and looked at the string of Christmas lights he'd tossed on the bushes a couple of weekends ago, pitiful compared to the neighbors' decorations.

"I can't," he said, then started walking towards downtown.

ROCK THIS TOWN

Thanksgiving dinner was good—but, after two days at home for the first time since late August, when he'd left for his freshman year of college upstate, Carl was already sick of hiding out in his room avoiding his family and felt about to explode if he didn't get out of the house—

He called two of his new college buddies who lived on Long Island, Frank and Joe, and invited them to crash at the house overnight so they could hit the bars up near the Massapequa Park train station, which, during high school, he'd never had good enough ID to even try to get into, but now they all possessed freshly altered New York State driver's licenses, thanks to a girl in their dorm who "chalked" them with pencils and Aqua Net and had changed the *3*s in *1973* to *0*s, making them all 22.

After Frank and Joe arrived, they piled into Carl's '81 Oldsmobile Cutlass Supreme—"The Green Car" for its shade of GM Forest Pine, which had belonged to his grandfather, who died of cancer less than a year after buying it—and made the two mile ride up to Massapequa Park, just north of Sunrise Highway, parking in the shadows at the far end of the holiday-deserted train station, behind one of the huge concrete supports holding up the elevated eastbound and westbound tracks of the L.I.R.R. Babylon branch.

* * *

They began the evening on Park Boulevard—the closest thing there was to a "Main Street" in the Greater Massapequas, which, otherwise, was mostly strip malls and mall-malls—and went into Kokomo's.

It was the heart of Saturday night, yet the dive was nearly empty, save a couple of middle-aged men sitting separately down at the dark end of the bar, and a young red-haired guy passed out at one of the little circular tables in the back, near the restrooms.

The bartender—in her 40s or so, attractive, facial features a bit hardened, dyed blond hair, tight black jeans, raspy smoker's voice, heavy local accent, black concert t-shirt from a 1984 Billy Joel show at Madison Square Garden—looked at their ID's and could tell something wasn't right, but shrugged it off and let them stay. She made them guess her name by pointing to her *eye* and then *lean*ing against the bar—

"Eileen!" she said. "Get it? Eye, lean—I know, it's corny. Please don't leave. What'll it be? The first round is on me! I'll even throw in some hot wings!"

It wasn't long before they realized why she was so anxious for them to stay, the place dead and the two guys down the bar totally creepy, staring straight ahead with several shots of whiskey lined up next to their beer glasses, waiting for it to be time to throw back the next one—

"How long has this place been here?" Carl asked, he and his friends smoking Marlboro "Reds", Eileen smoking Marlboro Lights 100s.

"Since the sixties. This place used to be wild, rock stars would hang out here—Vanilla Fudge, the Good Rats, Blue Öyster Cult, Lou Reed, Candy Darling—she grew up a couple of blocks from here. And then in the late seventies and early eighties it was known as 'Cocaine-amos', which was fun for a while, but then it got really nasty and gross. The current owners took it over five years ago and cleaned it up, but, as you can see, it hasn't really caught on—"

Pitcher after pitcher they drank for two hours and downed about a hundred wings, Eileen not charging them but accepting their tips, each throwing in a buck per pitcher.

In the back, the red-headed guy began to stir and rose from his table, then staggered towards the freshmen—

"I know you," the guy said to Carl. "Your name is Carl. You used to be friends with that loser Eric."

"Go back to sleep, Kenny," Eileen said.

"Hey, Kenny," Carl said, remembering Kenny Brill from eighth grade art class, a kid who bragged about how much weed he smoked, and by tenth grade was rumored to be snorting heroin and supposedly went crazy and broke all the windows in his house, then at some point stopped showing up at school. "It's good to see you. I always wondered what happened to you."

"I got hooked on the H-train, brother. Bad news, man, bad news. Can you spare a buck or two so I can buy a drink?"

"Kenny, I've warned you about harassing my customers," Eileen said. "If you don't leave them alone, I'm gonna throw you out."

"Alright, alright," he said, then staggered back to his table.

* * *

After bidding Eileen good night, they headed down to Front Street and into Gannon's Station Café, where there was a crowd, but they were older, their parents' age and above, and they must not have been used to young guys coming in because the old guy behind the bar didn't even card them. They ordered a pitcher of Budweiser, then retreated to the CD jukebox towards the back, where Frank put in a dollar for five plays, making the first selection "Revolution 1" from the Beatles' *White Album*, then the next four selections, "Revolution 9"—

"I think we're in a cop bar," Joe said. "A lot of mustaches in here."

About two minutes into the first playing of the eight-plus minute "Revolution 9", some guy with a bushy "street-sweeper" cop-stache and a really bad hairpiece came over, clad in Augusta green sharkskin suit and extra-wide brown-and-tan-striped tie with silver clip, holding a Rob Roy and an unfiltered Pall Mall—

"You punks think you're funny playing this hippie garbage?" he asked, gravel-voiced.

"Pardon?" Frank asked.

"On the jukebox. This isn't music. This is hippie garbage."

"We just picked the first song," Joe said. "Someone else came over and picked this one—"

"I know you're lying, punk. I've had my eye on this jukebox all night. This punk over here—" pointing at Frank—"put in a dollar, and chose five songs. This is the second song. And I use the term loosely, because it's not actually a 'song', but a piece of hippie garbage."

* * *

After a hasty exit from Gannon's, they headed back up the block towards the Front Street Pub, where about a hundred or so Harley-Davidsons were parked, many on the sidewalk and the rest on the street, some extending into Front Street's westbound lane—

"Let's go there," Carl said.

Frank and Joe exchanged glances, then said, "Sure."

There was a bouncer seated on a barstool outside the

door, a large, bearded biker guy with the name "Barf" patched to his leather vest. A rockabilly band was playing inside. He didn't ask for ID, but informed them of the $5.00 cover to get in.

"They sound like the Stray Cats," Joe said.

"They are the Stray Cats," Barf said.

Inside, the backs of their right hands now marked with giant black **X**s from Barf's Magic Marker, there they were, up on a small platform stage, Massapequa's own Stray Cats—Brian Setzer picking his Gretsch, Lee Rocker slapping his standup, Slim Jim Phantom banging his drums. The floor was packed with biker guys, most clad in leather jackets and vests patched with Pagan cuts, dancing with their old ladies.

The freshmen drifted towards the floor until they were suddenly seized by three leather-clad women, who, like ninjas, swiftly slapped a handcuff onto each of their wrists, then attached the other cuff to the brass rail on the bar—

"This juke joint has a three-shot minimum," said a woman with short black hair and a lot of makeup, tight leather pants, like Joan Jett, but a little off.

The bartender, who looked similar but different, like Pat Benatar, lined up nine shot glasses, filling each with Cuervo Gold and a little splash of Tabasco, a concoction known as a "Prairie Fire"—

"Finish three each and you can stay," Joan Jett said.

The three freshmen exchanged glances and shrugged. With their free hands, they raised their first glasses for a toast, then threw them back. Seconds later, each vomited at their feet, the red splatter glowing from the Tabasco and the earlier hot wing sauce—

Pat Benatar screamed, surprisingly loud and high-pitched. The band, in the middle of "Rumble in Brighton", brought the song to a stumbling halt. The bikers and their old ladies flashed angry looks towards the freshmen—

"Looks like we got a few lightweights over at the bar," Setzer said into the microphone, his voice echoing loudly through the big amps, followed by feedback. Rocker and Phantom chuckled, but the bikers and their old ladies started yelling, and it looked like it was about to get ugly—

"Get them out of here!" Joan Jett ordered the leather-clad women, then turned to the Cats and yelled at them to "Start playing!" The band broke into "Rock This Town" and everyone on the floor started dancing again, while the lads were uncuffed and escorted out—

* * *

Minutes later, in the darkness at the far end of the train station, after retrieving from the Oldsmobile an eighth of weed and a little brass pipe purchased at the "gift store" on Main Street upstate, the freshmen smoked a bowl they far from needed, which made them not high but once more nauseous. Joe puked again, and at some point, Kenny Brill found them and they let him have a couple of hits, then gave him some money, and that was the last thing Carl would remember until they had somehow arrived back home and were trying to get into the house without making noise, and then Frank and Joe passed out on the floor in his room—

* * *

Carl opened his eyes. It was 6:47 and starting to get light. Frank and Joe were gone. The house was quiet. His head was throbbing, his tongue stuck to the roof of his mouth. He felt like he was going to puke. With great effort, he pushed himself up from his mattress on the floor and went out to the hallway window to see if their cars were still there. They were gone, but his Cutlass was parked at a near-45-degree angle in the driveway, one of the tires on the front lawn—

"Shit!" he whispered, tiptoeing out the door while trying to extract the keys from his pocket. Having no recollection of driving home, he checked the front bumper for blood, which, fortunately, there did not appear to be. He then got in and turned the ignition, backing out of the driveway and pulling it back in straight.

After cutting the engine, he remained motionless in the cold quiet of the car's interior listening to himself breathe, until he slammed the steering wheel with the hand bearing the black ***X*** on its backside—

"Idiot!" he shouted, eyes stinging with tears, then whispered, "Never do this again."

ADAM ROAD WEST (PART III)

May 19, 1992

Lolita, with t-shirt from her lover's body shop in hand and .25 caliber automatic tucked barrel-down into the back of her pants, stood at the front door of the house at the end of Adam Road West, next door to Massapequa's legendary Biltmore Beach Club, then looked back at the Firebird parked on the street, Peter behind the wheel but distracted trying to find something on the radio while Howard was in one of his endless commercial breaks—

She rang the doorbell. While waiting, she looked nervously at the Beach Club property next door, until she heard someone inside. The door opened and it was *her*, the wife from the framed family photo in Joey's office at the body shop. Lo showed her the t-shirt, saying it belonged to her non-existent "sister", whom she claimed Joey was having an affair with. Lo didn't really know what she was saying, only trying to escalate the situation to where she would get worked up enough to pull the gun from her rear and crack the housewife in the head with it, then shoot her in the face. The housewife went down and Lo ran back to the car, Peter yelling through the open passenger window, "What the hell did you just do?"

Later that evening, several blocks away, Carl, just arrived

home for the summer after his freshman year of college upstate, and who'd earlier popped a tab of blue telephone acid he'd found in his wallet, was seated on the legless easy chair in his bedroom staring at the television when *News 12 Long Island* ran a story about a shooting in Massapequa on Adam Road West. He recognized the Beach Club in the background next door to the house where the shooting had occurred, which itself looked oddly familiar, then a medicine man appeared in the background, clad in "wifebeater" tank top and sandals with black socks, dancing on the lawn behind the *News 12* reporter, who didn't seem to notice—

The next afternoon, in his orange jumpsuit at the Metropolitan Correctional Center in Lower Manhattan, freshly convicted of murder and other crimes and now awaiting his sentencing date, John Gotti, satiated after a chicken-fried steak and biscuits smuggled in from Cracker Barrel, was seated in front of the rec-room television watching the news, *Live at Five* on Channel 4, and recognized the driveway of the house from which they were running a story about a shooting that had taken place the day before, next door to the Biltmore Beach Club—

"Paulie 'Pork Chops'," he chuckled. "They'll never get me for that one."

PLATFORM DIVING

Bobby showed up at a little after eight and Carl unwrapped the aluminum foil, revealing the three white tabs of cardstock each smaller than a fingertip with blue telephone receiver printed on them and laced with lysergic acid diethylamide-25.

"Are you ready?" Carl asked Bobby, who'd never tripped. Carl had done it for the first time two weeks earlier at college upstate and had purchased several extra tabs to bring home to Long Island for the summer.

"You guys said it was mild," Bobby said.

"It was, but it's loaded with speed, so it'll last eight hours and then it'll take you four hours to fall asleep. The difference is, last time we were up at school and could just wander off campus into the woods and go back to the dorm and do whatever. Now, as soon as we put these things on our tongues, we have to get the fuck out of here because my mother and stepfather are in the den directly below us and they aren't gonna move until the Carson monologue is over."

With a pair of tweezers, Carl placed one of the tabs on the tip of Bobby's index finger, then picked up another and put it on his own.

"Don't leave me hangin'," he said, then put the tab on his tongue.

Bobby did the same, then stuck out his tongue to show

Carl.

"Alright," Carl said, setting the timer on his Casio watch for thirty minutes to remind them to swallow the tabs, "no turning back now. Let's get the fuck out of here."

He refolded the aluminum around the last tab for future use, then retrieved his bowl, "Amanda", and the fresh dime bag he'd purchased earlier that afternoon and stuffed both into his half-full pack of Marlboros.

To get out of the house from his room, they had to go downstairs and pass through the TV den, where his mother and stepfather had just returned with fresh cocktails during a commercial break from *Dr. Quinn, Medicine Woman.*

"So, where you headed off to?" his mother asked.

Concerned that the tab on his tongue would fly from his mouth as he spoke, Carl, semi-ventriloquistic, answered, "Taco Bell."

"Taco Bell? Since when do you like Taco Bell? You always hated when I made tacos."

He shrugged.

"What are you going to do after that?"

He shrugged again and said, "Bowling."

"Bowling? Where? Hopefully not at 300 Bowl."

Carl shrugged and, fortunately, his stepfather cleared his throat to indicate he couldn't hear the TV, so his mother told them to have fun and, moments later, they were sitting in Bobby's white Toyota Celica.

Bobby, hand on key ready to turn the ignition, asked, "Are we really going to Taco Bell and Bowling?"

"I just said that to get out of there," Carl answered, "but, I actually don't have any better ideas at the moment, so, sure. Let's go get some tacos."

The nearest Taco Bell was in Seaford, the next town over. They went through the drive-thru and ordered Chilitos, crunchy tacos, and extra-large Mountain Dews, and Bobby parked in a space overlooking the Burger King next door. They had to wait six minutes before eating so they wouldn't swallow the tabs too soon.

After they'd finished eating and smoked a bowl, Bobby asked, "So, are we really going bowling?"

"Sure, why not," Carl answered. "Are you okay to drive?"

"Yeah, for now, anyway. But I don't know how long that's gonna last."

"Well, alright then. Let's just go bowling and see what happens."

Bobby pulled the Celica onto Sunrise Highway, but, moments later, Carl instructed him to pull into a 7-Eleven.

"We need supplies," he said to Bobby, "and we'd better get them before you can't drive anymore."

They purchased large coffees heavy on cream and sugar, a pouch of sour apple Big League Chew gum, a one-subject college-ruled spiral notebook, a two-pack of blue Bic Cristal pens, two bottles of Coke, four packs of Marlboros (box), the current issue of *Playboy* (featuring *Playmate of the Year* Corinna Harney and an interview with Ralph Nader), and a twelve-pack of Old Milwaukee (cans), which would likely require an ID check. Carl's New York State driver's license was altered, which worked at the college bars upstate, but, on Long Island, there was always the fear that some asshole would take it and turn it over to the police. The burnout dude behind the counter, though, gave him a knowing smile and didn't even ask for ID, and, moments later, they were back in the Celica heading east towards 300 Bowl.

Carl hadn't been to this place since eleventh grade, when he worked there for less than two months and was deservedly fired. Two days before the termination, though, he'd been tipped off by a coworker that they were gonna give him the ax at the end of his next shift, allowing him to exact revenge in advance. During this last shift, he unplugged the freezers with the snack bar burger patties, French fries, and pizza; he squirted ketchup and mustard into the finger holes of the balls on the racks and into the toe space of as many pairs of shoes as he could; he mixed a bottle of vanilla syrup they used for the egg creams into the tank of the lane oiling machine; and he pilfered a case of Miller Genuine Draft longneck bottles from the bar and stashed it behind the dumpster of the mattress store next door, where, after the firing, it was waiting for him to haul three miles home on the handlebars of his Centurion Accordo *Tour de France Limited Edition LXE* 12-speed racing bike. The following afternoon, the owner called his house screaming at his mother that he was going to sue them for everything they had and was considering filing charges with the police, but then nothing ever happened.

He knew it was unlikely the owner would be there late on a Saturday night, or that he would even be recognized now with his goatee, long hair, Rasta hat, and burlap hoodie. The place was crowded with Saturday night daters and families, and, to his relief, he didn't recognize the guy behind the counter. They had to wait several minutes for a lane to become available.

"I think I'm starting to feel something," Bobby said, looking a little paranoid.

They were eventually assigned a lane down on the lower level. There was a group date happening on the pair of lanes next to them, one of the women looking familiar to Carl.

"Shit," he said.

"What?" Bobby asked, seated at the scorekeeper's table.

"That woman over there, the one with the dark hair—she works at the employment agency I temp for."

They watched them celebrate after one of the other women rolled a strike.

"You wanna split?" Bobby asked.

"Nah. I think I'm alright. Let's just bowl. I used to have a

179 average."

"Jeez. I think it would take three games for me to score that."

On these very lanes, before his brief employment here, Carl was a decorated youth league bowler who once, on a Friday afternoon fueled by Twix bars, French fries, and vanilla egg creams, rolled a 220, the high game of the league season, for which he received a giant trophy. Now, however, his bowling skills had abandoned him and he was frozen in his stance on the approach. Sixty feet ahead, the pins were swaying in unison.

"You okay up there?" Bobby eventually asked.

Carl noticed the woman from the employment agency looking at him.

"My old pitcher's elbow is acting up," he said, then put the ball back on the return rack. At the scorekeeper's table he said to Bobby, "We need to get the fuck out of here."

Minutes later in the Celica—

"Dude, I don't know if I can drive," Bobby said.

"There's a train station right up the road," Carl said, lighting a cigarette. "Half-mile at most, straight shot east on Sunrise until you have to make that left turn. There's a little cop booth at the station, so be careful, but, if you can make it into one of those spots, it's free parking all weekend, and then we can just ride the rails until sunrise."

It was approaching midnight and there was little traffic on Sunrise Highway. The cop cruiser wasn't parked at the booth and Bobby made it into the station parking lot without incident.

The Babylon branch of the Long Island Rail Road is an elevated line that runs parallel to Sunrise Highway westbound into Queens and eastbound out to Montauk. Toting their supplies in a gym bag from the trunk, they rode the escalator up to the platform, where only a few people were waiting on the westbound side. The quiet was nice after the noise of the bowling alley.

"I'm definitely feeling something now," Bobby said.

"Me too. But we've got a long way to go. I think we should board the next train that pulls in, whichever way it's going. We'll either wind up in Manhattan or Montauk. Or Brooklyn."

"Okay. At this point, I'm following your lead."

"The acid will lead us."

"Wonderful."

They went inside the vacant, urine-stink waiting room and smoked a bowl, then went back out to the platform and lit cigarettes.

Sometime later, a pair of white headlights appeared in the eastern darkness, their silent, seemingly eternal approach hypnotizing them.

The train arrived at high speed, the breeze pushing them backwards.

It rolled to a stop and the doors slid open.

"Are we really doing this?" Bobby asked.

"I see no other alternative," Carl answered. "We must board this train and let it take us there."

"Where?"

"Wherever we're supposed to go."

"Wonderful."

The train was mostly empty, but, to stay out of view of the doors at either end of the car and also make a quick escape if necessary, they stood in one of the vestibules where the sliding doors were. Several stations later, the conductor still hadn't appeared, but then, through the dirty window on the door at the eastern end, they finally saw his zombie-like form approaching from the next car.

"Let's keep moving ahead and get off when we get to the front of the train," Carl said.

They pushed their way through the heavy doors at the

end of each car until they were at the front of the train as it arrived in Rockville Centre, the town where Carl had been born nineteen years earlier. The conductor was still a car behind and had to open the doors, allowing the trippers to disembark without paying fare.

Inside the train, the bells started ringing and the doors slid closed. The conductor, arms resting on open window, was looking at them, but said nothing.

"I'm pretty fucked up," Bobby said as the train pulled away.

"I think we're starting to peak," Carl said.

They sat on the platform and packed a bowl, and each cracked open a can of Old Mil.

"I think my beer is breathing," Bobby said, his can resting on the concrete dripping with condensation.

"Holy shit, it is," Carl said, both leaning in for a closer look.

They smoked and drank until headlights appeared in the west.

"Should we go back?" Bobby asked.

"No fuckin' way, man. We don't want to be trapped with the swine in that electric missile while we're peaking."

They concealed their beer and the bowl before the train pulled in. Several people at each door stepped from the cars onto the platform, then quickly disappeared into the stairways.

An hour passed and they smoked cigarettes and stopped talking when Carl started losing track of where he was and what he was doing there. He was also starting to mistrust Bobby and was aware that Bobby was starting to mistrust him, but he knew it would be dangerous to reveal his suspicion, so he tried to focus on his anchors to reality, the sipping of the beer, the smoking of the cigarettes, the occasional car going by down below, the pen, the notebook.

"I feel like we're being watched," Bobby said.

"It's just the acid," Carl said, as much to himself as to Bobby.

"No, man, look behind you."

There were two men standing in the stairwell, one appearing to be in his forties and the other in his early twenties, the latter holding a boom box that he placed on the platform and pressed PLAY.

Bells started ringing. Pink Floyd's "Time" from *Dark Side of the Moon*. Carl had listened to the same CD when he tripped upstate.

"What the fuck?" Carl wondered aloud, then stood.

"What are you doing?" Bobby asked.

"They're sending us a message."

"What?"

"I want to go over there and find out what it is."

"What? Are you crazy?"

"Yes."

The younger guy pressed STOP, then the older guy yelled, "Yo!"

"I'm going over there," Carl said.

"What if they're killers?"

"They're not killers."

"What if they try to mug you?"

"Then they'll be disappointed. But they know we're tripping. The acid has tapped us into their frequency."

"Well, it's all you, man. I'm staying right here."

"Suit yourself."

Near the stairwell, Carl approached the men slowly.

"Dude's high on acid," the older guy said.

"For real," the younger one agreed.

"How can you tell?" Carl asked.

"Clear as day, man. Two college boys sitting on a train station platform at one in the morning, smoking weed, drinking Old Milwaukee, writing in notebooks—"

"Whoa," Carl said.

"That's right, G," the younger guy said, "we just blew your mind."

"You did, man. We were hoping just to chill and not be noticed."

"Not be noticed?" the older guy laughed. "It's impossible *not* to notice you."

"Do you guys hang out here a lot?"

"Yeah, dude. This is like our living room. You guys are our guests, and I see you brought beverages."

"Yeah, man. You guys want an Old Mil? We also have some weed if you want to smoke."

"Now you talkin'," the older guy laughed.

Carl turned and waved at Bobby, who remained motionless.

"Your boy might be having a problem," the younger guy said.

"Well, do you guys wanna join us over there?"

"No way, man. You guys are sitting right out in the open. It's okay to make a little noise up here, as long as they don't see you from down there. Stay outta sight and bring your boy over here."

Carl headed back down the platform to the soundtrack of Grandmaster Flash & The Furious Five's "The Message" playing on the boom box.

Bobby's teeth were clenched and he looked paranoid.

"You alright?" Carl asked, realizing he too had a bit of jawlock. "I think it's time for some sour apple gum. But those guys over there are cool and invited us to hang out."

"Hang out?"

"Yeah, man. This is, like, their living room."

"Maybe we should stay over here."

"No, they said it wasn't safe here out in the open. We need

to get out of sight."

Bobby didn't respond.

"Okay," Carl said, "just get up and follow me."

Bobby stood and Carl picked up the gym bag and they headed over to the stairwell.

The older guy's name was Earl, and the younger guy was Johnny.

Carl packed Amanda and offered it to Earl.

"Why you call this bitch 'Amanda'?" Johnny asked Carl, inspecting the green, orange, and yellow tie-dye pattern on the rubber grip around the chamber.

"I had a crush on Amanda Whurlitzer from *The Bad News Bears*. The novel based on the screenplay. I read that first, then saw the movie later with Tatum O'Neal. I also like the Boston song."

They passed the bowl and sipped their Old Milwaukees, except Bobby, staring at the large cross atop the bell tower of St. Agnes Church across the street.

"Is your boy Bobby alright?" Earl asked.

"He should be. We're peaking."

"How come you're not staring off into space?"

"This is his first time. I tripped on this same stuff once before."

"Got anymore?"

"No. I got this stuff upstate. This was the last of it."

"How'd you wind up here anyway?"

"We were driving around, then Bobby couldn't drive anymore, so we got on the train and it took us here."

"Where you from?"

"Massapequa. But I was actually born here, Mercy Hospital, 1973. And now I'm back. The acid has brought me full circle."

"Is Bobby from Massapequa too?"

"No. He's from Lake Grove."

"Lake Grove? Where the fuck is that?"

"Out east somewhere in Suffolk."

"You guys know the next eastbound ain't gonna be for another two hours?"

"Shit," Carl said. "Well, the peak will be over by then."

They finished the beer and weed as the sky changed by degrees from black to blue. Eventually Earl and Johnny left, leaving the trippers alone to ponder the sky turning ever bluer behind the white cross atop St. Agnes across the street.

"I think I'm coming down," Bobby said.

"I'm definitely coming down," Carl agreed, "but we're still gonna be pretty wired for a while because of the speed."

Down on the street there hadn't been any vehicles for a couple of hours until a *Newsday* truck slowed and dropped several bundles of newspapers in front of a still-shuttered newsstand.

"It has officially changed from late to early," Carl said. "We just spent the night at a train station."

"Wonderful," Bobby said.

"If we hadn't taken the acid, we would have gone on thinking these were mere train stations, and not places that some people use as living rooms. There might be a Johnny and Earl at every station, and we never would have known. We have been ignorant, but the acid has opened new doors for us and we will never be the same."

They were hungry, but there was nothing open in the vicinity of the station. All they could do was sit on a platform bench like regular passengers and wait for the next eastbound train, lungs hurting, but still chain-smoking cigarettes. An hour later the train finally arrived and this time, wired and exhausted, they took a seat and paid for tickets, longing for the relief of sleep that seemed far in the future if their brains would only slow down.

Bobby was okay to drive and they went to 7-Eleven for

buttered rolls and coffee hoping the caffeine and food would relieve the exhaustion, which it did a little. Afterwards, Bobby dropped Carl off at his house, then headed back to Lake Grove.

It was just before six and Carl managed to make it through the house without waking anyone, a relief because he knew he was a grimy trainwreck and surely reeked, though he couldn't tell himself.

Exhausted and wired, he turned on MTV, which was playing the trippy new Beastie Boys video, "So What'cha Want".

"I want sleep," Carl scribbled in the notebook, but then there were no more words and all he could do was stare at the TV until, as the rest of the house began to stir, sweet relief finally came.

THE DISAPPOINTMENT

It had taken two extra months of summer sessions, but Carl finished his bachelor's degree within four years.

He'd been home at his mother's house nearly two weeks when he finally called his father. The last time they spoke, Carl had asked him for another $200 to make it through the last month up at school. His father suggested he find a job. Carl hung up on him.

This time, his father congratulated him, without enthusiasm, and with sarcasm. This was followed by a long, uncomfortable lull, during which Carl listened to the subtle deviations in the phone line background noise, including what sounded like a cry for help way off in the distance.

"Well," Carl finally said, "do you want to go to lunch or something?"

"I presume you expect me to pay."

"I haven't found a job yet."

* * *

They met at the Taco Bell on Merrick Road in Merrick, the approximate midpoint between Carl's mother's house in Massapequa and his grandmother's house in Franklin Square, where his father, since the divorce over a decade ago, had been living in his childhood bedroom.

Carl ordered two Chilitos, two soft tacos, and a Mountain Dew. His father ordered two crunchy tacos and a Diet Pepsi. They sat at a booth overlooking the parking lot and the Burger King next door. Neither unwrapped their food.

"So," his father asked. "Are you even going to try to find a job?"

"I've already been on two interviews in the city and I faxed out 24 resumes yesterday."

"If you had graduated on time, you would have started this process two months ago and probably would have had a job by now."

"I worked my ass off to graduate in the summer so I wouldn't have to do another full semester, which you would have had to pay for half of. I thought you'd be happy to be off the hook."

"Yeah, off the hook alright. I'm still paying for your sister's college, which already looks like it's headed for the five-to-seven year plan, and I suppose I'll have to pay for your brother's too, if he makes it through high school. Off the hook. It sounds like you're the one who's happy to be off the hook. Now you won't need me anymore. Not even a thanks for all I've done to pay for your education. Just like your mother. Such a disappointment. And what was your major again? English? What the hell are you going to do with that?"

"Did you just call me a disappointment? After I just graduated college? Oh, thanks for paying for half of it, by the way."

His father didn't respond.

"You're right," Carl said, sliding out of the booth. "I don't need you anymore."

SHIRTSLEEVES

In an industrial section of south Nassau County, Carl finally located the address that the temporary staffing agency had given him for the one-week data entry assignment at the Drisdon Plumbing Manufacturing and Supply Co., Inc.

The building was a weathered brick factory with an attached office. Just inside the main entrance was a lobby that appeared not to have been renovated since the 1960s or earlier, the bare décor consisting of four wood-framed chairs with cracked leather upholstery, a glass coffee table, and a fish tank full of green, primordial water with a dead koi floating on the surface.

He reported to the receptionist and was told that Maria would be out in a few minutes. He sat across from the fish tank, the filter still running, until Maria arrived, a woman appearing to be in her forties but seeming older, her dark, scraggly hair streaked gray, no makeup, metal-framed glasses taped together on one side, thick homespun sweater smelling of cat litter and cigarettes.

"The agency said you were proficient in Lotus 1-2-3," she said, not returning Carl's smile, which disappeared as he vaguely recalled listing it in the "Skills" section of his résumé, having once used the spreadsheet software for three minutes in the "Computer Lab" at college for an accounting class assignment.

"Uh, yeah," he said.

After deciding he was adequate, she led him past a row of cubicles to the office of Bob Drisdon III, the fourth generation of Drisdons to lead the company. In the middle of the room was a large walnut desk flanked in the rear by a pair of brass-poled American flags, and, on the wood-paneled wall behind the desk chair, a sepia oil painting of the founder, Boris Drisdon, a clean-scrubbed man with confident expression and hair parted straight down the middle, wearing an impeccable, pinstriped three-piece suit, appearing very much a businessman of his time who knew what the hell he was doing. There were other paintings around the room of yachts and beachside houses and some framed group photographs from the family compound in Montauk, and a large section of memorabilia from the Detroit Lions football team. The room left little impression of actual work being done within it, except in one of the corners, where, behind a sea-green privacy screen like those in elementary school nurse's offices, there was a small desk with desktop computer and rolling desk chair, next to which was a small folding table with a laptop and a metal folding chair that reminded Carl of a kiddie-table.

"You'll be sitting here next to me logging these invoices into Lotus 1-2-3," Maria said, showing him the stack of cardboard Banker's Boxes stuffed with hardly legible, handwritten, carbon copies of invoices from the past thirty years that Mr. Drisdon had tasked her with entering into the computer.

"Okay," Carl said.

"And Mr. Drisdon will be coming in and out all day. Don't say anything to him unless he addresses you directly, and don't look him in the eye."

"Uh, okay."

He sat at the kiddie-desk and she showed him how to enter the information into the spreadsheet—company names, addresses, dollar amounts, part numbers, etc.

"You do the next one," she said.

She talked him through it and had him do the third one on his own, which he completed without error. Then she let him start working alone but watched him while she started working on her own stack of invoices.

"Don't make any mistakes," she said after he'd hit the backspace button a few times.

"I'll try not to," he said.

Except for the buzz of the fluorescent tube lighting and soft tick of the wall clock, they worked in silence, which was fine with Carl, content to lose himself in the monotony until lunch.

At around 10:30 appeared Bob Drisdon III, a pudgy, middle-aged man with graying hair wearing an outfit from professional golfer Payne Stewart's line of "plus-four" knickers in the color scheme of the Detroit Lions—blue sweater vest with family crest on the left breast over silver golf shirt, blue flat-cap hovering over puffy pink cheeks—a comic contrast to his great grandfather in the painting and perfect complement for the "shirtsleeves-to-shirtsleeves" adage.

Maria tensed before he even spoke. Carl felt his eyes on him for a moment but managed to stay focused on the invoices and computer monitor.

Smirking, sarcastic, Drisdon asked Maria, "Are you done yet?"

"Mr. Drisdon, this is going to take weeks, maybe months to finish. There are tens of thousands of invoices."

"Well, hurry up then, and don't fuck this up the way you fuck everything else up."

"Yes, Mr. Drisdon."

"I'll be back in an hour."

Carl and Maria settled back into their quiet routine, but Carl had lost focus and Maria had to correct a couple of his mistakes.

"Does he always talk to you like that?" he asked her, but she ignored him and kept working.

At lunch, Carl went to the McDonald's drive-thru and listened to sports talk radio while he ate until there was a commercial break. In the silence he considered using the pay phone attached to the side of the restaurant to call the employment agency and tell them about Drisdon's inappropriate behavior and how he didn't feel comfortable going back, but, needing the money and not wanting to get thrown back into the temp pool waiting for a new assignment, he decided to go back and tough it out.

Back at the office he saw that Maria had eaten at her desk while continuing to work, her unzipped handbag on the floor revealing a pack of Carlton 100s, a brand he remembered from magazine ads when he was a kid but had never seen anyone in present-times smoking.

They worked quietly until 1:30, when Mr. Drisdon made his next appearance, now clad in white whale-cord pants and white polo shirt with family crest on the breast and light blue sweater tied loosely around his neck.

"Are you done yet?" he asked.

"We're working on it, Mr. Drisdon," Maria said without looking up.

"Remember, no fuckups. If you fuck this up, I'm going to have to write you up again."

"Yes, Mr. Drisdon."

He left again and Carl looked at Maria.

"How do you put up with that asshole?" he asked her.

She stopped typing and glared at him.

"Please stop talking and get back to work," she said.

At 4:00, Drisdon came back, now wearing a pinstriped

softball uniform with the full company name embroidered in baseball script across the front—Drisdon Plumbing Manufacturing and Supply Co., Inc.—and the family crest on the cap.

"Done yet?" he asked.

"Not yet, Mr. Drisdon."

Carl was starting to pound the keys as he entered the data.

"What's his problem?" Drisdon asked Maria.

"Please stop pounding the keyboard," she said to Carl.

"Just make sure he doesn't break anything or fuck anything up," Drisdon said, then abruptly left.

This time Carl glared at Maria, then went back to work. Drisdon didn't come back. At exactly 5:00, Maria said he could go, and she signed the daily time sheet that the employment agency had given him.

"Good night," Carl said. Maria didn't respond.

Back at his mother's house, where he'd been living for the past several months since graduating college, there was a note waiting on the kitchen counter telling him to call Barbara at the employment agency ASAP.

"We received a call," Barbara started, surprising Carl with her serious, unfriendly tone. "Is it true that you called our client, Mr. Drisdon, an 'asshole'?"

"Uh, no," Carl said. "Not to his face. He came in and started cursing at Maria, so, after he left, I asked her how she put up with 'that asshole'. He wasn't in the room."

"But you did refer to him as an 'asshole' to one of his employees in his own office."

"Did Maria tell you this? Or did she tell Drisdon and he called you?"

"It doesn't matter. Your assignment has been terminated and we are cancelling your contract. Because of your misconduct, you are now banned for life from Dunlop-Dunhill

Employment Services and its regional affiliate and associate companies nationwide. Your final paycheck will be mailed to your home address. Please do not contact us again unless you don't receive the paycheck."

"The guy came in cursing at us and treating us like children."

"Our decision is final."

"Can I appeal?"

"No."

"Well, then, Barbara, I would like to reiterate that Bob Drisdon III is an asshole, and, on that note, I will bid you adieu. Have a nice life, Barbara."

He hung up.

The check arrived in the mail the following Tuesday.

Eighteen months later, Dunlop-Dunhill Employment Services was charged by the IRS with tax fraud and the company filed for bankruptcy. In the months that followed, many of its regional affiliate and associate companies nationwide would do the same.

Three years later, Bob Drisdon III suffered a massive heart attack on the 13th fairway of the Garden City Country Club and passed away. His son, Robbie, inherited the company and sold it for $10 million, which, within six months, he'd lose day trading penny stocks and foreign currency.

Leaving Here

Carl was in his room, just having finished packing. In the morning he would be leaving for good. The house was quiet, his mother and sister at the mall, his brother downstairs watching TV, his "stepfather", Rick "The Dick", out in the yard doing something.

He'd been dreaming of this day for thirteen years, since 1983, when he was ten and his parents divorced at the beginning of the year, and, at the end of it, his mother married the man with whom she'd been having the affair. The lovers bought a house out in Massapequa, almost Suffolk County, and tore Carl from his life and friends in West Hempstead, none of whom he'd ever see again. Exiled in a higher tax and social bracket, he loathed everything about his new life, from the boozy Biltmore Beach Club scene his mother and Rick threw themselves into, to the broader suburban mall culture of The Greater Massapequas. He'd spent his adolescence counting down the years until he was finally able to escape to college upstate, only to find himself back four years later, the party over, less than broke, in a physical condition his doctor called "somewhat concerning". He quickly realized he had to get the hell out of this place as soon as possible and started jogging, and quit smoking every couple of weeks. He got a job in the receiving department of a financial prospectus warehouse out in Melville and started saving money. He read the rest of the good Kerouac novels and some of the really bad ones, as well as *Ulysses*, *Don Quixote*, and *Gravity's Rainbow*. He drafted the first ten chapters of the novel that was going to make him famous, and revised a few short stories he'd written in college. Finally, a year in limbo later, he'd saved enough and quit his job, and now it was only a matter of hours before he finally set out on the road to live his Kerouac fantasy, driving his grandfather's Oldsmobile towards a new life out West in the Emerald City of Seattle, where Pearl Jam lived—

The quiet was broken by his brother shouting and storming up the stairs, Carl thinking he was about to be attacked—

"Rick's passed out in the yard!"

"Call 9-1-1!" Carl said without hesitation, aware that Rick had recently been having chest pains and seeing doctors and that there was a history of heart disease in his family, yet he still continued to drink and smoke. His brother got on the phone in the kitchen and Carl went through the open sliding glass door out to the yard, and there he was on the grass, flat on his back, eyes wide open to the sky, but no life in them—

"Rick! Rick!" Carl said, but the eyes did not react, and the body remained still. He lightly slapped his cheek a couple of times, but it seemed futile. Carl's brother said an ambulance was on the way, then started relaying CPR instructions from the 9-1-1 operator. Carl tilted Rick's head back and held his nose, gave him mouth-to-mouth, then started pushing on his chest, but nothing was happening. At one point there was a slight gurgle, but he didn't come back. Hearing sirens in the distance, Carl kept pumping, then his brother tried, until the ambulance got there and they stepped aside, knowing the medics wouldn't be able to bring him back either.

* * *

Several days after the funeral, when things had finally quieted down and people stopped bringing food to the house, Carl and his mother were sitting out on the front steps, smoking cigarettes, listening to the Neil Young concert from Jones Beach Theater, "Like a Hurricane"—on clear summer nights, the music would sail four miles across the Great South Bay into the backyards of Biltmore Shores, sounding like a radio playing low, except the echo of the drums across the water had that sound that only live music has, and Neil himself was at the other end of it—

"What are you going to do, Carl?" she asked.

"I can stick around," he said. "I was thinking of asking for my old job back, saving a little more money, maybe give it a go next year—"

"No, Carl. You should go now."

"What about you?"

"I'll be fine. I just need time. A lot of time, probably. You've been wonderful these last two weeks, and I thank you for that. But you have to go live your life."

"Are you sure? I can stay—"

"Go, Carl."

* * *

There was no speed limit in Montana. Setting out, Carl hadn't wanted to push too hard his well-rusted 1981 Cutlass Supreme, the car his grandfather had bought less than a year before dying of cancer, now known as "The Green Car" for its shade of GM Forest Pine. He'd been careful thus far, but, after crossing the border into the Big Sky, he started going faster, not realizing it at first, on a long Interstate straightaway where it felt like he was hardly moving. The needle started dancing at 90, and at 95 the whole vehicle, weighed down by novels and a Brother WP-760D word processor, started shaking, but he was too close to 100 not to try and pressed pedal firmly to floor until the old beast made it, just prior to passing over a slight rise and sudden dip that sent her airborne, engine revving as tires lifted from asphalt, Carl finally free—

WAITRESSES OF THE NORTHERN TIER

At the truck stop next to I-94 in Beach, North Dakota—

"Can I refill that pop for you, hon?" the waitress asked.

Carl, seated alone at a booth with a large black telephone on the table, looked up from his burger and fries to the nametag pinned to the breast of her old-fashioned pink waitress uniform—"DINAH"—then continued up to her eyes.

"Pop?"

"Your soda-pop," she said, looking at his glass of melting ice cubes.

"Oh. Yeah. Sure."

"You alright, hon?"

"Yeah, just a little tired from driving."

"Where you headed?"

"Seattle."

"Another Seattle. Lots of people headed out that way. Even people from around here are goin' out there because they can't stand it here. Where you from? Somewhere on the East coast, I'll bet."

"New York."

"I knew it. Why'd you leave?"

"I was born in the wrong place. To the wrong family."

Dinah smiled.

"You talk like a New Yorker, but you seem different than the others I've seen passin' through."

"I actually grew up on Long Island, just outside of the city."

Dinah leaned in.

"Why are you lookin' at me like that?" she asked.

"Like what?"

"You're lookin' at me funny. I don't mean in a bad way, but like you're seein' a ghost or something. I admit, I didn't have time to shower this morning and I'm a little wrinkled after doin' this for six hours and countin', but I've seen all sortsa types passin' through here and they usually look at me a certain way, but not like the way you were just lookin' at me."

"Sorry. You just look a lot like someone I know. I used to know."

"I knew it. Is she dead?"

"Uh, no, not that I'm aware. She was my first crush."

"Ah, now we're gettin' somewhere. Was she your girlfriend?"

"No, though I wish she had been."

"Let me guess. She broke your heart and you never really got over her after all these years."

"She did break my heart, but I got over it. And there were plenty of others after her who broke my heart, ignored me, wanted nothing to do with me, or didn't know what the hell they wanted from me. But you really do look a lot like her."

"What was her name?"

"Maggie."

"Was she pretty?"

"Of course. I thought she was the prettiest girl in the school."

Dinah smiled.

"What's your name, hon?"

"Carl."

"Carl. I like that name. It's like a racecar driver name. Is that your green Cutlass out in the lot?"

"Uh, yeah. It was my grandfather's car."

"And he's dead?"

"Uh, yeah."

"Sorry, Carl. But it's cool that his car is still going. You don't see many like that anymore. I'll be right back with your pop."

She took his glass and floated past the booths of mesh-capped truckers to the soda fountain behind the counter, where she got him a new glass and scooped some ice into it and began filling it with Coca-Cola, glancing at him a couple of times while doing so. Moments later, she was back at the table placing a fresh pop and unwrapped straw next to his plate.

"Too bad you're just passin' through," she said. "I just got divorced and I'd go on a date with you."

"Oh. Sorry. I mean about the divorce, but thanks for saying that."

Speaking softly, she said, "If you're willin' to stick around for a little while, my shift ends at three, and I'll have an hour before I have to start getting dinner ready for the kids."

It was half-past noon.

"Well, I am a little ahead of schedule," he said, looking at his watch. "Maybe I could stick around for a bit. Is there anything fun to do around here? Where are we again?"

"Beach, North Dakota. And, no, there's not a single fun thing to do around here, at least until three o'clock."

* * *

By 1:30 he was back on I-94 racing through the scrubby badlands of eastern Montana smiling at the nice little memory he was taking with him of the waitress at the truck stop who looked like Maggie from seventh grade, the great clouds in the Big Sky hovering before him, the Rocky Mountains waiting beyond the horizon, and, at the end of I-90, the dawn of his new life.

Yet, there was something nagging at him, that this was not yet a "memory" but an active thought buried alive, and that there was still time to go back and turn that nice little moment into the ultimate Kerouac road experience.

Jack would have gone back.

* * *

By 2:00 he was back in Beach, population 913, touring the town from behind the wheel, past the little stores and the grain co-op and the railroad tracks, until he found himself back at the truck stop. He parked with the tractor-trailers and tried to take a nap, but he was running hot.

At 2:55, he got out of the car and went inside. Dinah smiled when she saw him and he smiled back as he headed towards the men's room. After he came back out, she passed by with a tray of dirty dishes and told him to wait outside, she'd be out in a few minutes.

Outside, he lit a cigarette and was still smoking when she came out. In the bright sunlight she looked less like seventh-grade Maggie and more like a twenty-something divorced single mother waiting tables for a living at a truck stop in the middle of nowhere.

"I'm glad you came back," she said, lighting a GPC 100 cigarette, which, despite his own habit, he couldn't imagine his sweet little Maggie doing. "Just follow me in my truck, it's a quick drive."

She headed across the lot to a dented, mud-splattered Ford F-150 pickup. He got into the Cutlass and followed her through town to a small house on Third Avenue overlooking the grain co-op, where, in the driveway, was parked another beat up F-150.

She pulled into the driveway and he parked on the street. She was still smoking her cigarette when she got out of the truck.

"Looks like my ex is home early," she said. "But don't mind him. The ink on the divorce papers is dry."

"He lives here?"

"Yep. He has his own room in the back."

He followed her into the small house. The front door opened into the living room, where, on the weathered plaid couch, sat a man wearing a white cowboy hat, white button-down western shirt, brown jeans, and white cowboy boots.

"Well, what do we have here, sugar?" he asked, smirking.

"Leave him alone, Buck, I mean it," Dinah said.

"Just askin'."

He looked at Carl.

"So, where you from, cowboy?" he asked.

"New York."

"New York? Only pussies come from New York."

"Buck!" Dinah exclaimed, then turned to Carl. "Don't mind him, he's just between jobs at the moment and a full-time loser."

There was a knock on the front door and it opened before anyone moved to answer it. In stepped an overweight, overbleached blond-haired woman in a white leather cowgirl outfit and a long cigarette dangling from her lips.

"Ma," Dinah said, rolling her eyes.

"Hey, sweetie," she said, removing the cigarette from her mouth and hugging Dinah, who didn't hug her back. She then shot a sharp look at Buck, who made no move to get up from the couch.

"Find a job yet, Bucky?" she asked him.

"No, ma'am."

"Figures."

She then turned to Carl.

"And what do we have here? Another quickie from the truck stop?"

"Shouldn't you be at the bar giving boners to drunk old farts?" Dinah asked.

"Yeah, but a pipe burst in the men's room over there and now there's shit all over the floor and Fred had to shut down until they clean it up. He might even have to call Servpro. He probably shoulda done that before this happened."

A crying toddler burst into the room and hugged Dinah's leg.

"He needs a diaper change," she said, lifting the boy. She then said to Carl, "This'll only take a minute, then we could go to my room."

She disappeared into another room with the kid, leaving Carl alone in the living room with Buck and his ex-mother-in-law.

"You like football, Carl?" Buck asked.

"Uh, yeah. Cowboys fan, actually."

"Cowboys? Why, fuck them Dallas Cowboys. This is a Green Bay Packers household, son. And if you think they got a frozen tundra over there in Wisconsin, why don't you pay us a visit come mid-January. You'll want to kill yourself within a week. And that ain't no joke. You really will want to commit suicide."

"It happens a lot in these parts," Dinah's mother agreed, nodding, exhaling.

Carl looked at his watch.

"I just have to run out to my car," he said. "I'll be right back."

He opened the door and slipped out, closing it gently behind him.

* * *

There was no speed limit in Montana and he made it to Billings just after sundown.

At Boomer's Diner across the street from the Days Inn, he was waited on by "BECKY", who looked like Nancy from eighth grade, the plain girl who liked him before she went Sandra Dee and turned hot.

* * *

The next day, lunching at a Pizza Hut in Missoula, he was waited on by "BARB", who strongly resembled Cara from that steamy night during the summer before tenth grade.

* * *

That evening at the Denny's next door to the Super 8 in Spokane, he was waited on by "JENN", who strongly resembled Colleen, the girl he worked with at the All-American Burger who'd chosen a loser over him, and whose sweet sixteen party he crashed.

* * *

The next day, lunching at The Brick in Roslyn, he was waited on by "MAGGIE", who strongly resembled actress Janine Turner, who played bush pilot Maggie O'Connell in the now canceled prime time CBS drama *Northern Exposure,* which had been filmed in town.

"Oh, wow," Carl said, "you're— "

"Maggie," she interrupted, "and my real name isn't Maggie and I don't really look like this. I just get great tips when I dress the part."

"Oh. You look just like her."

"Get over it, Carl."

"What? Wait, how do you know my name?"

"The Emerald City lies before you. The new life you've been longing for. The clean slate."

"This is fucked up."

"It's not fucked up, Carl. This is the normal. The fucked up is now thousands of miles behind you. And you want a cheeseburger with no onions, fries, and a pop."

"Uh, yeah."

"And, after you finish lunching, you will get back in the Cutlass and, without looking in your rearview mirror, continue over the Cascades, to your damp, overcaffeinated paradise."

She leaned in, hypnotizing him with her glowing blue eyes.

"Carl," she said, "you will let go of the old."

"I will let go of the old."

"You will open your mind to the new."

"I will open my mind to the new."

"And, when she appears, you will let her in."

"When she appears, I will let her in."

"You will not run."

"I will not run."

www.ingramcontent.com/pod-product-compliance
Lightning Source LLC
Chambersburg PA
CBHW030622310726
48979CB00003B/834

* 9 7 8 1 9 4 6 0 9 4 0 8 7 *